HUNGRY BONES

LOUISE HUNG

SCHOLASTIC PRESS / NEW YORK

Library of Congress Cataloging-in-Publication Data available

ISBN 978-1-338-83258-7

10 9 8 7 6 5 4 3 2 1   24 25 26 27 28

Printed in Italy 183

First edition, October 2024

Book design by Stephanie Yang

FOR MY MOM, MY DAD,
AND ALL OF OUR GHOSTS

BEFORE

Everything is black. I blink a few times to make sure my eyes are open. They are.

I smell metal. And something else . . . something musty, earthy, sharp.

Hunger. I have never felt such hunger!

My hands fly to the space around me. I scratch at walls above and below, to my left and to my right. This is a box. I am in a box.

I stretch and push against the walls, but they are resolute and do not budge. Every way I press, the box refuses to yield. This box is too small. I am being squashed. Is this what baby chicks feel like when they are too big for their shells?

I can't catch my breath. Are the walls collapsing? Is my chest? I claw around me and the terrible sound of fingernails scraping on metal makes me shudder.

I have to get out. *I have to find food.* Why am I here? *Who put me in here?* Is this some kind of trick?

1

"Help! Hello! Is anybody out there?"

I cry and wail as loud as I can, until my throat is on fire, but my voice goes nowhere. As soon as it leaves my lips it is gobbled up by the dark. My screams are extinguished. In this wretched box I am alone, without even my own voice for comfort.

Will I die here?

The thought doesn't cross my mind that I am already dead.

I can't be stuck here. I have to get out.

I feel around, looking for a latch or a hinge, anything that I might use to pry open my cell. The box is cold, the walls smooth. Rolling around below me like so many sticks and stones are loose items of various sizes: long, short, round, angular, tiny, as big as my head—a description I shortly realize is alarmingly apt.

Groping through the dark, I find a large ball. No . . . a rock?

In the blackness, my fingers follow the contours of the rock, finding several holes and crags. Smooth pebbles lodged in a crevice . . .

I gasp.

This is not a rock.

This is a skull.

1
MOLLY

"It's a left here! *A left!*"

Mom blows past Charlotte Street and almost into the path of a giant silver Suburban. The driver lays on their horn with just a little more enthusiasm than is totally necessary.

Welcome to Buckeye Creek, Texas.

Swearing under her breath, Mom slams on the brakes and throws our overworked fifteen-year-old Subaru Forester into reverse. Some kids hanging out on a nearby porch turn to stare as our loaded-down car squeals and lurches into the turn. I slouch down and pray we won't go to the same school. We probably will.

"Howdy, Charlotte Street! Nice to—ooh, Molly! Check out that cool squirrel!" Mom almost swerves into an average squirrel that's just trying to have an average squirrel day.

This is what it's like to road trip with Dot Teng, Adventure Mom. Freeway exits are missed; "scenic routes" are taken. We don't get "lost," we "find new destinations." You'd think with cell phones and Google Maps, taking a two-hour "detour" would be near impossible, but my mom has a habit of ignoring directions and then getting so far off the map that the Australian lady in her phone gives up and goes on a Marmite break.

Okay, it's not all bad. Since my mom doesn't do anything in a straight-forward way, we basically ate our way across Texas on our way to Buckeye Creek, a town just outside Dallas. Have you ever had migas? Legit Texas barbecue? Kolaches? As cranky as I was with Mom on our road trip from our last home in Bell Harbor, Maine, to our new home, the food definitely made Texas a slightly less bitter pill to swallow. Slightly.

Yeehaw, the Teng girls are Texans. For now.

This banquet across Texas where my mom pretended her credit card wasn't nearly maxed out was all a distraction. A distraction from the fact that Team Teng—as Mom likes to call us—was split on this decision. As much as I want to make my mom happy and be the sup-portive daughter for yet *another* move, I can't do it anymore. I didn't want to leave Bell Harbor.

But that's what the Teng girls do. We move. Once my mom decides we're moving, all her excitement and energy goes into that new place. She basically strikes a mental match and burns our old home to the ground.

At my ripe old age of thirteen, Mom and I had moved eight times.

Texas makes nine. When people ask me where I'm from, I take a deep breath and watch their eyes grow wide.

"Well, I was born in Los Angeles but we moved to Honolulu when I was five. We lived with my mom's auntie and uncle for a while. That didn't work out, so we moved back to California—Oakland—then Vancouver in Washington State, not Canada, then actually into Seattle. When I was eight, we moved from Seattle to St. Louis, Missouri, for a year, but *that* didn't stick, so then we moved to Chicago, then all the way to Brooklyn, New York, for a little more than a year, and then to Bell Harbor, Maine."

Now I get to add "Right now I'm from Buckeye Creek" and the stinger I like to tag on at the end, "But ask me again next year." It's a crowd-pleaser.

My mom says I'm sentimental. She's not wrong, I guess. Sometimes I wish I had my mom's spirit of adventure. My spirit, I think, is a homebody. If only we could settle on a home.

You see, I notice things. Things other people don't. This is the part where people usually look at me like I'm pathetic or in need of help. (Which one are you?)

Have you ever watched one of those murder mystery movies where the clues to the mystery are all out in plain sight, you just need to know what you're looking at?

Well, I always see the clues, even if most of the time I have no idea what mystery they belong to. I'll walk into a room, and there are things I see that other people don't. Not *invisible* things, more like my attention will be pulled to an old doorknob or an unremarkable vase. Unremarkable to everyone but me.

It's like the thing is waving its hand in the back of the classroom shouting, "Pick me! Pick me!" and if I do, it shows me its history—in feelings, in little bits of memory. It can be overwhelming. If there are too many things that want my attention or something catches me off guard, like the trash room light switch did in St. Louis, it makes me want to barf or pass out. I call it "the zaps."

When it's bad, I can turn into this zombie girl for days. Kids at school think I'm on drugs; teachers think there's something wrong with my home life. In reality it's just that some needy object wanted to suck my life force or show me some old-timey lady's eighty-year-old memories. It's rough because we tend to live in old buildings in big cities where generations of people have lived. Mom is thoughtful about buying new stuff that doesn't have a history, but sometimes buying secondhand furniture is unavoidable.

But Bell Harbor was different. Even though I was surrounded by old things all the time, the stuff felt less pushy. Much like the vibe in Bell Harbor, the old coatracks and vases and plates and cups and books were a lot more chill. They let me ignore them. I kind of got the feeling they wanted to be left alone too. Maybe that's just small-town Maine life for you; live (die) and let live.

In Bell Harbor I felt normal. I wasn't the spooky girl. Okay, I wasn't *just* the spooky girl.

Now, once again, I'm that weird girl who's an easy target.

"Is this bananas or what? Look at these old houses! Who knew the Southwest wasn't all coyotes and dirt!" Mom snaps me out of my moody reverie, ogling Buckeye Creek like it's Bel-Air.

I admit our new neighborhood isn't terrible. While it's a little run-down—a sagging porch here, chipping paint there, potholes that could use some patching—it looks like a neighborhood that might have been special a hundred or maybe even fifty years ago.

The hulking Victorian-style houses that seem drab and tired now still have ornate stained glass windows peeking out from over doors or from high-up attics. The wraparound porches that tilt at odd angles whisper of a time when long lace dresses swept across their boards.

Crossing one more intersection, we go all the way down the street to a dead end before Mom pulls into a driveway on the left and turns off the car in front of a big white house with light green window trim. This can't be the right house—it's huge. But Mom yelps with glee. "It's even better than the pictures!" she says, and hops out, practically skipping to the front door.

With two stories, plus what looks like an attic, the house reaches for the sky. Like other houses in the neighborhood, it looks old and creaky, but cared for. Mom and I have always lived in studios or one-bedroom apartments; sometimes we can find a cool living situation like our barn apartment in Bell Harbor. But a whole house? How can we afford this?

I get out of the car and crane my neck up to take in our new house on Charlotte Street. I wish I could be excited, but nothing about this feels right.

2
JADE

I am dusting my belongings when I hear the car out front. I go to the square window that overlooks the front of the house and look down at a big black car with all manner of possessions tied to the top.

New people.

It's been weeks since anyone has set foot in the house, and I was anticipating a long, hungry fall and winter ahead of me. The last people moved out rather abruptly after one of them walked in on me nibbling a cookie she'd left out. I don't know if she just saw the partially eaten baked good hovering in midair or if she actually saw some diaphanous, spectral *vision* of me, but Miranda's artificially tanned skin turned pale and she backed out of the kitchen, bellowing.

I wasn't sad to see them go.

Nonetheless, the worst part about people moving out of the house on Charlotte Street is the quiet. I know it sounds absurd, but it really gives me the creeps. Once that front door locks for the last time and the Living are off on their way, the silence that settles in is so heavy. The volume turns up on all my senses. Little noises startle me; I see shapes scurry past doorways. Or maybe it's just wishful thinking that another ghost has moved into the house.

By now, a lot of the people who have lived here must be dead. Would they be so thoughtful as to come back and haunt me?

The next worst thing is the hunger. After all these decades I'm still always hungry; it's inescapable. When people are around, I can usually pick over their scraps or leftovers—their trash if I'm desperate. A few times I've been lucky and someone purposely left me food: a person who thinks themself attuned to the spirits or a child who wants to share. I'm not picky; I'll take anything. I just can't go and take their food myself from the fridge or pantry. It's like there's an unseeable wall between me and the food. So scraps, trash, and handouts are my menu.

Though the gnawing in my stomach never truly goes away, when people are around I can eat enough to ignore it. But when the house is empty, I feel like I'm on a ticking clock. It's only a matter of time before the hunger becomes all I can think about, all I can feel. On a few occasions it's gotten so bad all I want to do is scream and scream so I feel anything besides hunger.

It's when I'm slowly losing my mind from hunger that I feel the least human. My humanity is always holding back a monster that wants to take control. I don't know where the monster came from, but I know I wasn't always this way. I also know that I need the Living and they have no idea.

I wonder if other ghosts have this problem. If there *are* other ghosts.

But seeing two young women exit the car and look up at the house—one grinning, one looking glum—my stomach and my interest are piqued.

Young people are always more clumsy with food. More scraps for me!

Replacing my belongings in the spot under the floorboard, I clutch my most precious possession, a red lacquer comb, and make my way to my vantage point on the staircase landing to see what these two will do.

You can tell so much about a person from the way they walk through the door for the first time.

Some people burst in with no regard for the souls going about their business behind the door. More than once I've been puttering around the living room trying to remember if I've stashed a morsel behind a loose baseboard or in the hall closet when someone blusters in and almost wrenches a few frantic beats out of my cold, dead heart!

Others come in and immediately start talking about what they're going to change. Paint this, tear down that, update everything.

But the woman who walks into my house this time is another kind. She looks around at my house like it's a treat. Tall, with shiny black hair that's cut at all sorts of jagged angles, broad shoulders, and long limbs, she fills the entryway with her excitement.

Also, can it be? Nobody who looks like me has ever lived in this house.

I inch down the stairs and lean over the banister to get a closer look at her.

Just as I get in close enough to see her long straight lashes and the smattering of freckles across her nose, she steps aside and there is a girl in her place. I can't help but stumble back.

I swear she looks right into my eyes. *Can she see me?*

The girl's gaze passes me in an instant, but I can't tear my eyes off her. She too has long limbs like the woman, but her body and features are round, chubby where the woman is all angles. She wears black denim shorts and a loose yellow tank top with what looks like a black cat silhouetted on it.

This girl looks like me. Not literally—my hair is very long and straight, while hers is shoulder-length and wavy; I'm short, she's quite tall; most everything about me from my frame to my nose to my mouth is small, but this girl could be imposing if there wasn't a shrinking quality about her. Like she's afraid the house might bite. And while my eyes—an exception to the architecture of my being—are big, dark brown ovals that take up a lot of space on my face, the girl's dark eyes are small, round, and piercing. All the same, I see myself in her.

Dozens of people have moved in and out of this house. I've examined so many faces, but none shared a hint of me in them. For my entire phantom existence on Charlotte Street, it always seems like everyone else has someone, *their people*, but I do not. There have been times I've not only wondered if I am the only ghost in the world, but if I'm also the only ghost with my eyes, my mouth, my nose, my skin, my hair.

But to see so much of who I am reflected back to me in the girl's face, her *being*, opens up a part of me. I may be the only ghost in this house, I may even be the only ghost in the whole world who looks like me, but out there, walking around in the world, are living people whom I share something with. It sounds so simple, and maybe for people who get to live out there, it's no big thing, but to me it's comfort. Maybe, outside this house, I belong somewhere.

Her gaze sweeps across the stairway and up the stairs. Something catches her eye and she moves toward the staircase. It's as if there's a weight on her. If a sigh came to life, it would look like this girl. I follow her gaze and see my comb sitting on a step. I must have dropped it while transfixed by her. She reaches for the comb.

The monster in me stirs. I spit out a growl.

No.

3
MOLLY

There *was* a comb. One of those old-fashioned Chinese lacquer combs you can buy in Chinatown. It was shiny and red and looked totally real. And it was right there on the landing.

But now it's gone.

Just as I was about to grab it, I got a blast of icy air in my face, a blast so strong my breath caught in my throat and I had to turn my head away. When I looked back, the comb was gone. It wasn't a hallucination, it wasn't my imagination—my hair was still settling when I opened my eyes.

I peer over the edge of the stairs to see if I accidentally knocked it over. No comb. I check behind me, thinking maybe I swept it down the stairs. No comb.

Looking up into the gloomy upstairs hallway, I feel my eyes straining, but there's nothing to see. Just the feeling that someone is staring back at me. A floorboard creaks from above and I squint.

"What are you doing?"

I jump when my mom speaks up next to me.

"Bah! Nothing. Looking. What are *you* doing?"

Mom cocks an eyebrow. "Uh, okay . . . as totally awesome as this staircase is, do you wanna tour the rest of the new abode with me?"

Squinting into the shadows one more time, I try to shake off the chills prickling my spine, and nod an "Okay" to my mom. Turning to walk down the stairs, I *know* I'm being watched.

At the door to the kitchen, I throw one more glance up the staircase. Is that a shadow leaning over the upstairs railing? I stop in my tracks, a knot tightening in my stomach. *It's just an old house with weird nooks and crannies that cast weird shadows and you're exhausted and hungry and—*

The shadow pulls back from the railing.

Something halfway between a groan and a squeak makes its way out of my nose. *Please not this house, please . . .*

"Molls? Don't you think?"

I snap back to my mom standing in the middle of the long, narrow kitchen. "What?" falls out of my mouth.

"I said, with all this counter space, we'll finally be able to make all those movie feasts we talked about. Are you okay? You look a little pale."

"I'm fine," I say, in a very not-fine croak, and try to look excited about the counter space. I have to admit the kitchen is pretty amazing. "Movie feasts" are when we've watched a movie like *Crazy Rich Asians* and want to try to make all the foods in, like, the night market scene—previously impossible in the single-burner kitchenettes we typically have.

But this kitchen looks all shiny and new, with poured concrete counters and sparkling white subway tiles. (The fridge alone looks like it costs as much as the rent on our last place—it has one of those dispensers for water and ice on the front!)

One end of the kitchen has a giant window that looks out to the street; in front of that window is a heavy-looking wood table, with four matching chairs. I run my hand over the smooth, cool table and relax a little. No zaps.

"Come on, let's check out that dining room—Molls, we have a dining room!—and while we're looking around, maybe we'll find an AC unit. It's like a furnace in here."

When I first walked into the house, the heat made my eyes water. But now, following Mom into the dining room, the sweat dripping down my back is icy, like I'm walking through the freezer section in a grocery store.

4

JADE

I follow the girl and the woman into the dining room. After the close call with my comb, I ran it upstairs to the safety of my attic before returning. I was pleased to hear them talking about "feasts" already.

I watch them examine the three square windows that look out to the backyard—once green with a little vegetable garden, now barren and patchy.

Across from the windows is a wall with dark wood built-in shelves. Nothing ornate, but everybody always marvels at them and all the possibilities. For the Living, this house is always full of possibilities.

"These are amazing!" the mother exclaims. "There's room for all our photos and treasures and then some."

Next to me, the girl briskly runs her hands up and down her arms, her mother's enthusiasm absorbed by the blackness of her mood. "It looks like where an old white lady would display her crystal chickens."

How did she know?

"Oh, good god, Molly—"

Molly.

"—are you really going to pull this moody teenager stuff now? We've got this big, beautiful house with these big, beautiful shelves. Can you just be nice to your mom and be excited for, like, thirty minutes? I promise after that you can egg my car or something."

This woman is her mother?

The girl—Molly—prickles. "Why does everything always have to be a joke? Dragging us thousands of miles from the only place I ever felt kind of normal isn't a joke!"

Molly heaves a frustrated sigh and stomps out of the room, across the hallway, and into the living room. I have to quickly hop out of her way so she doesn't walk through me. I hate it when that happens.

"Oh, come on, Molls! I'm just trying to lighten things up!" Her mother follows her, rolling her eyes, and I follow them.

We join Molly in the bright living room. Molly stands at the bay window with a built-in seat—one of the few parts of the house that predate me—cracking her knuckles. The snaps and pops make my flesh crawl—a very real sensation for me despite being devoid of actual flesh.

Her mother puts a hand on her shoulder but she shrugs it away. "Okay, yeah, you're mad. I get it. Bell Harbor was great, I know, but I promise Buckeye Creek is going to be great too—wonderful even! We're in a bigger city, there are more opportunities here, and most importantly we're near *family*. Please trust me, Molly. Team Teng forever?" she asks hopefully.

I move to peek at Molly's expression and notice her eyes flicker in my direction. Hope surges in me for a second, but her gaze remains unseeing.

Conflicting emotions battle across her dark eyes; she chews on the inside of her round, flushed cheek. "You never even talk to her," Molly says without turning around to look at her mother, her voice low and full like the lump in her throat might choke her.

Molly's mother moves around her and sits in the window seat. She gestures for Molly to sit next to her. Molly takes a step forward, but then thinks better of it and stays standing. "Well, that's kind of the point, isn't it? To fix things, to talk again. We've been so far apart, for so long, this could be the chance for us to figure stuff out and be a family again. With your grandparents gone, I worry about Bobbie. She's all alone; she doesn't have anyone on her team. I thought maybe we could add her to ours."

Who's Bobbie?

"Even though she hates you," Molly says, the vitriol behind her words freezing both me and her mother.

"Molly," her mother says with a sharpness I had yet to hear from her.

Molly softens and raises her eyes to her mother. "That was mean, I'm sorry. I get it, I really do, but it still doesn't change the fact that I didn't want to move."

Oh dear.

Her mother looks injured. "I thought you liked our adventures?"

An exasperated "Aaaargh!" escapes from Molly, accompanied by an enormous eye roll. She paces the room, the setting sun casting harsh angles of light and dark across her face and legs. "Adventures are when you backpack across Estonia or go cave diving in Cuba! Nobody wants *home* to be an adventure! Home is supposed to be reliable, easy, boring."

The mother furrows her brow in genuine concern. "You want our life to be boring?"

"Yes! Sometimes? It would be amazing to wake up and just *know* my own zip code, like a regular, *boring* person. I'm running out of space in my brain for new addresses!"

"Molly," her mother says, her good humor starting to unravel a little, "you have to understand that Bell Harbor just wasn't going to work long-term. If we're going to fix our family, if we're going to make our mark on this world, tiny Bell Harbor ain't it. I promise this is the right move."

Molly stops moving and levels her gaze at her mother. "And you're

20

telling me *Texas* in the conservative South is *it* for a Chinese American, never-married single mom who's a failed actress? Half the state doesn't even want us here—here being *America*."

If I wasn't already invisible, I'd want to disappear.

For a moment Molly's mother looks like she might cry, but instead she steels herself and goes to her daughter. They stand facing each other, the room vibrating.

"It's the *Southwest*, not the South. And for your information, there are, like, literally a million Asians in Texas. The haters can suck it. Look, I know this isn't easy, and it's kind of scary, but sometimes life is about running toward things that scare you. I've got a good feeling about this place, kid. Come on, Molly, I need you on my team. Who else do we have if we don't have each other?" She tiptoes into a smile, hoping Molly will follow.

"Mom." Molly speaks slowly. "I'm always on your team, forever and ever. But it doesn't always *have* to be you and me against the world. We can have a community; we can make plans that don't involve packing tape and boxes; hell, you could maybe go on a second date once in a while."

"*Hey,*" her mother says, this time with mock sharpness. She smiles reassuringly. "We'll make plans. I've already got so many plans for this house."

Molly's eyes don't hide her doubts, but she offers her mother an olive branch in a smile. "I just want to be normal."

"Normal is overrated." Then, taking a breath to clear the room and turn the page, she crosses to the giant front window and spreads her arms wide. "Just look at this! Can you believe we get to live here? It feels like we've accidentally moved into somebody else's life!"

Oh, the Living. It's my turn to roll my eyes.

5

MOLLY

She always does this. Just when I think I've got Dot Teng where I want her, she disarms me and sweeps me up into her fantasy world of big dreams and grand adventures. I would feel manipulated if I didn't think she believes everything she says. My mom is a lot of things, but she's not a liar. She sees everything as an opportunity. I see everything as something to be navigated. Maybe that's why everyone loves my mom and everyone feels uncomfortable around me—I'm the weird reality-check girl. Nobody likes reality.

Especially when that reality involves dead people's memories.

But I have to admit (aside from the staircase), this house is pretty uneventful so far. It definitely helps that it seems like almost every inch of this house has been newly redone to make it look kind of aggressively HAPPY. I'm not going to lie, it's a relief. I'm less likely to get zapped by new house parts.

We leave the living room and squeeze into the downstairs

bathroom under the stairs. It's also brand-new and spotless (the sink still has protective plastic on the faucets) except for a candy bar wrapper that's been shredded like an animal got to it and dropped between the wall and the toilet. Probably left by whoever installed the sink or something.

We wriggle out of the hot bathroom and into the cooler but still toasty hallway. "So, how can we afford this whole heckin' house with your meme money?" I ask.

"It's not *meme money*; you know I curate and execute a brand-forward content experience blah blah blah thingy for my clients."

"I've never understood what that means."

"It's a whole thing," she mumbles as she wipes the sweat from her face with her shirt. "This place might be big, but it's apparently hard to rent? People move out a lot. The owners let me have it for almost nothing."

"Why is it hard to rent? It looks like the owners put a lot of work into it." Mom starts to climb the stairs, but I hesitate.

She pauses on the third step. "I don't know, maybe it's because it's on a dead end? All I know is that the dudes made me sign this bizarre agreement where if we break the lease before the year mark, I can't disclose any issues with the house under penalty of lawyers eating my firstborn or something."

"*They made you sign an NDA?* And you did it?!" Something about signing a nondisclosure agreement for a house is extremely unsettling to me. "Mom! That's some straight-up murder house stuff!"

"I'm sure it's just something silly like the shed being over the property line or lead paint that hasn't been brought up to code." Mom waves me off and continues up the stairs. "Come on, there's three bedrooms up here. And there's got to be an air conditioner that works *somewhere.*"

"It's Texas. It's hot. *You* chose it," I call after her, but don't follow. I'm left alone looking up into the deepening shadows, the last fingertips of sunlight splitting the upstairs into brightness and black.

With all the newness around it, the staircase stands out as undoubtedly original to the house, the dark, heavy wood glowing from years of use. It doesn't seem to belong in this house anymore. All those hands that have come, gone, and clung to that railing over the years— the decades. Oof, that's a lot of zap potential.

I tell myself I'm being ridiculous, but my gut won't let my feet start up the stairs. The stairs lead somewhere I don't want to go. Don't ask me to explain that—there's just this major difference between the downstairs, all light and windows, and the upstairs. Upstairs, there's something waiting in the gloom.

6
JADE

I know she can't *see* me, but the way the girl's eyes search the crevices of the stairway, I wonder . . .

I slowly raise my hand and give a little wave. Nothing.

"Hello?" My own voice sounds strange and hollow after all this time alone. I know this is a pointless endeavor, but I try again, louder. "Hello!"

Nothing. Or maybe . . .

The girl remains unmoving, cautious. She stares at nothing, convinced there is something. She doesn't flinch or follow the sound of my voice with her eyes, but her brow furrows oh so slightly. Her lips part by a sliver.

Or am I imagining this? The thought that this girl could somehow, in some way, hear me is too frightening to believe and too tempting to ignore. I've believed people could hear or see me in the past, but it was usually a passing thing, if not a total misunderstanding. When you want so badly to be noticed, your mind plays tricks on you.

MOLLY

Geez, I am being such a baby.

Looking up the stairs into the recesses of the old house, it's like all the cells in my skin and eyes and ears have come alive and are shouting, *It's not what it seems!*

But what does it "seem"? I can't put my finger on it. There is nothing there, but again I feel my eyes straining to adjust to the dimness upstairs like the camera on my phone trying to focus. Focus on what, though?

The strain makes my eyes feel heavy, like I have rocks in my head. My stomach does a flip.

"Who's up there?" I mutter without thinking.

JADE

It seems like hours go by before the girl takes her first step onto the staircase, the second step creaking when it takes her full weight. Her hand reaches for the railing, but then as if thinking better of it, she returns it to her side. Slowly, carefully, the girl climbs the stairs, her eyes continually searching for something that ought not to be there.

Me. I ought not to be here. But here I am.

Her gaze is a magnet to me, but she can't see me. I've gotten very familiar with that searching look the Living send my way. Looking but not seeing.

She finally makes it to the top of the stairs and we stand mere feet from each other. Somehow, the hairs on my arm rise as if electrified. I didn't know I could do that! A gasp escapes my mouth.

MOLLY

The moment I get to the second floor, my skin springs up in goose bumps and I stifle a shiver. Why is it so dark up here? The light from the bedroom windows is just gobbled up by the shadows.

"Molls, is that you?" Mom calls from a room to my right. I stand alone, my eyes still searching.

Then there is a gasp. Clear as can be. Right in front of me. I freeze.

I glance toward the room Mom is in and then past it to a bathroom at the end of the hall. Nothing there. Looking to the left, there are four more doors—three of which are open. Two of the doors go to what look like bedrooms, one is a linen closet, and at the end of the hall there's a tall, skinny door with an antique doorknob and large keyhole under it. The attic, I'm assuming. This is the one door that's closed.

I've never lived in a home with a second floor, let alone a third. Cool. Kind of freaky, but cool.

There's nothing over on the other side of the hall, especially nothing that could gasp. I can't help but laugh to myself; I'm being so dramatic.

I take a step toward the room my mom is in and my eyes finally find the thing they've been searching for. Blocking my way, a darker shade of shadow rises before me. A shadow where there shouldn't be a shadow.

And there's that *feeling* again—the feeling of being looked at, scrutinized. *Is it tilting its head?! Does it even have a head?*

The air feels prickly around me, like a thousand tiny jellyfish are stinging my arms. I glance down reflexively and when I look back up it's my turn to gasp.

The shadow is leaning in, *inches from my face.*

"Molly?" Mom peeks her head out from the room. "You okay?" I see genuine worry flit across her face.

I exhale. The shadow is gone, like someone turned off a TV. Was it ever really there? The suffocating heat of the upstairs envelops me. My eyes relax. Is the hallway brighter? The only thing left is a headache.

"I'm good. Just taking in this giant, ridiculous house." *Be normal, Molly, be normal.* "So, uh . . . do we even have enough furniture to fill one room?"

Mom lights up. "Sure don't! But isn't this wild? Think of the possibilities. Part of the living room could be a studio for me. You have your own room now, we have a room for guests. It could be cowgirl themed! We're adulting now, kid!" She pops back into the room. Yes, of course, all those adults with *cowgirl guest rooms*, though I know she's thinking of one specific guest: Bobbie.

"You can hear yourself, right?" I say as I follow her into the room by the bathroom. I can't help but toss a look over my shoulder into the hallway.

The room is a big rectangle with robin's-egg-blue walls and two giant windows looking out past the dead end of the street to a patchy-but-grassy park beyond. What it lacks in view it makes up for in brightness. The whole room is bathed in early twilight gold.

"I'm going to pull the Mom Card and say this is my room." She grins, spinning in the middle of the room like the dancer she once was. "I should save up for a king-size bed."

"Go for it," I say. Honestly, this room feels overwhelming to me. "This whole room is almost as big as our Bell Harbor apartment."

"I know. Everything's bigger in Texas. Let's go pick out your room!"

We go down the hall to a smaller room opposite the stairs, next to Mom's room. It has a big window that goes almost all the way to the ceiling and the same robin's-egg-blue paint. There's another room across the hall that is a little bigger but has only one small window that is shaded by the neighboring house.

As silly as it sounds, I am sort of nervous about having my own room again, and the more light I can get, the better, so I take the room next to Mom's. This whole house feels like the shadows are just waiting to creep in.

After Mom gushes about the linen closet and how we should definitely acquire some legit linens, we make our way to the attic door at the end of the hallway. Mom tries the doorknob, but it's locked. "I think I have the key for this . . ." she says, patting her pockets.

The door is almost comically eerie. A darker gray-blue color than the other doors, the wooden boards are slightly warped and crooked. *Oh come on*, I think. *What Disney executive paid for this set piece?*

But even as I snark on the attic door, I know I can't go up there. Not yet. Every cell in my body is, like, NOPE.

"Um . . . I know this sounds weird but, uh . . . can we save the attic tour for later?" I ask, hoping my mom's adventurous spirit won't (again) make me go where no Teng has gone before.

She opens her mouth to object, then thinks better of it. "Yeah. I'm hungry anyway. Should we go choose our pizza?"

As we head down the stairs, I glance back toward the attic door. For a moment, I get that heavy feeling in my eyes again.

7
JADE

As unexpected as Molly and her mother are, I'm heartened by the life in my house again. They are a curious pair, but it's a welcome distraction from my own company. Plus, they are ordering pizza. Pizza means leftovers, crusts, and crumbs!

As the Tengs—as I've learned they're called—went back downstairs, Molly threw a glance over in my direction and I noticed an ever-so-slight pause. Could it be possible that this girl sees me? Some vague figure that resembles me? I need to capitalize on this opportunity to be seen, fed, or—hope against hope—heard, before they move out.

They all move out. Or die. Either way, there are boxes involved.

By now, most of the people who have lived here have died. Some in this very house! But I'm still the only ghost here.

I've tried so many times to get the attention of the Living, but even when they know I'm here they don't understand.

Kids are most likely to notice me. They're the ones who pay attention to a curtain billowing without a breeze, steps on the staircase, or a shadow out of the corner of their eye.

About forty years after I woke up in the box, Celia Lotkins noticed me.

Little Celia would play with her blocks on the landing between the first and second floors, spreading them out to make walls and crude castles. One day she built a tower of blocks and when I leapt over it— out of boredom, just to see if I could—her big blue eyes followed me up and over. She giggled and clapped her plump hands.

I ran up and down the stairs; I twirled circles around Celia; I waved at her while perched on the top-floor banister. Celia's eyes never left me as she squawked and pointed at me with glee. I stuck out my tongue and she grinned. She grinned *at me*!

I don't know if you can understand how thrilling it is to have someone smile at you after decades of being nothing but a "trick of the light." *Maybe I am still human!* I thought.

From then on, Celia became the closest thing I'd ever had to a friend, at least that I can remember. She couldn't hear me and I'm not sure what she saw when she "saw" me, but my presence made her happy. In turn she gave me back some version of a life. Granted, it was a life that revolved around a small child, but a confirmation of existence nonetheless!

I'd act out silly charades for her or we'd play hide-and-seek. I may have been thirteen (I'll forever be thirteen) and she five, but I loved nothing more than romping through the house with Celia. We would have continued on indefinitely, or at least until Celia grew up and moved out, but her parents started to worry.

It's always the parents who get in the way.

It started with Lorraine Lotkins noticing that Celia wasn't looking at the pictures in the book she was reading to her. Celia was looking at me. I'd been acting out scenes from a story about a witch, a girl, and a little dog too. Mrs. Lotkins closed the book and regarded her daughter. "Celia, sweetie, what are you looking at?"

Glancing from me to her mother, Celia answered, "It's just Evangeline with the long black hair. She acts out all the characters for us, Mama. Why don't you ever watch?"

From then on, Mrs. Lotkins discouraged Celia from mentioning "Evangeline." Whenever Celia's eyes wandered to me and we shared a secret snicker, Mrs. Lotkins would tap her on the hand or head and say, "What have we talked about, Celia?" With a deep sigh, Celia would reply, "There's no such thing as Evangeline."

The last time Celia saw me, or at least acknowledged seeing me, was when she was eight and came home crying one afternoon. Maisie, the girl next door, had teased her for being a baby and having an imaginary friend.

Mrs. Lotkins lifted her pencil-thin eyebrows and told Celia matter-of-factly, "Well, the only way to not be teased about having an imaginary friend is by not *having* an imaginary friend."

Something wavered in Celia, like a light going out. It was painful to watch. She hung her head and went up to her bedroom. I raced up the stairs behind her.

Sitting face-to-face on the round green rug that warmed the floor by her bed, Celia looked me in the eye with the mournful countenance of a person firing a beloved housekeeper or nanny.

"I'm sorry, Evangeline," she said. "You have to go away now." With tears falling down her cheeks, she stood up and walked away from me. She didn't look back.

Of course, I couldn't go anywhere. Celia simply chose to believe I did. People really like to think they can "release" spirits from places whenever they feel like it.

Celia never did see me again. Well, that's not true; maybe she could *see* me, she just never *looked* at me again. Now and then I'd catch her eyes dancing over in my direction when I walked past or flopped onto the sofa, but I was never sure if she was making the effort to ignore me or if I was just a rogue shadow that her eyes reacted to.

I became just a hazy piece of childhood memory to Celia Lotkins.

Something she might look back on with curiosity or even affection, but no more real than the Wicked Witch of the West.

Celia moved out when she was seventeen. Her family soon followed.

I suspect Celia is long dead, possibly a ghost now too. If she is a ghost, if such things actually exist and I'm not a special exception to some cosmic rule, I wonder if anybody can see her.

And I wonder if she remembers me.

8

MOLLY

After finally figuring out the wall-mounted AC units in the big bedroom, the guest room, and a corner of the living room, Mom and I order pizza from a place called Nash's Old-Fashioned Pies. It's on a three-page list of local restaurants, shops, and attractions that the house's owner typed up for us. On the first page is a handwritten note:

Hello, Dorothy and Molly!

Welcome to Charlotte Street. :) We hope you love your new home as much as we love it. Bradley and I felt so safe and cozy in the house, we just know you will too. We're just so excited to have y'all bringing some new energy to the house! If you have any questions or have a maintenance request, feel free to call or email anytime. And don't mind the attic, it's an old house and the boards like to moan and groan!

All the best,

Tómas

Wow. They are really laying it on thick. I've never lived in a place where the landlord wrote us a note, let alone one hoping "we love our new home." Maybe they really are desperate.

Mom and I unload our car as we wait for the pizza. It doesn't take long since we only have a bunch of boxes and bags, a couple of air mattresses, and no furniture. Nothing makes you feel like you don't belong like moving into a giant house with no stuff to put in it.

Mom runs upstairs to put her soaps and creams and shampoos in the bathroom, and I wander around the first floor again. The window in the living room looks straight out of the 1800s. The wooden bench is the same dark wood as the staircase, with little willow trees carved around the base. We've never had anything so *elegant* in our home before.

I know I should be careful, but it gets *so old* always having to tiptoe around antique things. Can't a girl just sit on a window seat?

I sit down tentatively on the polished wood of the bench and relax a little as it squeaks but nothing else happens. I lean back and let my hands catch my weight on the seat.

A current of energy surges through me. It knocks the air out of my chest as cold sizzles up my arms and into the back of my skull. The room turns bright and blurry as images swirl in front of my eyes.

Lots of voices. A floor-sweeping blue dress. "... they really must go."

"Look what you've done!" Anger. Fear. The sound of glass breaking, dim yellow light sparkling in the fragments. Ragged, rasping breaths fill my ears like they come from inside me.

The flash of a face with long hair, dark eyes, and pale skin. The kind of worry that ties my guts in knots.

My head snaps forward like I've been shoved from behind, and I find myself sprawled on the floor in front of the seat.

Welcome to Charlotte Street indeed. I've been zapped. The house zapped me.

My head throbs and I fight to steady my shaking hands. As far as zaps go, this wasn't that unusual. Not fun AT ALL and definitely makes me want to barf—but nothing that weird. Except . . .

Except there are tears flowing from my eyes. I have no idea why. It's like feeling an echo of some intense emotion, but I can't quite touch it. It's lingering. I feel like I've been kicked in the ribs.

Normally when I get zapped it's a lot to deal with, and my brain feels like it's run a marathon, but other people's feelings don't really stick around. It's more like I'm being shown what they felt—happy, sad, terrified. But once I snap out of it, the movie is turned off. I'm drained and spacey for a while but all I feel are my own feelings.

This time is different and it's freaking me out. Something got under my skin.

As I'm staring at the bench wondering if it's some sort of portal to another dimension or something (OF COURSE we would live in a portal house if that's real), the doorbell rings. It's the pizza.

"Molls, can you get that? It's already paid for!" Mom calls from upstairs.

For a second I consider just saying "Screw it" to the pizza and continuing to lie on the floor trying not to hurl, but if I did that my mom would get all worked up over my zap. Being the dutiful daughter, I drag my butt off the floor to open the door for the pizza delivery person.

While Mom has gotten really good at taking care of my post-zap symptoms—the barfyness, the spacing out, the out-of-body feeling of it all—she really hates acknowledging the zaps. She knows it happens, she knows what it is, but she won't talk about it. I think it scares her. I think it might be the *only* thing that really scares her.

And that kind of scares me.

9

JADE

I have a multitude of questions.

Did she see me in the hall?

Did she *hear* me in the hall?

What happened in the living room?

All I know is that she looked so ill standing there embracing a pizza box, I leaned in to make sure she was okay. While I don't exactly "breathe" the way the Living do, respiration is an old habit and some-times when I'm nervous I still hold my breath. While I was inches from Molly, examining her, I realized I was holding my breath, so I exhaled and watched the wispy hairs around her face gently lift.

She exhaled too and seemed to relax a little, the corners of her mouth sliding up the tiniest bit.

For a moment we seemed to breathe together. Could she possibly have felt my breath on her face? I've never affected someone like that before.

The moment was broken when her mother appeared. Molly snapped to and looked around, confused, a little wild-eyed, but didn't say anything. Taking the pizza from her, her mother carried it into the kitchen and began digging around in a cardboard box.

Following them into the kitchen, I ponder what this could possibly mean for me. In the span of an afternoon I've gone from a figment of people's imagination to a bona fide presence. At least to one living girl. I've never particularly wanted to be a scary ghost, but for now I'll take acknowledged and spooky versus unseen and polite.

But I need to conduct some tests. I need to discern the limits of Molly's abilities. The prospect of a project, something to fill my brain with purpose, thrills me.

Molly sits at the table and her mother fishes mismatched plates out of the box. I'm delighted that they chose Nash's Old-Fashioned Pies. They always use so much cheese it gets everywhere, and there will be whole globs left over for me.

While Molly's mother chatters about couches and something called the "Discount Rodeo," Molly appears to be only half listening. No better time than the present to start my experiment. I decide to start simple, with the obvious.

"Hello, Molly!" I call out as loud as seems reasonable. No response. I try again a little louder. "Hello!"

Molly continues to stare into the middle distance, chewing on her lip, lost in thought. I need to break into those thoughts, get her attention.

I gather the energy to nudge a plastic water bottle on the kitchen table. It tilts over and Molly absent-mindedly reaches over to right it. I suppose a fallen water bottle isn't exactly a haunted house horror.

Molly's mother puts a ceramic plate near the edge of the counter while she digs deeper into the box. I take the opportunity to lift it up, holding it in midair for just a second, before dropping it. It crashes to the floor and shatters.

Molly's mother curses and Molly chides her mother for not being careful, but neither of them seems the least bit troubled. I suppose a broken plate is a nonevent to clumsy people.

I stomp around the room, wave my hands in front of Molly, lean my face right up to hers again. Nothing this time. Not even a blink.

I plop down on the floor for a moment to think. What was different about the other times?

Moving objects always drains me a little. I'd blustered all around the kitchen and no living soul was the wiser. During the encounter by the door and in the upstairs hallway, everything had been quieter—tuned in.

Could it be that simple?

I go and stand near Molly. She gazes right through me.

Clenching my fists, I pull as much energy as I can to myself and focus on Molly. I imagine a pale light starting at my toes and growing all the way up to my head. A low hum fills my ears like electricity building. Keeping my focus, I take a deep breath and shout one short word.

"Molly!"

Molly sits bolt upright in her chair. Eyes wide.

1Ø

MOLLY

Will I ever feel comfortable in this big old house? It seems like every time I turn around, something is trying to get my attention. Is this what having a puppy or a toddler feels like?

The first night in the house (after the staircase, window-seat, and kitchen incidents) was . . . fine. We ate the extra-large pizza with extra cheese, peppers, onions, jalapeños, and anchovies—our favorite—in the living room fort while watching movies until late. Every time the house creaked or the air conditioner kicked on, I jumped a little bit and did a quick scan of the room. I'm not exactly sure what I was looking for, but I couldn't help but be on guard for any otherworldly surprises. Mom kept asking if I was okay and I kept telling her I was. I know she doesn't want to hear about spooky things and I don't really feel like talking about it.

We dragged our tiny air mattresses into our respective rooms and said good night around two o'clock in the morning. Mom asked me if

I wanted to sleep in her room with her, since that's what I'd been used to for so long in our studio apartments, but I didn't want to give in to my nerves and get in the habit of sleeping *with my mommy* no matter how nervous I am.

At first I try to fall asleep listening to my favorite podcast about crows, but after spending the day listening so hard to all the sounds, I really crave silence. So I turn off my podcast, close my eyes, and wait. That's another problem: Silence means hearing every little thing.

But I need to sleep. Tomorrow, Mom wants to get up at a reasonable hour and find real mattresses, buy groceries, and maybe get a couch for us. It is going to be a whole day of running around and if I don't get some sleep I will have no patience for the Dot Teng Experience.

But you know what's worse than hearing the scary thing? It's waiting to hear the scary thing. Every time I start to doze off, a motorcycle or car rumbles by in the distance and my eyes fly open, sure there's *something* glowering at me from the dark.

I try the slow breathing exercises Dr. Sardee in Brooklyn taught me. Breathe in for five seconds, exhale for eight seconds. Inhale for six seconds, exhale for nine seconds. Seven seconds in, ten seconds out, and so on.

I concentrate on breathing and feel my heart slow and the muscles in my neck uncoil a little. Closing my eyes, I try to rationalize all that has happened to me today. In my world, the easy answer here is "a ghost," but I really, really want a less horror-movie way to explain it. This is what I come up with:

1. Exhaustion. I've been in the car for days with my mom. That would mess with anybody's head.

2. Faulty wiring. The internet says there's a thing called a "fear cage" where you think you're dealing with ghosts when actually there's, like, electromagnetic energy or microwaves or something flying through the air and therefore your brain tricks you into feeling spooked.

3. Maybe it was a fluke. Just my normal (if you can call them normal) zaps, only more intense because nobody has been in the house for a while. Like building up a static electricity charge that needs to be released.

I am feeling pretty good about my list, my heart slowing down to almost sleepy rhythms, when a sound makes me perk up again. My heavy eyelids pop open and blood surges through my veins to my head and hands. All five foot eight inches of me tenses, waiting for another sound. I don't have to wait long.

Thwap! A sharp slapping sound slices through the silence of the house.

Shhhh-ccccrrrreeeep. A scraping sound follows. I take a gulp of warm, stale air and consider what to do next.

Then I hear, clear as can be, a hacking cough outside my bedroom door.

"Mom?"

Nothing.

"Mom? Is that you?"

Nothing at all.

Just let it go, just let it go, just let it go. I will myself to close my eyes and accept this all as just another part of this fever dream of a house. But I can't let it go. I crawl off my air mattress and toward the door.

Sitting on my knees by the door in my giant University of Hawai'i Rainbow Warriors T-shirt, I reach for the doorknob, turning it as slowly as I can to crack open the door.

There is nothing. Faint yellow light comes up through the stairway from the streetlights out front, allowing me to just barely make out the railing, the top few steps, and the linen closet across the hall. My mom's gentle snoring drifts out into the hallway from the gap under her bedroom door.

I'm turning back into my room when movement in the fuzzy blackness catches the corner of my eye. At first I think I'm seeing things, like how if you stare at something long enough in the dark it looks like it's moving. But there is no mistaking it: The attic door is closing.

The same attic door that was locked earlier in the day.

Now there is definitely someone closing it from the other side.

No, no, no, no, no. My head is buzzing and my hands are frozen.

I am not breathing. Afraid I might pass out, I let out a big exhale but stop midway.

Despite the oppressive Texas heat, my breath hangs in the air, a milky cloud, like it did on winter days in Maine. An icy cold creeps from the direction of the attic. Without thinking, I whisper into the dark, "Hello?"

The door pauses. *Whatever is on the other side of the door heard me.*

Each of us is waiting to see what the other will do.

Not wanting to find out who is surely hearing my heart beat out of my rib cage, I pull my door shut, shove my backpack against it, and dive under the covers, my air mattress squeaking in protest as it skids across the floor.

11
JADE

A chunk of pizza crust lodged in my throat. That sometimes happens when I haven't eaten any real food for a while; my throat shrinks. Another reason why I tend to stash food around. I'm afraid if I go too long without even nibbling on something, my throat will get so small that I'll never be able to stretch it out again. I'll starve and become the monster.

After spending some time digging through Molly and her mother's leftover pizza—thank goodness for lazy people who just leave pizza boxes out in the open—I dragged myself upstairs to doze in my attic for a while.

But that confounded crust wouldn't go down my throat, so I found myself coughing as I walked through the dark house. Finally, with one big, forceful hack in the upstairs hallway, the pizza crust flew out of my throat. Though I wanted to find it—I'm not one to waste even a morsel of food—I heard someone stirring in the bedroom down the hall.

I crept through the dark. I started to close the attic door, pausing when I thought I heard a noise, before pulling it firmly shut. Climbing the stairs, I heard a door close, then a thud. I just about popped out of my skin.

These people! Will I ever have peace again?

12

MOLLY

". . . gotta be something better than this, there's gotta be something better to do . . ."

Before I open my eyes, it almost feels like a normal Team Teng morning. Mom in the shower belting out show tunes, me still in bed *wishing* she wasn't in the shower at—I crack an eye open to look at my phone—7:07 a.m. belting out show tunes. No matter where we move, there are constants: Mom rises early, Mom sings loud, Mom will come over and sing AT ME to get me out of bed if I don't do it myself.

I let out a huge sigh and open my eyes. *Fine, I'll be awake.*

The room is bright, bare, and foreign. Since there are no curtains on the windows, the morning sun feels inappropriately cheery, filling every inch of the room with heat and light. I already feel the sweat gathering in the folds of skin on my back and around my pits. Fun.

I roll off my air mattress and heave myself to my feet. Stepping out into the shadowy hallway, I am surprised by how much cooler it is. Without even thinking, my eyes travel to the attic door. I can't fight the goose bumps that pop up despite the sweat dripping down my back.

The door is closed, just like we left it. Just like it should be.

Did last night even really happen? It all feels far away—the cough outside my room, the attic door closing. It was probably just my sleep-deprived brain messing with me. My stomach whines and I'm not sure if it's from hunger or from the knots that are bumping around in there.

Surprisingly, I don't have a lot of experience with actual hauntings. I mostly just get zapped. And I really have no interest in finding out more about *the afterlife*. As far as I'm concerned it is what it is when we die—living is too complicated for me to worry about ALL THAT. So whoever or whatever is out there, I hope they're picking up on my big "not interested" energy.

I head downstairs in my pajamas to munch on some cold pizza for breakfast. I know some people think it's gross, but I almost prefer cold next-day pizza to fresh pizza. Thumping down the stairs, I pass the front door and, yawning, shuffle into the kitchen.

Weird.

The huge pizza box that Mom and I left out last night because it was too big to fit in the fridge is partially ajar and hanging halfway off the counter.

I walk over and lift the lid. The portion of pizza we left last night appears mostly untouched except . . . it looks like a piece is missing?

Huh. I clearly remember that exactly half the giant pizza was left. It was unusual that we didn't make more of a dent in it.

Inspecting the rest of the kitchen, I find no other evidence of middle-of-the-night snacking. In fact the counter and floor are totally devoid of crumbs. Very unlike Dot Teng to leave no trace. The hairs on my arms rise up for what seems like the hundredth time since moving in.

But what am I freaking out about? A clean kitchen? Mom probably just got up to gnaw on some pizza before she showered. I hear her coming down the stairs.

"Hey, Molls?" she says as she comes into the kitchen.

"What's up?"

"It's fine if you eat upstairs, but can you not just throw your left-overs on the floor? I found this in the hallway by your room. Let's maybe not be total trash pandas in this new place."

She holds up a chunk of pizza crust between her thumb and pointer finger. I can see teeth marks in it.

The events of last night come barreling back into my head and all of a sudden I put together what logically couldn't have happened but somehow definitely did.

The missing pizza slice, the *spooky* lack of crumbs, the crust chunk in my mom's hand: Someone—or some *thing*—had been munching on our leftover pizza, brought it upstairs, then *coughed it up outside my door.*

I feel all the blood drain out of my face.

"Molly? Babe? You look like you're going to barf."

13
MOLLY

Mom and I spend most of the day looking at stuff for the house. Sometimes shopping with my mom can be fun. She's like a magician pulling rabbits out of a hat—if the rabbits were clearance rack surfer cat pajamas. But today my heart just isn't in it.

We've barely lived in Buckeye Creek for a day and I already feel like this place doesn't want us. I mean, I don't really believe in omens, but something about walking into your new house and getting zapped, goose bumped, and shouted at by a disembodied voice doesn't really make you feel welcome.

As we walk the aisles of dusty discount stores, all I can think about is how stuck I am. Stuck in the house, stuck in Texas, stuck doing whatever Dot Teng wants to do, as usual.

When I was younger I used to wonder if she was actually my sister just pretending to be my mom because our real mom had to go to Neptune on a secret Space Asians Mission. At least if Dot Teng was my sister, the resentment might make more sense?

We're at this stuffy furniture warehouse called the Discount Rodeo when Mom stops to look at a low wooden coffee table with roses carved on the legs. As she talks at me about the "ren faire vibes," my blood starts to boil.

The anger I've bottled in the name of being supportive of my mom comes bubbling back up, and before I can find it in me to shove it down again I snap, "I don't care what table we get!"

Mom cocks her head at me. "Is something wrong?"

"Of course!" I yell, and stomp away to the mismatched chair section, arguably the most depressing corner of any discount furniture store.

Of course. This is the refrain I've been thinking my whole life.

Of course I'm the dork with the cool mom who everybody loves but nobody has to live with.

Of course I'm always the new kid.

Of course I always stick out as not only the new kid but *also* the Asian Girl. This isn't always a big deal, but when it is, *it is*. It's a very distinct feeling to be singled out not by name but by your race.

And of course, *the biggest of course*, is the fact that I'm the ghost girl. The zombie girl. The girl who isn't quite right. Tears burn my eyes. I feel so pitiful, standing there crying in front of all the lonely chairs, that even more tears fill my eyes and spill over in torrents.

"Molly, love, what's going on?" Mom creeps up behind me but keeps her distance.

"Nothing. It's fine. Go get your table."

"Things are obviously not fine. Talk to me? Please?"

I take deep breaths and try to loosen up my throat so when I speak I don't sound like I'm being strangled.

"I'm not your mascot," I manage to say in the most measured tone I can muster.

"My mascot? I'm sorry, you're going to have to catch me up because I still don't know what's going on. I mean, it's fine—I'm cool being the crying Asian ladies with the chairs. Constance Wu will play me in our movie."

And just like that I am even more furious.

"Can you go thirty seconds without making a joke? I know you think it's cute but it's really condescending. I'm not your pal, I'm not your 'adventure buddy,' I'm your daughter, and it would be really great if you could just be a *mom* for once in your life!" The tears flow down my cheeks, under my chin, drip under my shirt and onto my chest.

"I'm still lost. I thought we were having fun?" Mom sounds genuinely hurt.

"You always think we're having fun! Do you really think it's fun

58

always being confused and broke and having all eyes on you? Actually, I bet you love it—you get to be the center of attention!"

"Now wait just a second, Molly, you have no idea—"

I can't listen to her excuses. "No! You always just *decide* what's best for us, but you never *ask me*. If we really are 'Team Teng,' shouldn't I get a say?"

Her eyes are black and her jaw sets. Her voice comes out low and soft—never a good sign. "Okay. Tell me what you want."

"I want to go back to Bell Harbor!" I yell. I wonder when the Discount Rodeo management is finally going to do their job and escort us out. "Living there was the closest I ever felt to normal. Do you know how amazing it feels to be just another kid? But no, you couldn't bother to talk to me about our thousandth move. You just *informed* me. Maybe that's the only parental thing you do. You just tell me what to do." Yikes, maybe that was going too far. I see her flinch at that one.

But I can't stop now.

"I'm just so unhappy and I'm so stuck and I'm so scared. I don't want to be the I See Dead People Zombie Girl again! Nobody wants to be that girl, Dot!"

Uh-oh. She hates it when I talk about dead people. And she really hates it when I call her Dot. HATES IT.

"WATCH IT!" she snaps. "We're not having this conversation in the misfit chair section of the Discount Rodeo. Get in the car *now*." She throws me the keys. "I'll be right out."

Tears blurring my eyes, I stalk past her and out the front door to our car. Even with the windows down I roast in the unrelenting heat of the Texas sun. The heat comes from all sides—the sky, the concrete of the parking lot, the oven of the car, and from the rage that roils off me.

Mom staggers out of the Discount Rodeo dragging that Medieval Times–looking coffee table with her. She shouts at me to open the trunk, then slams the table into the back with the other random crap we acquired today. She bungee cords the door down and climbs in on the driver's side. Her expression is stormy, her eyes slightly red.

We drive home in silence, both of us preparing for the next round.

14
JADE

Molly and her mother went out for the day so I finally had some time to sit in the quiet of my house. They haven't even been here for a full day and it feels as if it's been weeks!

Some people move in an orderly fashion—boxes labeled BEDROOM or KITCHEN, a plan for all their furniture. Others have so many belongings that their lives just seem to explode everywhere. But Molly and her mother are an interesting hybrid: They have so little but their presence is so big.

In the living room, mismatched pillows and a couple of blankets make up what they called a "pillow fort" last night. They propped a laptop on a box and watched movies together. By the end of the night, mother and daughter lay curled up side by side, lit only by the glow of the laptop screen. I watched them from the murk of the hallway.

The gulf between my life and death felt bigger than ever.

I don't remember my mother, but I know I had one. It's as if I know the memories are there, but I just can't reach them. I don't remember my mother hugging me, but I know she did. I don't remember my mother brushing my hair out of my eyes, but I know she did. I don't remember my mother telling me she loved me, but . . .

Then it dawns on me: Molly can see *and* hear me. If Molly will talk to me, pay attention to me, maybe she can help me figure out who I am? There has to be some clue about me out there somewhere. If I can just learn a little bit about myself, I'm sure I could crack open the door to my memories.

I trot into the kitchen to snack on some more pizza and contemplate this idea.

With great concentration, I lift the lid to the box and take a crust. I don't want to frighten Molly yet again, so I try to be tidy. But as I stand gnawing on the cold, chewy bread, I change my mind. With a great burst of energy, I push the pizza box off the counter.

If Molly is going to help me, first she has to acknowledge that I exist. She knows something is going on, and whether she likes it or not, I need her to admit that her house is haunted.

I am putting the finishing touches on an "eerie pile of junk" in Molly's room when I hear the front door slam and footsteps run up the stairs.

Exhausted from planting "ghost evidence" around the house all afternoon, I was looking forward to retiring to my attic for a rest when Molly bursts into her room and slams the door.

Her face crumples and tears fall down her chubby cheeks as she slides to the floor, her back to the door. Despite my distaste for the drama that the Living seem so fond of, I can't help but feel sorry for Molly.

The front door slams again and Molly's mother calls out, "Molly! Where are you? We need to talk." We hear her move around the downstairs before the weight of her footsteps makes the stairs creak. We hear her on the other side of the bedroom door.

"Molly, can I come in?" The mother's usual playful, musical quality is not there. Instead she sounds like most of the mothers I've seen over the years. Serious, measured.

Molly doesn't answer. "Molly, please." The doorknob rattles.

"No!" Molly cries, and grabs the doorknob in her hand to still it. "This is *my* space in here and I at least get a say on who comes in."

The floorboards on the other side of the door squeak and there's the soft thud of her mother seating herself on the hallway floor. "Fine, we'll talk this way. But we're talking."

With everyone seated on the floor, I sit down too, a couple of feet away from Molly. I think about finding a tissue or handkerchief to hand to her, but remember that a floating hankie might not be what she needs right now.

"I wish I'd known exactly how angry you were about this move." Her mother's voice comes in clear from the sizable gap under the door. "But, Molly, I'm not a mind reader."

Molly bristles. "You're right, you're not a mind reader, *I am*. I mean, I read the minds of dead people, why can't I read yours? And maybe you would have known how much I didn't want to leave Bell Harbor if you had asked."

Seeing the tumult of feelings that cross Molly's face, I suddenly feel very bad about my haunting hijinks.

"I'm sorry you're hurting, but I'm not going to apologize for making decisions that I think are best for us. Let me tell you, kid, that's the hardest thing about being in charge, making sure this little world I've created for the two of us doesn't shatter."

Molly rubs her eyes and takes a deep breath before speaking. "But that's exactly it. You think that by moving us all over the place in search of better things, you're making our world bigger, when in fact you're shrinking it down to just you and me."

"I've always kind of liked it just you and me," her mother says gently.

"I love you and me too," Molly starts. "But sometimes I feel like you want it to be the Dot and Molly Show forever. Maybe you don't need more than this—us—but I'd love to build a world with you *and* friends *and* a school that I go to for more than a year *and* be part of a community."

Dot is silent for a long while. Both Molly and I watch the door, the tension growing with every second. I'm surprised at how invested I am. I know they are arguing, but in this moment I feel such jealousy. Did my mother and I ever argue like this?

When her mother finally speaks, her voice is heavy. "I'm doing my best, Molly. Really I am. But I guess I've been a little one-sided with things, I can admit that."

I scoot closer. Molly and I now sit side by side, the two of us leaning into her mother's words.

We hear her take a deep breath. We lean in closer. The smell of living wafts off Molly—tears, deodorant, perspiration. I take a moment to still myself; I think about moving away so I don't make her breath puff out in clouds. It's not the time for that.

"I hear you, I really do, but—" Dot sighs and her frustration seems to seep under the door. "You have to understand that we can't just up and leave Buckeye Creek, this house, this lease. We can't afford it. At least not yet. So here's what I'm willing to do."

Molly cocks her head, her brows raised.

"It's the beginning of July now. We give it until the end of October— let's say Halloween. If things still suck for you by then, we'll go back to Bell Harbor."

"Really?!"

"NO!"

Molly and I speak simultaneously, my "No" notably being heard only by me.

Her mother continues, "But you've got to really try to make this work, Molls. Seriously. No moping around for the next few months acting like this is a prison sentence. If you don't give Buckeye Creek an honest try, I swear I'll lock you in the attic and homeschool you until you're twenty-three. Got it?"

Molly rolls her eyes, but I can see her melting. "What about Bobbie?" she asks.

Who is this Bobbie?

Silence.

"Mom?"

"I'll worry about Bobbie. It'll be fine," Dot says too quickly, her voice tight.

Molly nods to herself, understanding something I don't. She sits very still, her hands in her lap, her eyes on her hands. She's turning a decision over in her head.

They can't leave! In a little more than three months I have to get a girl who refuses to acknowledge me to pay attention to me, then help me . . . do what? I don't even know yet. To me, three months is the blink of an eye.

My head begins to hum. A growl trembles deep in my belly.

Molly looks up and says, "Okay, I'm in," and reaches for the door-knob. *No!*

The growl tumbles out of my throat and I also reach for the door-knob. I'm not sure if it's me trying to stop Molly from leaving or the monster afraid for its food source.

Molly's head whips around—she heard the growl!—just as our hands simultaneously touch the doorknob.

For an instant, it's as if my bones are on fire.

15
MOLLY

A small bed in a mostly empty room.

A scream bouncing off the exposed beams of a wooden ceiling.

Blackness. A scratching sound. A musty sweet smell.

A woman reading a book to a little girl.

A window with antique wavy glass; something red and slick and cool sliding through my fingers.

I only touched the doorknob for a few seconds, but in those seconds I felt and saw giant icebergs of somebody else's life, hinting at something huge and daunting under the surface.

Shrouding all the images that tumbled through my head is the overwhelming feeling of loneliness. No, loneliness isn't enough of a word. It's *longing*. Waves of it crash down on me. I long for something or someone I've lost.

And I am hungry. Starving. The need for food wraps around me like a thorny blanket. I feel wild, like I could chew the flesh off my own bones. Whose messed-up memory did I discover?

Falling back, my hand pulls the door open and I crumple into a pile as my mom rushes to my side. My heart races, my hands tremble. Before I can stop myself, a big open-mouth howl tumbles out of me. It starts in my stomach, rips through my chest, fills my throat, and is released into the house.

Collapsing into my mom, I howl until I think I might throw up. And then I do. The wail quickly shrinks to a sob, then a whimper. I wonder if our neighbors can hear us: those weird screaming Asians. I hope we don't hear sirens in a minute.

The mourning feeling finally starts to trickle away and I lift my head to look up at my mom. She looks down at me, her long hair falling like curtains around our faces, making a "hair fort" that surrounds us. Her shampoo smells so good. Mom used to hide us in the hair fort when I was little and scared to go to sleep in the dark.

"Hey," she says. "That was a rough one, huh?"

I nod. She always knows a zap when she sees it. She puts her forehead on mine and we breathe together for a little bit.

"My pits are sweaty, how 'bout yours?"

I take inventory of my armpits. Yep, sweaty. I nod again.

"Mine feel slippery. What do yours feel like?"

I wiggle my arms a little. "Squishy," I say.

"Gross," Mom says, and smiles. "Texas smells like old window screens. What do you smell?"

I take a few deep breaths. "I smell peppermint shampoo, BO . . . and barf. Sorry."

"Hey," Mom says, and bumps my head gently, shaking the hair fort walls. "Some of the greatest times of my life have involved barf and BO. This one time in college—"

"Okay, okay," I grimace. "Let's keep it PG."

"You're of age, I can get as PG-13 as I want, daughter."

"No you cannot, parent."

Mom rolls her eyes and raises the walls of the hair fort. A cold breeze blows through the room—it must be the air conditioner, right?—and brings us back into reality.

Sitting up, I see my mom can barely hide her fear. I can only imagine what I look like. Despite how frustrating the last couple of days have been, I'm really glad to have Dot Teng as my mom.

"I'm okay, really," I croak unconvincingly.

"What did it this time?" she asks. "I'm so sorry, Molls, I really thought since the owners had redone everything, there wouldn't be anything to . . . you know . . ."

"No, no . . . it wasn't . . ." I trail off as I remember the doorknob. *I've already touched it lots of times. Why now?*

Then I remember the growl, hot on my neck just before the zap. This was different.

"It was a . . . a random zap; sometimes it happens," I tell her, trying to sound like I'm telling the truth. Mom doesn't look convinced. "It's just been a while since I was zapped," I lie again. "Plus, I'm tired and with all the stuff today . . ."

Mom starts to ask more questions, but I cut her off.

"I'm sorry we fought," I say, changing the subject. "I like the plan. Until Halloween. Go team." And I give my mom a weak thumbs-up. She smiles, clearly relieved on all levels.

"I'm sorry we fought too. I promise, whatever comes next is going to be good."

I nod, trying hard to believe her.

Mom takes a huge breath and tries to look unruffled. "Okay. This is what we're gonna do: We're gonna clean you up, we're gonna clean me up, I'm gonna haul that stuff in from the car, and then I'm going to make, like, a million scallion pancakes and we're going to eat every last one of them. Yeah?"

I nod. "I can help."

"Just go hop in the shower and I'll do the rest." She stands up and offers a hand to pull me up too. I hesitate.

"I'll walk you to the bathroom and make sure nothing happens between here and the shower, okay?" she asks, reading my mind.

While I am still angry over having no say about leaving Maine, I can't help but feel real affection for my mom. Nothing seems to faze her—not moving, not uprooting our lives, not starting over and over and over again—and sometimes it's pretty great to have a mom who can watch her daughter basically get possessed by an inanimate object and not have a meltdown herself.

The shower feels so good and erases the goose bumps that cling to my skin. And while I start to feel better, I can't get the doorknob out of my head. I leave the bathroom and head to the kitchen, but I stop at the top of the stairs. I have to know.

Turning, I go through the open door in my bedroom and grab the doorknob before I chicken out.

Nothing.

16
JADE

In the safety of my attic I sprawl across the warm floorboards, tears soaking into the old wood, then vanishing. In the few seconds that Molly and I touched the doorknob at the same time, she tore something out of the depths of me. The monster emerged.

Molly and I both heard it! It's my greatest fear that one day, when this house falls down or it's condemned and nobody moves in to cook their meals or spill their food, the monster, with nothing else to eat, will consume me.

I crawl over to the loose board under the window and lift it open. Feeling around in the space underneath, I pull my treasures out and lay them before me. I run my fingers over my comb.

For as long as I've been haunting this house, I've been like a crow, stealing shiny treasures from the Living. A hairpin here, a button there, a piece of ribbon. Pretty little trinkets of life that have been forgotten by everyone but me. I can't grab big things like a book or a roast chicken, but small things—the crumbs—are mine for the taking.

I lie on the attic floor, rubbing my thumb across the comb's smoothness, and let myself cry, like a girl, not a monster. As much as I love seeing families in this house, and sometimes I can almost pretend they are mine, there are always the moments that remind me that no amount of wishing will make me belong to them.

Why did these two have to move into my house and turn my existence upside down? I could have really gone for another couple like Bradley and Tómas. They lived here for almost a decade and left about a year ago. They quietly read their books, did repairs, and held hands as they watched history programs on the television set.

Watching stories with Bradley and Tómas was the first time I really connected people and places to words like *Asian, oriental, Japanese, alien, yellow, Chinese.* I'd heard these words used over the years, sometimes with anger or disgust, but I'd never fully comprehended how I was a part of it. We watched shows about American history, and on the screen I occasionally saw images of people who looked like me. There were Chinese people who were chased down and killed; Japanese people who were imprisoned. People who looked like me were separated into categories of "good" and "bad." Seeing the things that transpired outside my door for all these years, I can't help but wonder how I got here.

I lie on the floor, turning over the comb. As if on cue, my stomach growls and I remember the "million scallion pancakes." No matter how distraught I am, the promise of food in the house comforts me. I'll stave off the monster inside me for a little longer.

Unless Molly somehow summons it again.

17

MOLLY

While I've come to a temporary peace with Mom, the house—or whatever is in the house—continues to be anything but peaceful.

After my shower, I felt wary but calmer. That is, until I came downstairs while Mom was in the shower and found the pizza box flung across the kitchen, the top cracked open.

For a second my heart started to pound again and my hands got clammy, but then I took a step back. Some *thing* is definitely messing with me.

In that moment I went from being scared to being mad. After years of dealing with attention-starved objects, dead-people memories, and zaps, I am in no mood to let a cranky old house with its needy old ghosts get the best of me. It can barf attack me all it wants, but I am not going to let it make me miserable. I am done with this ridiculousness!

Standing taller, I walked over to the pizza box and picked it up.

That electric feeling started to travel up my fingers, which was totally unexpected because to the best of my knowledge it was not an *antique* pizza box. But instead of letting it freak me out, I tossed the pizza box on the counter and said, "Not today, Ghosty!"

Thus began my great experiment: "Operation What If I Was Normal?" which is really "Operation Ignore, Ignore, Ignore."

Obviously I'm being very mature. Or maybe this is what all adults actually do when they get spooked. Ignore, ignore, ignore.

Of course the house isn't going down without a fight.

In the weeks following the doorknob zap there's been the "usual" haunted house stuff like footsteps where there should be none, lights turning on and off, and items getting moved around. Just yesterday I found half a jelly doughnut tucked into the corner of the downstairs coat closet that made my fingers tingle, and every night someone knocks on my bedroom door at two o'clock in the morning. The first couple of times I groggily opened the door thinking that maybe my mom needed me, but there wasn't anybody there. There never is. Or at least I don't look hard enough to find out.

I know Mom notices some of the haunted-house goings-on too, but I think she tries her best to look the other way so I don't panic (and neither does she).

A couple weeks after I took my stand against the pizza box, Mom and I are arranging her new bed frame and mattress in her bedroom when a pen on her desk flies across the room and lands on the bare mattress.

Mom and I stop shoving the bed around. We look at the pen, we look at each other, we look at the desk. There is no living person around who could have thrown that pen. So we keep arranging the bed, talking about the curiosity that is the Texas fast-food chain Whataburger.

What I don't tell my mom is that my stomach lurched when I looked over to her desk.

I saw the faint outline of a person, that same foggy outline I'd seen in the hallway the first day. I've seen it a few times since, but this time there was something different: Two eyes blinked at me from the void.

Two eyes that locked on me.

Two eyes that followed me.

Two eyes that were so *not* ghostly that it somehow made things worse. Those were human eyes, and those human eyes belong to some-one who is most definitely watching me.

I'm sticking to my plan. Ignore, ignore, ignore. But I can already feel it failing.

18
JADE

Fortune smiled on me in the form of a jelly doughnut. Normally, Molly and her mother eat every last scrap of sweets, but this time Dot rushed off somewhere and left the remains of the doughnut peeking out from the overfilled trash can.

I gathered my energy and grabbed the doughnut wedged under the trash can lid, hastily carrying it to the downstairs closet to stash for dessert. Even though my mouth watered at its sugary, fruity aroma, the thought of something so civilized as "dinner and dessert" delighted me. Snagging dinner leftovers from Dot and Molly—who are always leaving food unattended—is easy. However, sweets rarely escape their jaws.

But then Molly, in her "I don't believe in ghosts" charade, found my doughnut and threw it away.

I can't help but take this personally.

19
MOLLY

Two weeks after I came eye-to-eye with whatever it is I'm ignoring in our house, I'm in the backyard trying to make an ancient-looking lawn sprinkler work. In a bikini top and old cotton shorts, I'm determined to run through the sprinkler like an eight-year-old.

August in Texas is no joke. I've heard people say it's "hot as an oven," but this is the first time I've actually felt like a pie.

I am wrestling with the hose, trying to get it to connect with the sprinkler, when I feel a sharp stinging sensation on the top of my left foot, then my ankle, then my calf.

Dropping the hose, I look down to see a bunch of little reddish-brown dots moving all over my leg. I scream and jump up and down, swatting at the dots. This only seems to make things worse. My ankle feels like it's on fire and welts pop up on my fingers and wrist. I flail around the yard like a person possessed.

Out of nowhere a ratty beach towel hits me in the face and a voice yells, "Quick! Brush 'em off with that!" For a moment I stand there completely baffled. "Do it!" the voice demands, so I obey. I frantically brush the dots off with the towel and throw it across the yard.

"You've never seen fire ants before?" the voice asks. *Is the house actually talking to me now?*

"No," I growl, bending over to look at my puffy leg.

"Whoa, okay . . . sorry . . ." the voice says, and I hear someone moving away on the other side of the wooden fence. Since we are at the end of a dead-end street, we only have one neighboring house. A house that looks like a sibling to ours—three stories, old, a little hunched over—but their house is painted a vibrant sky blue.

"Wait! I'm sorry. Those were ants?" You know your life is bonkers when you assume all unfamiliar voices are ghosts.

"Yeah!" A wide vertical fence board lifts from the bottom, like a teeter-totter, and a face peeks out. A person about my age with long, dark wavy hair shaved on the sides, tan skin, and big hazel eyes looks back at me. "I'm Eleanor." Her high voice has that ever-so-slight sing-song twang I've noticed from people in the area.

I suddenly feel very self-conscious about being in shorts and a bikini top. "Oh—whoa. I'm Molly," I say a little too loudly. I instantly feel very uncool, like I do around most people my age.

My ankle throbs, pulling me out of my embarrassment for a

moment. I sputter and start to sit down on the grass to look at my leg.

"Wait! You might sit in another anthill! You do *not* want those ants in your pants," she warns from the fence. "Get the hose and run cold water on your leg; it's really the only way to stop the burning."

I hobble over to the side of the house to turn on the hose, then let the cold water flow over my leg. Without thinking, I let out a sigh of relief. Eleanor laughs.

"So I guess you're not from around here . . . ?"

"No, I'm not from around anywhere."

"Hm. A mysterious newcomer." Eleanor wiggles her eyebrows. "How's the leg feeling?"

I glance at my lower leg, which now has red bumps all over it. "Not great."

"Yeah, it's gonna start itching and then white pimple-looking things might pop up. *Do not pop them*, it makes it so much worse. Put allergy cream on it later and then an ice pack. It's gonna itch for a while, but you'll survive."

"Thanks," I say, self-conscious that my neighbor's first impression of me was as the rude, screaming ant-bite girl. "So, you live next door?"

Wow, why don't I just ask her if she enjoys blinking or breathing air?

My dumb question doesn't seem to bother Eleanor. "Yep, up until y'all moved in, I was the girl the neighbors gossiped about, but now you've stolen that honor from me. Welcome to the club."

"The club?" I ask.

"Yeah, the Buckeye Creek chapter of the 'But Where Are You Really From?' club. My mom's from Mexico and my dad's parents are from St. Thomas. It's all very confusing for people. You?"

Ah, yes, that club. "My grandparents were from Hong Kong, and I think my dad was second generation from a mainland Chinese family—I never met him—but I get '*konnichiwa*-ed' a lot."

She smirks. "So where are you really, *really* from?"

I decide to give her the simple answer. "We just moved here from Maine, but we move around a lot." At this point, in the shade of my house, I notice that Eleanor is still standing at the gap in the fence, leaning over from her yard at a weird angle. "Um . . . do you want to come over?" I ask.

Something passes over her face. "I'm good!" Probably seeing the awkwardness that is my whole person, she adds, "It's nothing personal. I just don't go near your house. No offense."

For a moment I forget the bites scorching my legs. "You don't?"

Now it's Eleanor's turn to look embarrassed. "I'm sorry, it's just . . ." She kicks the patch of dirt at her feet. "The last people who lived there, they were kind of friends with my parents. One of them, Miranda, would talk about how sometimes at night it sounded like there were people walking all over the house; there were random shadows every-where. Or she and Burt would argue about who ate the last piece of pie and then they'd find it in the hall closet with little bites that didn't belong to either of them."

I feel my face drain of color and hope Eleanor doesn't notice. *The doughnut in the closet. The pizza crust.*

"And before Miranda and Burt, there was this other family—the McBriars, I think?—that barely stayed a month. One day they were here, then all of sudden they just LEFT. Also . . ." I watch her decide whether or not to tell me. "A couple times, when there hasn't been anyone living in the house, I've thought I've seen a dark shape standing in the attic window." She looks guilty. "Sorry. I'm just kind of freaked out by your house. Since Tomás and Bradley moved out a year ago, nobody stays in it very long."

"Oh" is all I can say.

Carefully she asks, "Have you . . . seen . . . anything?"

I don't need to say a word; my face must say it all. "It's an old house," I offer limply.

She nods, like that's all the confirmation she needs. "Okay, well, I'll see you around, Molly. Be careful. You're going to BCMS? I'm going into eighth grade. You?"

Figuring that meant Buckeye Creek Middle School, I nod.

"Cool. We'll be in the same class. Okay, go take care of your leg."

She waves and swings the board in the fence down, once again leaving me alone with my big, stupid haunted house. I slump against the back door.

I can't decide what's more terrifying: living with a ghost or making friends.

2Ø
MOLLY

After dinner—fried rice and hot dogs, a Teng specialty—Mom went up to her room to work on some content gigs she'd recently picked up. I flopped down on our new used couch to watch videos on my phone and try not to scratch my bites (I looked it up; they're actually stings, and fire ants are no joke—*of course* I live in a place with giant killer ants).

Like Eleanor said to do, I slathered my leg in hydrocortisone. It's kind of exciting to have a potential friend next door, but I can't stop thinking about what she said about the house. I'm not the only person who knows there's something strange going on here. This is both affirming and alarming.

I must have dozed off on the couch, because I wake with a start—not sure if it's almost midnight or almost dawn. A glance at my phone says ten o'clock at night. That's when I notice how cold my left foot is. Did Mom put an ice pack on my leg while I snoozed? Do we even own ice packs?

I sit up and look at my leg. No ice pack, no cold cloth, nothing. I touch my ankle and it's freezing, like my lower leg was stashed in the fridge for a while.

"Mom!" I call upstairs. "Did you put an ice pack on my leg?"

"Did we buy an ice pack?" she calls back from her bedroom.

That answers that.

As I reach for my glass of strawberry soda on the coffee table, my hand passes through a breeze—I even see the dark hairs on my arm move like they're in front of a fan.

I yank my hand back. Then I remember something: Those ghost bro shows always talk about "cold spots" and ghosts sucking energy away from things. Of course! Why did it take me this long to put the pieces together? I am dizzy when I realize that while I slept, a ghost probably worked its GHOST POWERS on my ant stings. GHOST ICE PACK.

"Ignore, ignore, ignore," I mumble to myself as I get up and move away from the couch as fast as I can, almost tripping over the table. I turn to look at the couch.

Nothing seems out of the ordinary. The table, my glass, my phone next to the glass. Even though I can't see anything, there is electricity in the air, like when you scoot your feet across a carpet and get shocked when you touch metal.

My whole body waits, preparing itself for . . .

SNAP! The wooden blinds that cover the window over the couch go all the way up like someone yanked on the cord that raises and lowers them. My heart ricochets off the backs of my eyeballs.

Suddenly, I am face-to-face with my reflection in the dark floor-to-ceiling window. Seeing my eyes reflected in the mirrorlike glass, I'm reminded of the eyes I saw in my mom's room.

While I'm definitely surprised, *window blinds* are barely scary and can definitely be explained away. Maybe Mom didn't close them properly? I rub my arms and try to shake off the residual shivers.

That's when I notice something weird about my reflection.

It isn't moving.

It isn't *my* reflection.

21

JADE

It's working. Try as Molly might, she can't ignore me.

While I genuinely felt sorry for her—her leg was so red, bumpy, and miserable looking—I have to admit I wasn't acting purely out of the kindness of my heart. By just touching my finger to her foot, her ankle, her shin, I knew I'd make her flesh go cold.

My thinking was that if I helped her a little, showed her that I noticed her poor ant-stung leg, she'd finally have to admit I wasn't just some mindless phantom floating around the house torturing her with—what does she call it? *The zaps.*

What I didn't expect was that she'd see me!

It seems that if she *looks* for me or if she's given no other choice than to *contend* with me, then she *can see me*. There's so much potential here.

In the days following the "window incident," I've been following Molly around like a spectral puppy dog. *Look at me! Look at me!* I yap as she moves through the house. So far she either can't or won't see me.

It's another day where the sun is baking the house on Charlotte Street to a crisp. Molly rolls out of bed when the sun is almost at its highest and drags herself to the bathroom. I wait a moment, then take a deep breath and walk through the door.

I despise walking through doors, walls, really anything solid. It's not that it hurts, it just feels like my guts are being wadded up into a ball and my brain is being squished into my nose. It only lasts a second but it's very claustrophobic. Obviously it's a necessity when you're a ghost, but blessings to anyone who leaves a door open.

Molly slouches at the old white sink with metal knobs and draws a line of toothpaste on her toothbrush. I stand behind her and look at our two selves in the mirror. We are two faces that time never intended to meet. Two faces that could share an unknowable past.

I wonder if Molly knows other people who look like us. What is it like to live in a world where seeing people like you is the norm rather than an event?

I suddenly feel very tender toward Molly. It's such an odd thing to remember that I am both her elder and her peer.

Molly breaks my reverie as she spits in the sink and reaches for a bottle of face cleanser. When she bends down to rinse her sudsy face, I see my chance.

I dip my finger into a glob of dropped toothpaste, like an artist into paint.

22
MOLLY

STAY

I stare at the word written in toothpaste, frozen, water dripping from my face.

The handwriting is not how I'd expect a ghost to write. But what does ghost handwriting look like? I guess I'm surprised because it's so pretty. The *s* seems to swoop, and you can almost see the flick at the tail end of the *y*.

HOLY COLD SPOT, BATMAN. It must be in the bathroom with me *right now*. Someone is *watching me*. Isn't that a horror movie trope? I whip around to make sure there are no surprises behind me.

Nothing. No one. *Phew.* I exhale. But then I turn back to the mirror and actually jump. The word now reads:

STAY!

The cap to the toothpaste rolls around in the sink. It was perched next to the toothpaste tube just a second ago.

Ignore, ignore, ignore, I tell myself.

I grab a towel and wipe the message away without batting an eye (even if my fingers get a little tingly just being near the ghost writing). The mirror clean, I get my sunscreen from the medicine cabinet and slather it on a little too aggressively. I'm rubbing the sunscreen out of my eyebrows when I see what looks like a white blob appear on the mirror. More toothpaste.

I wipe it away with my finger. Nope, we're not doing this, ghost.

Another dot immediately appears in the exact same spot. I wipe it away again and grab my deodorant.

Blob.

Blob.

Blob.

Wipe. Wipe. Wipe.

"Cut it out!" I bark into the air.

I start to reach under my shirt to put deodorant on but freeze. Right in front of me the toothpaste tube on the sink oozes a big white glob. I can see where an unseen finger pressed the tube.

A bigger, more assertive blob of toothpaste appears on the mirror where my left eye is reflected. Then to my horror, I watch as a "+" symbol is slowly, carefully drawn, and then the letter *M*.

Then *O*.

Then *L.*

L.

Y.

Scrawled across my reflection is: a big blob of toothpaste, then +
MOLLY.

It hits me. That's not a blob. It's a dot.

The message says: Dot + Molly.

The ghost wrote the word *STAY*, then *Dot + Molly*—all in that lively,
swoopy handwriting.

I drop my deodorant on the bathroom floor and step away from the
mirror. The backs of my legs hit the bathtub, almost making me fall
into it. I feel like cold water is rushing into my skull and hands as I
gape at the mirror.

Whoever this ghost is, it knows me and it knows my mom. I can't
ignore that anymore. It isn't just some random memory attached to an
antique ashtray or doorknob. That I can deal with. This is actual intel-
ligence. This ghost *wants something from me.*

The dead person living in—I mean *haunting*—my house wants us
to STAY.

"Don't you know ghosts are supposed to chase the living *out* of the
house?" I say out loud. "Of course, of all the haunted houses, I had to
find the one with a ghost who wants me to stay put instead of 'get out.'"

From the emptiness of the bathroom, a laugh echoes across the porcelain tiles. It's right in my ear and around me, all at once, airy and youthful. I'm surprised by the anger that so readily bubbles up in me. I'm just so tired of everyone *needing* me to be in a place for them, but nobody asking me what *I* need. "No! Stop talking to me. Everyone needs to stop telling me what to do and where to live!"

I smear the message across the mirror and leave the bathroom. I'm not running, I'm not screaming, *I am in control.* Not my mom, not the ghost. ME.

I walk down the stairs and out the front door—my hands smeared with toothpaste, still in my shorts and pajama shirt, pausing only to shove my feet into a pair of rubber flip-flops. I let the front door slam behind me.

All the way down the stairs I hear a second set of footsteps following me.

23

JADE

I may have really bungled that.

24
MOLLY

I don't know where I'm going but it feels good to be alone. Oh shoot, wait . . . am I actually alone? Intelligent, literate ghosts are new territory for me. Can it follow me? I pause on the sidewalk to do a "ghost vibe check."

Nothing. No tingles, no electricity, no chills. I continue marching down Charlotte Street, into a shady, tree-lined section of the neighborhood. Free from the sun beating down on me, I slow down and look around.

We've lived in Buckeye Creek for over a month now, but I've never walked this way. I don't really walk anywhere. Everywhere Mom and I go, we go in our car. But I've learned from living other places that it's hard to really get to know a place unless you walk around it.

Big houses, some with two floors, some long low ranch houses, sit back from the street. There's evidence of people living their lives everywhere—soccer balls, a lone Frisbee, a sign supporting a city council candidate. I bet this was a really pretty neighborhood back in the old days.

I've heard my mom say that this is a "historic neighborhood." *Historic for who?* I wonder. While I've seen Latino families around and a Black couple walking their giant fluffy dogs—and Eleanor next door—the neighborhood is overwhelmingly white. I can't help but wonder how many people have noticed us, talked about us. *Those Asians in the house at the end of the street—in the house they shouldn't be able to afford.*

I mean, it's nothing new. Some of the places we've lived we're "The Asians." Not only that, but Dot and I don't always fit the mold of what people "expect" of their Asians. She's kooky and I'm spooky. We are hard to put into a box and I think that freaks people out. Well, certain people.

There's a big triangle of grass and a sign that says CHARLOTTE SQUARE. I guess "Charlotte Triangle" didn't have the same ring. I cautiously sit on a bench under a giant tree—I half expect a zap, but thank goodness there isn't one—in front of a rusty swing set with bright orange seats.

I need to think.

Watching a middle-aged lady in bike shorts throw a ball for her yellow dog to catch and return, I go over all the stuff that led me to be sitting here, sweating on a bench in my pajamas.

These are things I know:

1. There's a ghost in my house.
2. The ghost in my house knows me, knows my mom, and knows *stuff* about me and my mom. It's been listening . . . and watching. It iced my leg.
3. It wants me to stay.

But why?

My gut says something really bad happened to the ghost in the house, but I don't have a concrete reason why I know this. I just feel it—from the zaps. That growl from the big doorknob zap . . . that's not a sound a happy person makes. That empty, longing feeling from those memories are still rattling around in me—sometimes it's hard to tell what's my loneliness and what's lingering from the memories.

I think about how we can miraculously afford this place and how Eleanor said she'd seen two families flee the house in less than a year. Is the ghost dangerous? I mean, it *growled*, and I know it can move stuff around—could it hurt me or my mom?

Haunted houses always have secrets: secret passageways, treasure maps hidden behind walls, confessions written in blood under floorboards. If there's a ghost, there's a reason.

I haven't looked at every little nook and cranny in the house. The ghost has me at a disadvantage: It knows so much about me, but I know nothing about it. I need to level the playing field.

I know what I have to do. I have to go into the attic. It's the only place in the house I haven't been. And there's a reason for that.

And while I know it's what I have to do, I hate the idea. Like the feeling I have about the ghost and its terrible past, I know there's something in the attic. Someone. I don't think they want me up there. The house might have my mom's name on the lease, but this is definitely not *our* house.

But whose house is it?

That wave of dread that I'm getting all too familiar with passes over me once again. I'm going to have to investigate the attic and I'm not sure the ghost is going to be happy with that. The thought of it makes last night's burrito lurch in my stomach.

But wait—hold up. I'm the new Molly. The Molly who speaks up, the Molly who demands to be considered. Even if the ghost wants me to stay, *I* get to decide. And if I'm going to decide, I need more information.

I'm so pumped I stand up triumphantly—fists clenched, ready to take on my ghost—just in time to have the yellow dog's gooey, slobbery ball hit the side of my head with a moist *thwap*. The dog bounds past me, almost knocking me over.

"*OH MY GOSH*, I'm so sorry!" Bike Shorts Lady calls, running over. "Are you okay, sweetie?"

But I'm more than okay. I AM MOLLY TENG AND I AM POWERFUL. The dog toy to the head invigorates me. It jostles loose some hunk of courage in me. "I'm good! Thank you!" I say a little too sincerely and with way too much enthusiasm.

I reach down to pet the dog on the head before turning toward my house and striding forward to go meet my ghost head-on.

25

JADE

I hear Molly's slippers slapping the pavement before I see her stalking up the driveway. She throws open the door, barely pausing to shut it behind her, and storms up the stairs on what appears to be a mission. What is she up to?

At the top of the stairs she makes a beeline for her mother's room. I watch her go over to the nightstand and open the top drawer. After rifling through it, she comes out with a ring of large, heavy, old-fashioned keys.

No.

I lunge for the key ring but I miss and my fingers graze Molly's arm. Her whole person jolts as if she's tripped on an exposed wire, and she looks over her shoulder in my direction.

She walks down the hallway to the attic door and begins fumbling with the keys. I frantically grab at her hands but I'm not focusing and my hands pass through hers like air, like I'm nothing.

She shudders and I see her breath from the sudden cold as she exhales in annoyance, but she continues trying each key, attempting to get the lock on the attic door to turn.

When her fingers hold up the final key, I gather up every little bit of strength I have and grab on to it. For a moment the key is poised in the air. Molly's hand holds one side; I hold the other. An icy film forms on the key. It hangs in space, silence and stillness smothering the frantic energy ricocheting around the hallway.

"What are you hiding?" Molly says through gritted teeth, the color draining from her face and a tear falling down her cheek. The tear so distracts me that I lose the focus required to wrestle the key from her and she rips it from my grasp. I fall to the ground, a growl starting in the pit of my stomach and rising up out of my mouth.

Wiping the tear away, Molly puts the key in the lock, and after some effort, the antique lock turns.

26
MOLLY

The door to the attic opens with a groan and I'm hit with a blast of hot air. It must be over a hundred degrees up there. I hesitate, but it isn't just the heat that makes me pause. Whoever or whatever lurks in the attic does *not* want me up there.

When the ghost tried to take the key from me, it was as if something dripped down off it and soaked into my hands, my skin. The familiar zapping sensation made my hands tingle, but instead of a rush of random, dusty memories, the memory of someone's feelings crashed through me.

HungryHungryHungry. HELP. My stomach hurts. Blood in my mouth. Can't move. Where is this? Can't breathe. So dark, dark, dark.

"Why is this happening to me?"

I hear that growl from the Big Zap in the empty hallway.

NO. IGNORE. The ghost is just trying to stop me. I squelch the impulse to run, then push the door all the way open, the steep, narrow staircase like a throat belching blistering breath at me. Sweat drips off my arms and face as I climb the stairs, both from the heat and the knowledge that I am undoubtedly not alone. Whatever is with me is *mad*. But I keep climbing. More disembodied growls and hisses nip at my heels.

I can think of a thousand reasons why I should forget all this and go back downstairs and zero reasons why I'm standing in this attic unsure of what exactly a growling ghost can do to me. But then I see the sloping ceiling. The exposed wooden beams . . . I've seen those beams before.

They're the wooden beams from the zap. The Big Zap. This is the room from that memory. The empty room with the little bed.

I feel sick when I remember the scream that echoed off those beams.

I focus on breathing. This is real. Somebody's life was in this attic. And *something* happened here. I now have one compelling reason to stay and investigate.

A floorboard creaks behind me . . . on my left . . . on my right. In front of me. I'm suddenly super aware that I'm not standing in *my* home anymore. This is the ghost's home. And I was NOT invited in. "I'm just going to have a look around," I whisper. "I'm just trying to figure you out." The floor creaks in response.

I walk around the room.

The floor is made of faded wooden planks that extend from the back to the front of the house. The main part of the room is where the angled ceiling comes to a point. I have to be careful not to bump my head on the beams that hold the roof up. The whole attic smells like dust, mildew, and old things.

There's a cracked window that overlooks the backyard, and another window at the front of the house that looks out on Charlotte Street. The sun streaming through it reveals old-timey wavy glass.

What's left of my stomach lurches yet again. *It's the window from the Big Zap.* The window where someone watched a car drive away. I'm confused. Was I seeing the ghost's memories from when they were alive or dead or . . . both?

More new questions to add to the pile.

There are a few cardboard boxes shoved under the darkest parts of the roof, along with a couple of metal trunks, and a lot of broken lamps and furniture covered in dust. Like a rookie I run my finger along one cobwebbed trunk and feel electricity stab at my fingertips. For a split second I see a man raising a toast in a brown tweed three-piece suit, but I push the memory away and try to stay on task. He had tall puffy hair like he was from the 1960s or '70s. Not who I'm looking for. My ghost is much older.

I explore the attic for almost half an hour, sweating profusely and feeling vaguely nauseous. *Sweating Profusely and Feeling Vaguely Nauseous: The Molly Teng Story*—the title of my memoir. Finally when I start to see stars and my head feels as heavy as a bowling ball, I decide to take a break.

I sit down under the wavy-glass front window, my back against the wall, and let my head droop. Closing my eyes and taking some deep breaths, I almost wish the ghost would blow a breeze my way. I realize that I'm still in my pajamas and smell like hot garbage. I'd better at least change and put on some deodorant before my mom gets home or else she'll worry that I'm depressed. Which I am. But I don't want to talk about it with her.

After a few minutes I'm ready to give the attic another once-over. As I shift my weight and haul myself to my feet, I feel the floor under me move. I turn around and press the board beneath me. One side lifts up, like a lever—or a secret compartment! Finally!

Cold envelops my shoulders and my breath blooms in a milky cloud. Is that another growl or just a car in the distance?

But I can't help but smile. "Gotcha!" I say, and scramble to turn and inspect the board I'm sitting on.

Like the rest of the floor, this board is gray brown with age. It's thick and heavy. The ends are smooth and worn, probably from decades of having been lifted up. I press on the left side, and the right side swings up. I catch one end and easily pull the board up out of the floor. I'm trembling at this point, and the sweat on my body feels like someone has doused me in ice water.

But I'm not stopping now.

Moving the board aside, I look down into the floor. Shadows make it hard to see into the hole, but there is something in there.

A rumble to my left vibrates the air. That was definitely a growl this time. The temperature in the room is dipping; my teeth are chattering with every breath. The house, the attic, *someone* is telling me to stop, but I can't.

I reach my hand in. The growl gets louder—it's right in my ear. Just as my fingers graze something smooth—a purse? clothes?—the room shudders—it flips between sweltering hot and freezing cold—then out of nowhere there's a shadow and the outline of a person next to me.

I turn my head, like I'm moving through Jell-O, like the movie is in slow motion. But before I can see who's next to me I hear a shriek, clear as day:

"Get away from there!"

27
JADE

My own voices startles me. It bounces around the room. Nonetheless, Molly turns and looks right at me.

I cannot emphasize this enough: She looks *right at me*. I see the tiny movements of her sharp black eyes across my face, my arms, my hands, my torso, my legs, my feet—my whole person. This is not eyes searching, confused, not understanding what they're seeing. This is being seen.

Somewhere deep inside me I remember what this feels like. I am suddenly more human than I've been in over century. The monster shrinks and retreats into the dark cavern where it lives in me.

"You." She breathes the word.

"Hello, Molly," I say, still adjusting to the sound of my voice.

When I say her name her eyes widen. "Who are you?"

Perhaps the most difficult question she could ask. "I am the girl whose house you live in."

"Do you have a name?"

"I . . . I did—I do. But I'm not sure I remember it."

She gives a tiny nod. My eyes flick to the hole in the floor. She sees it. "That's yours?"

"Yes." I move toward it, to put the board back, but Molly takes a half step to block me.

"Not everything is yours; leave that alone," I say, my voice deep, ragged. Hands clenching, I feel the monster stir.

Molly lifts an eyebrow at me, but doesn't move. "*You're* telling *me* that 'not everything is yours'? Seriously? After you've been invading every inch of my life? YOU get to tell me that not everything is mine?" A laugh explodes from her. She isn't afraid of me. I don't know if I expected her to be, but it catches me off guard.

"I'm sorry, I didn't mean to torment you. I just needed you to see me, to listen to me, to . . . help me." I gesture at myself; I gesture at her. "I've been invisible for so long, Molly."

Something about saying her name again makes her shift her weight uncomfortably. She looks at the hole in the floor with my possessions and then back at me.

"It's all I have, Molly," I say, using her name on purpose. She steps aside and I rush over to replace the floorboard. If I had a heart, it would have finally stopped pounding.

Standing up, I face Molly again. "I suspect you have some questions for me."

She snorts. "Uh, you think?" On her exhale, I notice I can still see her breath. "What are you doing here?" she asks.

"This is my home."

"How long has it been your home?"

"For at least a hundred and twenty years, maybe longer."

"You don't know?"

Another difficult question. I find myself struggling for words. "I know I died here, but I don't remember anything before that. I suppose I must have lived here if I died here."

Molly's eyes grow big again and she sinks to the floor. I follow her and sit on my knees. "You . . . *died* here. You remember dying?"

"Mostly, I remember waking up dead. But fleeting moments of what it was like when I was dying sometimes come to me. Fear . . . confusion . . . love. I think—I *know*—someone loved me, even if I can't remember anything about them."

Molly's eyes soften and she swallows hard. "I know."

"What do you know?"

She hesitates. When she speaks, her voice sounds thick. "I see things, memories from"—she looks at me, unsure—"from *the dead.* It's like memories get stuck in things, furniture, walls. I've seen some of *your* memories. I felt them when . . . the doorknob . . ."

Molly looks to me, her expression asking me to confirm that the doorknob incident in her room was in fact me. I nod.

"I just didn't know the memories were from . . . dying."

"Oh," I say. It all makes sense now: Molly's behavior, her careful way of moving through the house, her refusal to touch certain things. "I'm sorry, Molly, that must be very frightening. It was never my intention."

"It's not you, it's just how I am. For some reason, I can feel and see the past. But I've never really seen a, uh, a—"

"—a ghost?"

"Yeah, I wasn't sure if that's how you identified, but yeah, I've never seen a ghost like you before, more like echoes of people. But I've touched the memories of a lot of, well, dead people. I call it 'the zaps.'" She laughs again; it's a nervous habit I've noticed in the Living.

"So it seems you may know more about me than even I do. What else would you like to know?"

She's careful. "Why am I seeing you like this? Why now?"

I think a moment. "I'm not sure. As you know, I've been trying to get your attention for a while, but you've been trying to ignore me. This is the first time that you've made the decision to acknowledge me. I tried to stop you from coming into my attic and you defied me. That's a form of acknowledgment. So I suppose the combination of me focusing my energy and you opening up to me with your unique abilities—"

"—flipped the spooky switch," Molly finishes, her eyes a little glazed, taking it all in.

"Well, I was going to say 'raised the curtain between our worlds,' but yes, 'spooky switch' works too."

"So now we can just talk to each other whenever we want like it's no big thing?"

I shrug. "I don't know. This is all new to me—you're the first Living I've ever spoken to. Well, the first Living I've ever spoken to who's really been able to *hear* me."

Molly's eyes widen. "So nobody's talked to you for a hundred years?"

"A hundred and twenty. But yes. Some people have seen me, but almost nobody *looks* at me. Do you understand?"

"I do. I'm sorry. That sounds really lonely."

I'm surprised by Molly's sincerity. With her sharp eyes on me, I feel exposed. More than I was ready for. I look down, suddenly bashful. "It is. Very."

"You growled at me," she says rather suddenly, her gaze meeting mine. We sit very still together.

"Yes. I'm sorry. I can't always control it. I mean you no harm. There are just things about me, about being a spirit, that are . . ."

How do I explain what I can't explain?

". . . unimaginable."

Please don't ask me more.

As if hearing my thoughts, she just nods the tiniest of nods and says softly, "Okay."

Taking a deep breath, she asks the question I knew was coming, the one I have the least good answer to. "So, what do you want from me? Do you just want someone to talk to or do you have UNFINISHED BUSINESS you want me to, uh, finish? *Do you need me to avenge you?*"

"What? No! Well, I don't think so?"

"You don't *think* so? How do you not know if you need to be avenged?"

"Because I'm not even really sure who I am. I don't know anything about who I was and why I'm stuck here."

Molly's interest is piqued. "What do you mean stuck? You can't leave the house?" she asks.

"No. Not at all."

"Not at all? Have you tried?"

Of course I've tried!

I go over to the front window and press my hand against it with all my strength. Nothing. My hand can't go through; the window doesn't crack or break. It's as if I'm not doing anything. Then I kneel down and reach for the floor—I just have to make the decision—my hand glides silently through the boards.

"It's the same with all the outer walls of the house. Even if the front door is open, it's as if there's a wall stopping me from leaving. I've tried squeezing into boxes or hiding in wardrobes when people are moving out—it doesn't matter. I can never make it past the walls of this house."

"Wow. That's legit ghost story stuff," Molly says.

Sitting back down with Molly, I continue. "But more than that, I have no idea who I am or where I came from. I was hoping you would help me figure out my past; maybe that will free me. Maybe my past is why I'm stuck."

Understanding lights up Molly's features. "That's why you want me to stay."

"Yes. I don't know how long it could take. If you leave in a couple months, that might not be enough time. I have a whole life to figure out."

Molly averts her eyes. She's silent.

"Also," I add, "before you and your mother moved in, I'd never seen another person who looked like me. I find your presence . . . comforting."

She cocks her head. "What do you mean?"

I'm embarrassed. I sweep my hands over my face, then gesture to Molly. "This . . . me. You."

Molly sits up straighter. "Wait, you've never seen another Asian person?"

"Not that I can recall. I've seen people who look like me on television, but—"

"—you watch TV?"

"When the Living watch television, so do I. I've seen almost every incarnation of television around!"

Molly ponders this. "I guess that makes sense. So wait, you've only seen Asian people on TV?"

"Yes." I hesitate. "You and your mother make me feel a little less alone. I'm sorry if I've been a bit overzealous."

Recognition and understanding fill Molly's eyes. "It's okay. I probably would have been pretty excited too if I thought I was alone in the world all these years. Besides, I'm kind of used to dead people messing with me. All the same, the bathroom is off-limits, okay?" She smiles, and as if on cue the sun shifts in the sky and the room is lighter and brighter.

The door slams downstairs and Dot calls for Molly. It's already late in the afternoon.

"I should go," Molly says as she stands up. "I'm sweaty and stinky and still in my pajamas. If my mom sees me like this she will freak out and make me talk about my feelings all night over gummy candy. She likes to think it's therapy. It only kind of is."

Molly brushes herself off and I stand too. As I stand, it hits me how drained I am. It's hard being seen and heard for so long. I wobble on my feet.

"Whoa, are you okay?" Molly asks.

"I'll be fine, I've just never done this before." I close my eyes and concentrate on the feeling of my feet against the floor.

"Could we talk more later? I really do need your help. Do you think . . . do you think you might be willing to stay?"

Molly starts to say something, then stops. I can't tell if she's angry or sad or scared. Maybe all of the above. She just sighs and looks at me with those dark, piercing eyes.

"It was nice meeting you," she says, and hurries down the attic stairs, locking the door behind her.

28
MOLLY

"Molls? What're you up to? I was thinking of making Food in a Pot tonight, what do you think?" Mom hollers up the stairs. I can hear her dumping her bags by the door. "Food in a Pot" is what we call rice, soy sauce, and whatever else we can find in the house that isn't too gross. It's good 71 percent of the time.

"Sounds great! I'll be there in a sec, I'm just changing!" I call downstairs as I grab some clothes from my room and run to the bathroom to splash water on my face and slather my pits in deodorant. I've basically spent the whole day anxious and sweaty (except when I was freezing) and it shows.

My hands shake a little as I wash up. *What in the holy heck-fire just happened?*

Was I really just chatting with a ghost in the attic? Is this it? Is this where I finally break with reality and Mom and I never leave this house and we adopt eighty-five squirrels and we become like some Asian *Grey Gardens*? (I know about that old movie because Mom dressed up as flag-dancing Little Edie for Halloween one year.)

Breathe, Molly, breathe.

There's a ghost in this house and it—*she*—needs my help. But what am I supposed to do? What *can* I do? I'm just the girl who gets zapped by dead-people memories; what do I know about being a ghost detective?

And she wants me to stay. Another someone who wants me to stay in Texas.

"Arrrrrrrgh!" I shout to nobody, and attack my right armpit in frustration.

I dry off anything that needs drying and throw on a pair of denim shorts and an old UCLA School of Theater, Film, and Television T-shirt I inherited from my mom. I still look like a swamp baby, but at least I don't smell like one too.

I come out of the bathroom and see my mom going into her bedroom. She pauses and looks at the dirty clothes in my hand and then back at me. Her left eyebrow arches. "You look weird."

"The wonders of genetics," I say back, trying to sound light and playful, but it comes out snarky.

"Whoa, tone it down. What did you do today?" she asks as she continues into her room, expecting me to follow her. I do, mainly because I'm afraid if I go into my room I'll be faced with our resident ghost again.

Mom heads to her desk and plugs a card reader into her laptop. She begins downloading photos of the vegan diner she took photos of today. Mom's already got a few jobs in the area creating content for local businesses.

"I just hung around, watched stuff online," I tell her, sitting on her bed.

She looks over her shoulder at me. "You're just getting out of your pajamas now? It's almost four o'clock."

"I'm on summer vacation, I'm supposed to be a slug," I say, willing her to stop searching my face for the truth she knows is lurking in there. "I walked to the park and played with a dog."

This relaxes her. Normal kid stuff. She turns back to her computer, moving files around. "I saw that Eleanor girl from next door; she seems cool. Why don't you invite her over sometime? You two can be slugs together."

"No," I say a little too quickly. Between how much Eleanor intimidates me and THE GHOST, that's more than I can handle.

Mom sighs. "Whatever you want, but you know you're always welcome to have friends over. I love that you've met someone here."

It's my turn to sigh. I know she's trying. She just really wants me to like Buckeye Creek. But after today's events, I'm definitely no closer to wanting to stay here—no matter how many people want me to.

29
MOLLY

After dinner, Mom wants to watch "something with Keanu Reeves," so we hunker down on her bed with her laptop. Our Food in a Pot masterpiece of frozen vegetable medley, some leftover fried tofu from a Thai food night that was almost unacceptably long ago, and lots of soy sauce and chili oil turned out to be one of our better dinners. When Mom pauses the movie to return some emails, I release a big, exaggerated yawn, tell her I'm wiped, and stand to leave.

"Do you need to talk about anything, Molls?" she asks, a worried-kitten look on her face.

I shake my head no. I feel bad, but her eagerness makes me want to talk even less. Even if I did want to talk to her, I know that ghost stuff really bothers her.

The closer I get to my bedroom, the colder it gets. My stomach flip-flops. By the time I step into my dark room I can see my breath in the light streaming through my window from the streetlamp.

That's not all I see.

She's standing by the window looking out into the night. She looks like a still from a movie. Not even a ghost movie, but some old, sad, romantic film. For a chilled, silent moment I notice how beautiful she is. She wears a plain light yellow dress. It looks like rough cotton, with short sleeves and a loose skirt that hits below her knees. It seems old-fashioned in that it looks practical, almost like a uniform, but made by human hands.

Long, shiny black hair falls most of the way down her back and she has giant, searching eyes that look like two silvery pools. Her features are delicate, like they were crafted rather than born. But all the same, she doesn't look innocent or frail. She gazes out the window and I'm convinced she's seeing back into the years she's been trapped here.

Wow, it hits me. Trapped HERE. In THIS HOUSE. Not even in this neighborhood or city, *this one house*. The outside world is like a TV show teasing her about the life she can't have.

I suddenly feel very sorry for my ghost—I realize that I do think of her as *my* ghost—and I start to wonder if helping her might be doable *before* I leave Buckeye Creek. A floorboard creaks beneath my feet and her head snaps in my direction. Something about the way she moves, too fast and too smooth and without any sound at all, is the eeriest thing I've seen in a long time. She's both very human and not quite.

She smiles. "I liked your *Food in a Pot*." She says the words like she's trying them out for the first time.

I connect the dots with what she just said. "You *eat*?"

My question seems to amuse her. "You make it sound so *creepy*. Of course I eat."

"How? Where does it . . . go?"

She moves over to my bed, climbs on, and sits on her knees. It pops into my head that she might have sat on my bed tons of times without me knowing it. Her expression darkens, almost like her face is retreating into shadow.

"I don't really know. I just know that I have to eat . . ." She trails off. "In that way I'm like some sort of an animal. Hunger is my only real companion, Molly." When she says my name, my skin prickles.

"Where do you get food from?" I ask.

She drops her eyes, retreating even more. "I steal leftovers and morsels that you leave out—like a creature, a rodent." She lashes herself with her words. "And I hide food when I think it will be scarce."

I remember the doughnut I found in the downstairs closet.

"Why are you always hungry?" As soon as I ask this question, I know I've made a misstep. Something in the room changes.

"I think . . ." She chooses her words carefully. "I think . . . I'm being punished."

The room gets colder. It's as if she's pulling the air in close to herself like a blanket. My jaw tightens to stop a shiver. Do I feel sorry for her? "What are you being punished for?"

She looks me square in the face and I'm surprised when I see pearly tears in her eyes. Ghosts can cry? I guess I've heard stories about doomed weeping women, but seeing a ghost girl's eyes brim with tears in real life feels way more tragic than I would have guessed.

"I don't know. I don't really remember anything about living other than a fragment here, a fragment there. But I must have done something terrible to be punished with such solitude, such unrelenting hunger. There's a monster inside me, Molly. I'm so afraid of it."

She stops and wipes her tears. The way she does it is like a little kid, big wipes with the back of her hand. She closes her eyes and takes a deep breath before turning her gaze on me again. It's jarring to see such troubled, weary eyes look at me from a face that appears as young as my own.

"Wait, the growling from earlier, in the attic . . . do you mean an *actual* monster?" There's no way that sound came from this girl crying in my bedroom.

"Yes. This is why I always have to find food. When I don't eat, the hunger takes over and I start to slip away. I turn into something else, an actual monster!"

She hangs her head.

Without thinking, I reach for her hand—like a friend. For a moment, when our hands touch, I get a jolt of hunger, fear, and mostly shame.

"There's nothing to be ashamed of!" I blurt out. "It can't be your fault!"

She looks at me quizzically. "I felt that," she says. "When you touched me, I felt a sharp, buzzing sensation and then . . . warmth. You understand loneliness."

I nod. "The zaps. Welcome to my world."

Something in her brightens. "Your world. I'd like that very much." She sighs. We sit in silence. She looks unsure. So I ask the question: "What did you want to talk about? You were waiting in here for me."

She looks relieved that I asked. "Will you help me find out who I was, Molly? Have you thought about staying? I know it's a lot to consider, but you're all I have."

I don't know what to say. I want to help, but how long would I need to stay? Could I figure out a whole life *and* afterlife in a few short months?

She sees my expression and her whole being droops. "Well, please think about it. I'm happy we spoke tonight." She starts to rise.

"Wait," I say again, reminded of one more question. "What do I call you? I know you don't know your name, but I can't just call you 'ghost girl.'"

I watch her think, her eyes seeming to search for a memory in the dark. "Jade. I don't know where that name comes from or why it's in my head, but call me Jade. At least for now." She sways in place again. "I need to go to my attic; it's been a long day." She stands and moves silently away from me, her steps just a little too fluid.

"Okay. Good night, Jade."

She smiles, looking like she might fall asleep on her feet. "Good night, Molly." And she walks through the cracked door into the dark.

3Ø
JADE

Sometimes I fantasize about what it would mean to escape this house. I imagine soaring, flying out into the world with the sun on my face and gusts of fresh, cold air lifting me higher and higher. All I'll have to do is think of a place and I'll fly there. I'll slay the monster in me with visits to hot dog stands and ice cream shops and strawberry patches. The growl in my stomach forever extinguished. I'll no longer be closed in by walls and dust and leftovers, my existence not an afterthought to the Living. I'll be free!

But the pearl of this fantasy is the belief that I will find my mother—her ghost. The one who loved me. If she's out there, I know she's waiting for me. Hidden behind the locked door of memories, I believe we promised to take care of each other. Perhaps this is whimsy, but it keeps me hopeful. Maybe she's trapped in a house of her own somewhere out there, dreaming of her escape. Maybe I can help her.

These are thoughts I only take out once in a while. This dream is so lovely, something so warm to curl up in, but when I have to put it away and cold reality sets in, the loneliness is never more acute.

But I'm daring to dream a little more lately.

This morning the house has been quiet for hours as I wait for Molly to wake up.

Finally, I hear her jostling around in the kitchen and make my way down there. I find her drizzling chili oil over a corn tortilla covered with cheese. Then she shoves the food into the microwave and hits start. She goes to the fridge and takes out an open can of cranberry sauce.

"What's that for?" I asked.

"Dipping sauce," she mumbles, and shifts her weight impatiently in front of the microwave.

"I've never seen anyone make such a concoction and I've seen some questionable recipes." But even as I say this I can feel my stomach coming to life.

"Oh please," Molly says, leaning down to look through the microwave window. "It's cheesy, it's spicy, it's sweet—what's so questionable about that?"

I laugh. Molly throws me a look. The microwave dings. "What?"

"Sorry, I wasn't laughing at you. I just like your confidence."

She rolls her eyes but she does it with a half smile and a snort. She gingerly takes the plate out of the microwave with an oven mitt and sits down at the table with the cranberry sauce, a spoon, and her quesadilla. She tries to pick it up a couple of times but it's too hot so she waits. "I don't know if anyone has ever described me as 'confident.' 'A team player' or 'accommodating,' but confident? I'm scared of everything."

I cross to the table and sit down. It's lovely to sit at the table with someone, almost as if we are dining together. Again, one of those familiar things I can't quite place in my memory. Molly plops a glob of deep red cranberry sauce on the pale yellow tortilla oozing with cheese and chili oil and carefully takes a bite. I watched her intently. Maybe too intently.

"You're watching me eat like it's a movie and every bite is a cliff-hanger. It's really intense."

I avert my eyes, feeling immediately embarrassed.

Molly notices my reaction and puts her food down for a moment.

"It must really suck to be hungry all the time. Sorry, I'm being self-ish." She rips a chunk off her quesadilla, cheese stretching as she pulls the piece away. Smearing cranberry sauce over the top of it, she holds it out to me. "Try it."

I have to stop the monster in me from tearing it from her hand. *I'm eating with someone, I'm sharing a meal, I am human, I am in control,*

I AM in control, I tell myself while gritting my teeth, and try to emulate all the people at dinner tables I've watched over the years.

I take the offering from Molly and bite into it with concentration—no frenzied gobbling, tasting it. The cold, sweet-tart taste of the cranberry sauce over the salty-melty-spicy cheese, chili oil, and tortilla combination is surprisingly good! Some chili oil drips onto my hand and I frantically lick it up. My eyes dart to Molly, who is watching me. Right, the Living don't usually panic if a drop of food doesn't make it to their mouth.

I eat the whole thing and Molly hands me another piece. "You're right, it's one of the best things I've ever eaten," I say.

Molly raises her eyebrows. "Wow, and you've been eating things since before my grandma was born. You like Flamin' Hot Cheetos?"

We spend the rest of the afternoon sitting at the table (!!) eating Cheetos, cream sandwich cookies, and licorice ("Red Vines are the only good licorice. Fight me on that," she says). I tell Molly about the people who have lived in the house before her. I tell her about Celia Lotkins; I tell her about the first time I saw a television, a computer, a smartphone.

"So you're like a really, really old lady in the body of a thirteen-year-old girl," she says.

"I guess," I respond. "I mean, I don't *feel* like an old lady?"

"Do you feel like a kid?" she asks, gnawing on a piece of licorice.

"I only know what it's like to be a kid, so . . . yes?"

Molly's mom gets home and hollers that she's going to hop in the shower—something about vegan cream cheese and a blender mishap. I stand up and am about to disappear and go back up to my attic when Molly stops me.

"Jade. I had a great afternoon with you. I really don't want you to be hungry or feel like a monster or anything, so, if you want, I'll bring food to my room tonight and you can have it."

A lump catches in my throat. Another first.

"I'd really like that, Molly. Thank you." I disappear from her sight and retreat to my attic. My stomach is purring and so am I. Is this the best day I've ever had? I can't help but grin and look forward to seeing Molly later.

31
MOLLY

After my mom got home, I tried to be as normal as possible and listen to her as she told me about a Chinese dim sum and barbecue place that opened up in the strip mall Buckeye Creek calls the International Village. It's mainly Chinese and Korean businesses with a couple of South Asian restaurants, a taqueria, a Caribbean food counter, a pho place, and a boba joint. The barbecue place might bring my mom on to create all their social media content and a website.

"I think the owner was a little judgy about the fact that my Cantonese is so bad and that I can't read Chinese, but I told them about making egg rolls and lo bak go for your por por's catering company as my after-school job and they warmed up to me. I should teach you how to make lo bak go, Molls, would you be into that?"

"Yeah, maybe," I said noncommittally. Lo bak go, these turnip cake squares (well, actually it's radish, and when I say "cake," it's more like really solid pudding—translation is an imperfect science) with pork or shrimp in them are a favorite of Mom's at dim sum, but I can't get over the firm-goo texture. My mom grew up making food next to my por por, my grandma, which I'm pretty sure is why most of the Cantonese she can speak is food related.

Mom finished up sending some emails while I got out the ingredients for our noodle dinner and started the water boiling. I don't know if we make Singapore noodles the right way, but it's a favorite of ours: fried noodles, veggies, a few scraps of char siu—Chinese barbecued pork—if we have it, those baby corns I love, egg, and a kick of curry powder.

Things with Mom and me have been . . . fine. It's a little tense. I can see her trying her best to make Texas cool and interesting for me— bringing me snacks from trendy cafés and proposing that we go to this big German water park place in New Braunfels before school starts. I'm not mad at her really, I get why she's doing it, but nothing about staying in Texas is exciting to me. All I can think about is going back to the peace and simplicity of Maine and continuing my life there.

I try to be nice to my mom, but I have to be firm with her. I'm finally standing up for myself and what I want. If I give in now just because I feel bad, I'm afraid I'll never have any say in my life until I'm eighteen and we've moved ten more times.

After dinner, I take my time cleaning the kitchen, setting aside leftovers for Jade as well as some candy and cookies for dessert. Has she ever had sour worms before? I throw everything under foil in the fridge and flop onto the couch for a while to look up stuff about ghosts.

From a blog called *Dallas Is a Ghost Town* I learned that when ghosts "manifest" they need to pull energy from the environment around them, so you get what they call "cold spots." The website says ghosts can be "intelligent hauntings" or "residual hauntings"— basically they're either ghosts with a brain who want something or ghosts that are just caught in a loop. Kind of like hitting rewind over and over again on a scene in a movie. Either way, it seems like if something bad happens, emotions get embedded in the place where it happened and a ghost gets stuck.

I wonder if that's what happened to Jade. She doesn't remember anything—how she got here, who she was—but something terrible must have gone down for her to be trapped in this house for over a hundred years.

Holy bananas, am I living in a murder house?

Just before eleven, I nuke Jade's noodles and gather everything on two plates to bring to my room. I am very conscious of the strong smell of the noodles as I carry the meal upstairs—I hope Mom won't come to my room asking for a bite. But as the smell wafts down the hall to her open door, she yells, "Ooh, good idea!" and I hear her head downstairs for her own late-night snack.

At eleven o'clock sharp there is a knock at my door. I am less startled by the fact that there is a ghost at my door (the room had already started to get chilly) and more that someone in this house actually knocks.

"Come in!" I call too loudly, and I hear Mom say, "What?" from the stairs. "Nothing!" I yell as my door creaks open and Jade steps into the room. The only sound that comes with her is the complaint of the squeaky floorboard by the door. It's funny how the floors in this house have always noticed her even if nobody else has.

Shutting the door, she stands nervously, smoothing her dress. The glow from my nightstand lamp illuminates half her face, making her look more like a ghost than ever before. She smiles politely, eyeing the food as if waiting for an invitation.

"Oh! Is this like a vampire situation? Do I have to invite you to eat in front of the living or something?"

Her brow wrinkles in confusion. "What? Vampires? No, I . . . I just . . . I'm not used to living people watching me eat. Today was the first time. Normally, eating is a stolen moment for me."

"Oh!" I'm surprised by how much this stabs me in the heart. "Well, I'm really excited for you to try this food. It's Singapore fried noodles, chocolate chip cookies, and sour gummy worms. Have you ever had sour gummies before? They're my favorite. In the gummy candy category," I clarify.

She takes a step closer, peering at the neon-colored candy. "I haven't, Molly. Thank you for sharing your favorite with me." I've never seen someone be so formal about sour gummies.

"Well, then—dig in!" I say, and push the plates toward her.

Jade tentatively walks toward the plates on my bed, her big eyes soft but locked in on the food like a cat approaching prey. Then everything happens so fast.

She pounces upon the noodles, the chopsticks I'd laid on the plate clattering to the floor. As she pulls the pile of noodles toward her, her small mouth strains to open as wide as possible. I can't help but stare, my own mouth hanging open.

Is this real?

Did her teeth spontaneously sharpen to points? Did her neck grow long and thin, the muscles and tendons popping as she struggles to inhale every little bit?

The most unsettling thing is her eyes. Her normally bright and curious gaze turns empty. Both her eyes, pupils and all, turn flat, opaque white. There is no gleam, no glisten. A deep, gagging growl comes from her curled lips.

An involuntary exclamation slips out of my throat. In an instant, Jade's empty eyes clamp on me and I instinctively back away from her. What is looking at me is not Jade.

Then I remember the monster she's mentioned before.

The sides of her pinched lips turn up in what resembles a smile. Her gaze is a steel trap holding my attention while her jaw churns the food in her mouth. A halting, rasping sound comes from her body and I realize that she—*it*—is laughing at me, *leaning* toward me; her clawed hand reaches out. I can't move, I'm transfixed.

One of those baby corns falls off the plate and lightning quick she catches it in her jaws. She is once again consumed by the food. I watch her, afraid to move.

And then, just like that, it's done. The plate is empty, and I mean *empty*. Not a drop of sauce, not a shred of a noodle.

My eyes meet Jade's, now back to normal.

I am so in over my head.

32
JADE

This is a nightmare. I am the nightmare.

Reflected in Molly's eyes, I saw the monster grinning back at me. I was so eager, so moved by the offering of food, that I lost myself for a moment.

Will I ever be human to Molly again?

I weep. There is that terrible feeling again—embarrassment. But this time, it is stronger. This time, it is shame.

I curl into myself, backing into the corner of the room. I let go of staying solid and feel my body fade. Forget about Molly's help; I will have an eternity of being a ghoul.

"Jade!" Molly's voice cuts through the noise in my head. I stop mid-disappearance, hanging in a gauzy, half-visible state.

"Jade, don't go. It's okay. Please . . . please talk to me."

I lift my head to meet Molly's imploring gaze. Does she mean it? Is this a cruel joke? I've seen the Living be cruel before.

She looks at me, unflinching. Those dark eyes of hers hold on to me and I will myself to a solid form. A long white cloud of breath comes from her mouth.

Molly picks up one of the gummy worms, an unnaturally colored blue-and-red confection covered in sugar, and holds it out. "The blue-and-red ones are the best. I think they're supposed to be strawberry and . . . and, uh, blue?" She laughs. "But they're really good. Here, try it."

I wipe my cheeks and move toward her, aware that my stomach churns and roars with every step. But I smooth my hair and think about the weight transferring from one foot to the other as I move—*these are human things, hair, walking, weight*—taking myself to the edge of the bed where Molly sits. I take the worm and carefully put it in my mouth.

A burst of sour and sweet explodes on my tongue as I chew. It's a delight! The sharp flavor is reminiscent of fruit but is also entirely unrecognizable. Without thinking, I giggle.

"Right?" Molly says. "What a totally ridiculous food, but it's so good! Do you want another one?"

I nod. "Please."

"It's cool, you don't need to be so polite. Sit down and eat dessert with me," Molly says, and points at a spot on her bed. I sit, and Molly and I eat the gummy worms in silence. I notice chewing; the roughness of the candy that dissolves away to stickiness. Gooey pieces adhere to my teeth; my tongue chases them. I am human! I am eating candy!

I also notice how long the silence stretches, another very human experience. There are things to talk about, but for a while the worms fill the void.

"What do you want to know?" I finally ask.

She is cautious. "So . . . that was the monster?"

I don't need to say anything.

She nods. "It just, like, comes out of nowhere sometimes?"

I chew a yellow-and-green worm slowly. "I don't know if it's really fair to say it 'comes out of nowhere' because it's always near. It doesn't come from nowhere, it comes from me. It *is* me. I don't quite know where I end and the monster begins."

"I'm sorry. That sounds scary."

How to respond to sympathy . . . I just whisper, "It is."

"How long have you been this way?"

"As long as I can remember. Ever since I've been dead."

Molly's eyebrows pop up. I forget how jarring it must be to hear someone talk about having died in the past tense.

"So you only remember being dead?" she asks.

I reach for a cookie. So does Molly. I hold the cookie in my hands, appreciating how perfect and round it is. I don't often get to admire my food. "I remember waking up in a box—"

"A coffin?!" Molly interjects.

"No, a dark, metal box. I was scared, I was bewildered, I cried for help. But nobody came. Just the hunger."

Do I tell her? Do I tell her what I've done? Molly sits motionless, waiting.

"You don't have to talk about it if you don't want to," she says. Her kindness overwhelms me.

"I—I do. It's just . . . everything I reveal makes me more and more of a horror. I might look like you, but I'm not like you. You won't want to help me."

Molly's brow furrows; she shakes her head. "Whoa. Just a sec. I don't know what you've been through, I probably can't fully understand it, but give me a chance. People act like I'm a 'horror' too. Sometimes I wonder if that's why we move all the time. Yeah, my mom likes her adventures and has some serious FOMO, but I also think that deep down she's scared for me . . . *of* me. She never wants to hear about what I see in the zaps; she just wants to hold my hand, wipe my tears, and move on. Which is great, but I feel like I have this whole life she doesn't want to hear about."

"And that life is seeing the lives of the dead?" I ask.

"Yes! Dead people have been my whole life, which most living people just can't understand. Or don't want to understand. It's hard to go about living when I'm always worried a dead person's memory might pop up and take over." She looks away on the last word. *Take over her life the way I have.*

"So you've always had these powers?" It's nice to be asking Molly about her life instead of explaining mine.

She shrugs but still doesn't meet my eyes. "Yeah. But it's not like I was bitten by a radioactive spider and woke up with great powers and great responsibility."

Molly looks at me expectantly. I am blank.

"Okay, so you missed *that* pop culture reference. My point is, I've always been this way; there were no before-times. Some of my first memories are of getting zapped. Like when I was five in Honolulu and my mom's family was visiting. That was my First Big Zap. Some uncle gave me a little toy horse to play with, said it was my por por's—oh, that's my—"

"—your grandmother, your mother's mother." I finish her sentence automatically. This is just a word I know. It floats to the surface with ease.

"Oh, you speak Cantonese?" Molly asks, surprised.

"I don't know. I guess so?" This is the truth, as I can't remember speaking the language, nor can I pull Cantonese words out of the air, but somehow hearing the word triggers knowledge I didn't know I had. Another thing Molly brings out in me. "Anyway, sorry, please continue, Molly."

"Okay. So I was given this tiny toy horse that was my por por's when she was a kid. It was made of dark, shiny wood and had a real mane and tail made of horsehair. I think it had eyelashes too. Anyway, as soon as I touched it, this jolt of electricity, like hot needles flying through my veins, went from my fingertips to my head and I saw an old lady in a blue Chinese padded jacket fall down. My wooden horse clattered from her hand onto a green tiled floor I'd never seen before. I heard a child crying and crying, hands grabbing for the old lady lying on the ground. I felt so scared in that memory; the child's voice kept shouting, 'Wake up! Wake up!' And then, before I could make sense of anything, I came back and got sick all over the horse. I think we threw it away."

I'm riveted. "Who was the lady?"

"That's the thing, I'm not sure. I've tried to talk to my mom about it, but she changes the subject. All I know is that after that, we saw our family a whole lot less. I think I might have embarrassed my mom. She doesn't even talk to . . ." Molly stops herself. "She doesn't even talk to all of them anymore."

My heart aches for her. "I'm so sorry, Molly. That's a lot to carry."

"It's fine. I'm used to it."

"So you don't know *why* you have these powers?"

"No clue. Sometimes I wonder if there's a reason I can do what I do. But most of the time it feels like a fluke, like how some people are born with webbed toes or a photographic memory—only I'm seeing someone else's photographs. I don't think of it as special; it just makes me different, which can suck sometimes. I mean, it's not like I have a superpower that can fight the forces of evil or change the world."

"You've changed my world," I say.

She sighs, but it turns into a laugh. "I guess you're right. I'm Molly Teng, Changer of Worlds!" She can't hide the bitterness in her smile. "Basically, what I've been trying to say is that if anybody is going to understand—even a tiny bit—what you're going through, it's me. I can't promise I won't be scared or will always know what to do, but that doesn't mean I can't be your friend."

Friend. She said friend. The word seems to catch both of us off guard. That small word feels so enormous.

I decide to trust my friend.

I tell her about the box, fighting to escape from it. The terror and confusion of being in a cramped, dark place. Wailing for help, thrashing against the walls, crying for something—someone—I can't remember. I tell her about the memories I can't catch—a gentle hand, a voice, sorrow, so much sorrow. I tell her of the murky snippets I remember from dying.

I tell her everything—well, almost everything. Some things are too . . . shameful. She may be able to look past the monster that shares my body, but she won't be able to look past the monstrous, desperate thing I've done.

Molly listens. I can't read her face. I think I've frightened her. And then I'm frightened.

"I think I was loved, but I can't remember anything about it. I think I'm being punished. I'd just like to know why. Who was I? What did I do to deserve this punishment?"

I wait, careful now. "I wonder if with your *gift*, you might be able to see things about me that I can't. There have to be memories about me in this house; we just need to find them."

Saying that aloud feels dangerous, but I can't take it back now.

Molly doesn't talk for a long time. It's past midnight. The candy and cookies are all gone. She crushes a crumb on the plate with her pointer finger.

"I'm really tired, Jade," she says, making little crumb piles on her plate. "We'll talk tomorrow, okay? I'm sorry, this is a lot and I need to be alone and think." The trepidation on her face is unmistakable.

"Okay, good night, Molly."

"Good night, Jade."

What have I done?

I let myself disappear into the night.

33
MOLLY

I could say I woke up feeling anxious, but that would mean that I slept.

After Jade left my room last night—I only know because I watched the door open on its own, then carefully shut (still creepy even if I know who it is)—I tried to turn off my brain and go to sleep. But that wasn't happening.

I lay there in the dark that was spliced by the light of the streetlamp and listened to the house creak, the AC struggle, and all the thoughts tumbling around in my head.

All the stuff she has had to deal with is SO beyond me. And the monster she shares a body with . . . I can't even begin to understand that. There's ghosts and then there's this. I don't know what Jade is.

But Jade's been so alone for so long, I can't blame her for so desperately wanting help.

I'd be lying if I said I didn't like her. Monster aside, she's so warm and inquisitive. What would it be like to see the world through her eyes? Just for a little while. And after so long on earth, it's amazing she's still so curious about everything. Jade and the sour worms is my new favorite thing. Yeah, she kind of needs to get on board with some boundaries, and that old-fashioned politeness is a little extra, but there's time to work on that.

Wait, what am I talking about?!

Not only am I not staying in Texas long enough to figure out an otherworldly 120-year-old mystery, but in order to do that, Jade wants me to use my, uh, "gift," as she calls it. The thought of walking around this haunted house getting zapped over and over and over again looking for pieces of Jade's story is more than I can handle. The little bit I saw on that first day, all those feelings, being sick to my stomach—I'm supposed to do that to myself again and again?

I want to shut down and pretend none of this happened, but . . . I'm all Jade has. I have my mom, and . . . well, that's it. But that's more than Jade has! I never thought *I'd* be the girl someone envies. But here we are.

Arrrrgggghhhhh. If only I'd stuck with Operation Ignore Ignore Ignore.

As the sun climbs higher in that big, wide, annoying Texas sky, I hear my mom galumphing down the stairs for her morning coffee and realize all at once that I need to get out of here today. I need to be distracted for a while—and Dot Teng is nothing if not good for distraction.

And yeah, I need to get away from Jade, so I can figure some things out.

Mom was embarrassingly delighted I wanted to come with her today. "You wanna be my assistant? I bet there will be some free char siu bao in the deal. It's like the old days when you actually liked me!"

I'm going to help her take some behind-the-scenes photos and video of the Chinese barbecue place in the International Village. That's one thing Buckeye Creek has over Bell Harbor, I guess: a Chinatown.

Loh Kitchen BBQ is in one corner of the International Village. Crammed between the Asian supermarket and a Chinese bakery, Loh Kitchen BBQ has a glowing sign with big English block letters and a glass front wall with the word OPEN in blue-and-red neon. Of course, part of the front window displays glistening barbecue duck and pork with that mouthwatering red-brown burnish. It reminds me of being a little kid in Honolulu or Seattle—getting together with family or friends at our favorite dim sum places and arguing over the check as we packed up leftovers.

We spend the day in the kitchen with the owners, sisters Hazel and Rose Loh. Mom takes pictures and grabs footage of the fifty-something-year-old sisters cooking in their small but ridiculously efficient kitchen.

Hazel and Rose move around each other like they have eyes in the back of their heads. Rose, petite and plump, will be thunderously chopping up a barbecued duck with a big, flat knife—my hands balling up into fists, thinking about how easily that knife could cut off my finger—and Hazel, long and lithe, will swivel around her with a container of rice flour, not spilling a speck. Then like magic she produces dozens of perfect ham sui gok—sweet, golden, chewy rice dumplings filled with salty pork.

"You want to try?" Hazel asks me, a gleam in her eye as she makes little oval bowls of dough for the filling.

"I don't—I'm not good at—" I start to explain, but in the blink of an eye she's put a chilled ball of dough in my hand and is showing me how to make it into a little nest for the meat. She commands, "No, more filling! Don't be cheap!" Hazel laughs and laughs, her gleeful cackle impossibly infectious.

After I make some very lumpy dumplings ("You take these home, nothing tastes better than food you made yourself"), Rose sweeps me away to help mix up her SECRET tofu skin roll filling. "Tastes just like my mother's fu pei guen. This is my favorite thing we make." (She even makes me close my eyes when she adds the SECRET ingredients.) I don't know what she puts in those rolls and I don't care. They are glorious.

The restaurant isn't fancy, but Hazel and Rose are experts and it shows—they work so fast and with so much precision. Rose makes perfect, pillowy char siu bao—barbecue pork buns—as she yells up front to a server about the napkin inventory while Hazel steams glossy cheung fun, rice noodle rolls with shrimp or pork, while teasing my mom about her "ABC Cantonese" ("ABC" is slang for American Born Chinese). It's like their hands have their own brains!

Now and then, Mom asks me to jot random thoughts down in her notebook for her. "Smells like a banquet, tastes like home"; "Texas barbecue has met its match"; "Don't ask for seconds, ask for *dim sum more.*"

"Oh, come on," I say at that last one, and she just laughs at me. "I'll make it pretty later," she says, and snaps a photo of Hazel hanging up a gleaming barbecued duck.

We pack up to leave Loh Kitchen BBQ, now with three bags full of crispy-skinned duck, barbecued pork, mostly-not-misshapen ham sui gok, a dozen fried tofu skin rolls, and, like, thirty char siu bao. Seriously. "You can freeze them and eat them later! They'll still be good," Hazel says when our eyes bulge at the sight of all those pork buns. Hazel and Rose say and do everything with such enthusiasm, it's impossible not to believe them.

I can't help but think about sharing those bao with Jade.

Before we leave, Mom goes to the back office to talk timelines with Hazel. I play on my phone in the kitchen until my ears perk up at a loud, deep voice at the front of the store. I peek around the burgundy half curtain that shields the kitchen from the counter where the cash register sits.

A tall man with light brown hair, a ruddy face, and a goatee stands at the counter glowering down at Rose. He wears the Dallas dude work uniform of a light blue button-down with no tie, open at the neck, and pleated khakis. "Do you un-der-stand," he barks at her, purposely dropping each syllable like a rock. "I. Want. More. Pork. Buns."

Rose, in her perfect-but-accented English, explains to him that there are only three buns to each order, it's printed on the menu. If he wants more, he has to buy another order.

"I'm not buyin' a whole 'nother order of pork buns, I just want one more. Now, I'll give you a quarter and you'll give me another bun. I don't care what you think you wrote in the menu." It isn't a question, it is a demand.

Rose holds firm and the man's nostrils flare. He swears and says something about how stingy all Chinese are. He leans into her—I'm afraid he might spit on her—and snarls, "Just give me the bun!"

I don't know what comes over me. I step out from behind the

curtain, my sneakers squeaking on the mopped floor. Rose and the guy look at me. Before I know what I'm doing, I speak.

"It's on the menu."

He waves me off. "Get back in the kitchen. Doesn't anybody here speak English?"

My hands ball up into fists again, but this time for a different reason.

"HEY. Don't tell me what to do and don't tell her what to do. And it's your own English that's lacking if you can't comprehend that there are *three buns per order.* Don't insult us with your quarter either. Either pay for another order of buns or get out."

Whoa. What am I doing? But I can't stop now. No way.

I look at Rose to make sure she isn't mad at the way I'm speaking to a customer, but she nods at me and turns back to the man, stone-faced. "You heard what the girl said." We glare at him. The power of the Chinese lady glare is mighty.

The man sneers at Rose and sticks his finger in her face, telling her that she's lost a customer. Then, just to complete the stereotypical racist white dude picture, he yells, "Go back to China!" as he walks out the door.

I would have laughed at the absurdity of him if my heart wasn't pounding so hard.

As we watch him drive off in—what else—a red pickup truck, I lean my head against the wall and proceed to stress-sweat. "I'm so sorry, Rose. I made you lose a customer!"

"Ai-yah!" she says. "That guy comes in here every few weeks and complains that we shortchange him or don't give him enough noodles. He bullies us until we give in just to stay safe, you know? But when the little girl with the American English yells at him, then he leaves! Ha! I tell you, this country. I'm glad to see him go."

"What a jerk," I say, and wipe my clammy palms on my shirt.

"Who's a jerk?" My mom appears beside me, having come out of the back office with Hazel.

Rose fills Mom in on everything that happened, Mom's eyes filling with more rage with every dumb thing the dude said. When Rose concludes with how he drove off all butt hurt, she says something in Cantonese, gesturing at me with a grin.

Mom's eyes go from warrior to weepy in a blink and she thanks Rose in Cantonese. "Doh jeh, doh jeh." Thank you for the gift, thank you from the heart. We all giggle a little at Mom's kinda wonky Canto, but the sentiment is real.

On the way home, Mom beams at me. "What did Rose say? She was talking about me, right?" I ask.

"She said, 'She is a good girl. Not afraid. You never have to worry about her.' And it just made me realize."

"Realize what?"

"That I've been worrying about you my whole life—finding the best place for us, the kids at school, the zaps. But you're tougher than you look."

"Gee, thanks." I roll my eyes.

"No!" She laughs. "I mean, there's so much I don't understand about you, kid. That I can't protect you from. Which, as a mom, is a freakin' terrible feeling! So I try to make the stuff I *can* control as good as can be. That's partly why I moved us around so much. I want you to have the best life possible."

"Oh" is all I can say. I feel like the worst person ever, but her honesty is bringing me down from the high of the day with the Loh sisters and back to the reality of our life at odds. All the same, I love her a lot in that moment. Can two things be true at once?

"So, I guess what I'm saying," she continues, "is that while I really do think being in Buckeye Creek is doing good things for us—for you—I get that you're wise and more mature than I've given you credit for. So come October, I promise whatever you decide, Buckeye Creek or Bell Harbor, we'll make it work. You've got a good head on your shoulders, Molls."

I know I'm supposed to have a moment with my mom, but I can't bring myself to cry or hug her like they do in sitcoms. I feel conflicted.

I can't stand the thought of my mom being right, of staying in Buckeye Creek with guys like that dude at the restaurant, of not going back to the ease and mostly normalcy in Bell Harbor. But being in Buckeye Creek, being in the house, meeting the Loh sisters, meeting Jade—these things are getting under my skin.

As we drive through the dimming streets of our suburb, down the massive winding freeway, past the mall and chain restaurants, then onto historic, tree-lined Charlotte Street, a wave of contentment washes over me. With a car full of Chinese barbecue and a day's worth of memories, I feel renewed.

While this should bring me comfort, it only confuses me more.

I've always wished my mom would let me make decisions in our life, and now that I've finally been given a chance to make a decision—THE BIGGEST DECISION—I'm having doubts.

Plus, I know Jade is waiting at home.

34
JADE

These days it seems all I do is wait for Molly.

I wait for her to wake up.

I wait for her to want to talk to me.

I wait for her to feed me. (Though the cereal she left out for me this morning was greatly appreciated.)

Is this what it's like to be one of those big slobbery dogs that sleep by the front door until their owner comes home? I wonder if I am the reincarnation of such a dog. Is there even such a thing as reincarnation?

But today feels extra urgent. What must she think of me? I obviously frightened her and then I had to go and ask her to use her gift—the gift she quite obviously doesn't see as a gift—to help me. Is it selfish of me to ask her to stay?

The car pulls up to the house just as the sun is dipping below the horizon. The sky is orange, pink, and purple and the insects are starting to strike up their chorus in the backyard. I've seen thousands of these evenings. I can practically count down to darkness by the second.

I watch from the living room window, careful to keep myself invisible as Molly and her mother unload bags from the car. Molly glances up at the window, and while I know she can't see me, I swear I see her grimace in my direction.

The front door opens and the house is instantly filled with the sweet, salty, sticky smells of barbecued meat. I've smelled a lot of barbecue over the years; people in Texas have an affinity for it. But this one smells different. There are different spices, some more assertive and pungent, some earthy, something floral hiding just beneath it all. As I inhale the aroma, it's like I'm tasting it. My stomach gurgles and I hush it. *"Molly will feed us,"* I whisper.

I warm with that knowledge. I am such a lucky ghost. I get fed on purpose!

Molly and her mother bring in bags and bags of food packaged in paper and Styrofoam containers. There's meat, dumplings, buns, rice—I've rarely seen so much carefully crafted food laid out on the kitchen table. Not a pizza in sight.

Molly and Dot dig in, filling their plates high and heading into the living room to watch a story—like they always do—over dinner. I wonder if they understand that the dining room is for more than strange souvenirs.

Molly hangs back for a moment and places a pork bun and another round golden treat on the kitchen counter. She whispers in my general direction, "The char siu bao and ham sui gok are amazing; take these, we'll eat more tonight in my room. See you around midnight." And she goes off to join her mom.

I pick up the fresh warm food and cradle it in my hands. So beautiful. *Char siu bao*—barbecued pork . . . or *fork roast bun*—once again the translation of the words floats to the surface of my mind. I'm remembering something from another life—*my* life.

I press the bouncy white bun. It will be such an experience! I can't wait!

I turn over the egg-shaped dumpling, the ham sui gok. It has a crisp golden skin, but it also feels soft and chewy. (Chewy foods are my new favorite!) *Ham sui gok . . . salty water corner.* These are things that my brain just knows.

Before I can marvel at my linguistic prowess for too long, my stomach roars and I gobble the treats down. I *did* try to slow myself, to savor the salty-sweet chewiness, but it was nearly impossible.

Molly and her mother eat in front of a laptop, watching some show set in the '90s. The 1990s. Dot exclaims, "I'm so old! I totally had those pants," and Molly occasionally points at the screen and says, "Oh my god, that is so YOU."

There is a lightness to their interaction. Something is different. There's less friction. Does this mean something?

By eleven o'clock they both start looking sleepy and Molly's mother hits pause on their show. "I'm gonna go read in bed; that Japanese sci-fi book I'm reading is really heating up. You going to bed?"

Molly melts onto the floor from the couch before standing up and stretching. "I don't even want to know what that means. No, I'm staying up for a bit; I think I'm going to have a second dinner."

"Again? Okay, but save me a few char siu bao." Dot kisses Molly on the cheek and saunters up the stairs to the bathroom, where I can hear her singing as she washes her face.

Molly goes to the kitchen, where she piles up a pair of plates with food. Going tentatively up the stairs, she flits to her room when she sees the bathroom door is closed and her mom cannot witness the plethora of food she's carrying.

At first she closes the door behind her, but before I build up the energy to turn the doorknob, she opens it just wide enough for me. A lump blooms in my throat. I go in, using the built-up energy to push the door shut, and sit down on the side of the bed Molly gestures to.

A plate waits for me and Molly is already nibbling on a bun.

"Isn't this the best!" she gushes.

My face might split from grinning, I am unencumbered by fear for a moment.

"It really is."

35
MOLLY

Jade sits down at the foot of the bed and, noticing how I have my knees pulled under me, she copies how I sit. Watching me, she picks up one of the ham sui gok and takes a tentative bite, her eyes darting around as she chews slowly, like she's experiencing every chew for the first time.

"You okay?" I ask, trying not to show that I'm thinking about the monster.

She looks up at me with eyes shining. She looks so much like a little kid sometimes, rather than a hundred-year-old ghost-lady-kid, it's disarming.

She swallows her food. "I'm more than okay! I think, right now, I am happy."

"You are?" Maybe I'm a little too surprised when I say this, and she stops like a deer in the headlights. "I mean, that's great!"

"You remembered me," she says, all lit up. "Even though you were cross with me this morning, you left me food. And then when you ate with your mom, you made sure I had food too. And now, like you said you would, here we are eating together. You *think* of me. That hasn't happened for so, so long. In fact, I have no memory of actually being *considered!*"

"Wait," I say. "I have a question. Why can't you just use your ghost powers to go into the fridge or cupboards whenever you want and get whatever you want? Why all the sneaking around and depending on people to leave out food?"

"I'm honestly not sure why things are this way," Jade says, a little worry crease appearing between her eyes. "I guess it's like part of whatever punishment this is. I can eat crumbs, I can eat things you give me"—her voice lowers—"I can eat garbage . . . but if I try to open the cupboard or refrigerator—which requires *a lot* of energy—it's like there's an invisible barrier, and that barrier is on fire. Once I was so desperate when a new family moved in, I tried to open a cupboard to get some crackers they tossed in there. But when I touched the cupboard door, it was like it was molten. Except the burning seemed to come from *inside* my fingertips—the closer I got to the food, the worse it got. I can't steal, I can only scrounge."

She won't look at me. "The food . . . it's not mine to have." Shame oozes from her, and I feel like a monster myself for asking.

"Oh," I say just to break the silence. I try to figure out what to say without sounding too awkward. "I don't want that to be your forever."

A thought travels across her face. "Molly, does this mean . . . that you'll . . . that you'll help me—"

"Wait." I stop her before she gets too far. "I have to say some things too. But I promise, it's not bad . . . I don't think."

How do I say this without sounding like a total cheeseball?

"Okay. So. Today I had to speak up for someone. I had to stand with somebody I cared about and not back down, even if it scared me. And, honestly, I *was* scared, but in my gut I knew I couldn't live with myself if I didn't help. So I did. I've never thought of myself as being strong or tough—my mom and I have always kind of shared this idea that I'm fragile, I guess? But today, somebody tried to bully me, get me to break, and I didn't. It wasn't even an option."

Jade just blinks at me.

"Um . . . okay, I can see you're confused. My point is that I'm tougher than I thought. And I really want to do what's right. So, while I'm in Buckeye Creek, I'm going to help you . . . with my, uh, 'skills.' Because you're strong too and you deserve to know who you are."

Cringe. I shove half a bun in my mouth to stop myself from rambling. I look at Jade. Iridescent tears trail her cheeks.

"Thank you, Molly. I can't believe it. Maybe the universe isn't punishing me after all." She searches my face. "You think I'm strong? After what you've seen of me?"

"Are you kidding!" I exclaim, spraying pork bun all over my bed. "*Especially* after what I've seen of you. You never give up! You've watched hundreds of people come and go, you can't leave this sweltering house, you hunt and gather food for yourself? AND you're going after what you want? There are living people who can't do any of those things. If it were me trapped here, I'd have chewed off my own arm to get out!"

The smile drops from Jade's face. Her eyes dart away from mine.

Uh-oh.

"Did I say something wrong?"

"There's just so much you don't know about me," she says quietly. "Sometimes to be strong, like you say, you have to do things that you . . . you . . . wish you could forget."

Molly, you dork! What have you done?

"Hey, Jade, it's okay. I'm going to help you. There's nothing you could have done that will scare me away now." I try to appear sure of myself, but now I'm really curious: What has Jade done that could be so horrible?

She seems to calm down a little and nods at me, forcing a smile. "Okay, Molly. Okay."

"Great. Then if we're going to solve your mystery, we probably need a plan, right?" I say, trying to ride the wave of confidence I caught today. Plans, right? That's what teen sleuths do? They find a mystery, make a plan, do the plan, solve the crime, and go to prom. My prom will be getting out of Texas.

Jade and I eat and scheme and come up with a plan where over the following weeks we'll explore every inch of the house "memory hunting." As much as I hate the idea of it, I'm willing to let myself get zapped so we can find some clues about Jade's past.

While Jade really wants to get started right away, I have to tell her to slow it down. I can't spend all day every day getting zapped! She looks at me blankly when I tell her she needs to chill.

"My brain will turn into oatmeal if we don't pace ourselves," I explain. "Also, part of solving a mystery is examining the clues, so if we find some information, we need to understand it. I know we don't have a ton of time, but slow and steady wins the race, right?" If I'm taking care of myself, I'm taking care of Jade. We have to be smart and not turn me into a permanent gruel-for-brains zombie.

Jade pops the last piece of ham sui gok in her mouth and bops up and down on the bed as she eats. "It's just so *cool*—"

(So cute when she tries out words from "the youths.")

"—to look forward to something."

"Yeah," I say, feeling full, sleepy, and relaxed for the first time in a while. "We can do this."

36
JADE

"I'm sorry! I can't let it zap me over and over again—which, by the way, is REALLY getting old today—but all I see is some old dude blowing out a lot of candles on a cake and a banner over his head that says 'Mort's Seventieth Birthday Bash.'"

Molly crosses her hands over her chest, her mouth in a flat line; her eyes seem to rest permanently mid-roll. We've been examining the built-in shelves in the dining room all afternoon—finding which of the original shelves remember things. I don't recall a time when the shelves haven't been in the house, so I assume they hold memories that could be important. Molly isn't convinced. For the past two hours every zap has been from a man named Mort, an electrician wondering about his pregnant wife, or Sandra Mitchell from the 1930s, who was *really* passionate about teacups. However, I don't remember a Mort, which intrigues me and seems like it could lead to a revelation.

Molly hates Mort. At least, Mort's family's fascination with his seventieth birthday.

"We've almost examined every section of the shelves! Please just that last corner? What if we skip over *the* shelf that holds the key to who I am!"

"Ugh, FINE." Molly grumbles and stands in front of the corner of the shelves closest to the living room. Taking a deep breath, she reaches for the lowest shelf and closes her eyes.

For a few moments it's like she goes somewhere else. Her eyes fly open but she is unseeing. They water a bit as her pupils dart from side to side, up and down. After nearly a minute she stumbles back as if she's been shocked. She sinks to her knees, her head in her hands.

"Molly . . . what did you see?" She takes deep breaths as the color returns to her cheeks.

"Mort . . . he . . . they . . . you're . . . YOU'RE MORT!" Her eyes are fixed on me. Neither of us breathes. Then she breaks into a smile and bursts into laughter.

"Gotcha!" she says, and lies flat on the dining room floor, her head under their newly acquired dark wood table. I don't know if I will ever adjust to Molly's sense of humor.

"I'm sorry, Jade, I'm not trying to be mean, but I'm wiped. We've been investigating for hours today! I need a break tomorrow.

Remember what I told you about becoming a barfing zombie with oatmeal for brains? Well, I think I've got the barfy part under control now, but I feel like I can't remember my middle name anymore."

I sit down under the table by her head. "What's your middle name, Zombie Molly?"

She opens her eyes wide and extends her arms straight up in the air in front of her like the walking undead. She says in a low monotone voice, "Mooooooort!"

I poke her shoulder with my hand.

"Hey! Watch it, Edward Chilly Hands!" This time we both let out tired giggles.

"But really, what is your middle name?" I ask.

"Mei, like my mom's sister's Chinese name, my auntie Bobbie. She used to be my mom's hero or something."

"Used to?"

"Yeah, they don't talk now. I'm not sure what happened. Something about Bobbie disapproving of something my mom did. Which, knowing my mom, could be anything. Bobbie is a big reason we moved to Buckeye Creek. My mom wants to fix things with her. She lives in Denton, so not far."

"Are you going to see her?" I ask.

"Mom keeps saying we're going to, but something always comes up. It's weird, I kind of think she's scared of Bobbie. She keeps wanting to pull the trigger, reach out to Bobbie, but then she freaks out and puts it off."

"Do you know why?"

"I don't. It's like when something really, really matters to you and the stakes are super high, it feels safer not to try and always wonder instead of trying and maybe failing. I think my mom is afraid of failing and then losing her sister forever."

I take this in. Another lonely person is added to the equation. It seems as if there are people everywhere searching for each other, yearning to connect. Is anyone out there thinking of me? After over a century, the odds are slim. The loneliness I've been able to keep at bay during my days and nights with Molly rears up and envelops me.

"Hey, helloooo, Jade?" Molly waves her hand in front of my eyes. "Where'd you go?"

"Oh, you know, Panama, Portugal, Macau, all with first-class passage!" I try really hard to sound jovial, not bitter. I take a big breath. "Okay, Molly Mei, where should we investigate next? I know you're tired, and you're right, you need a break. Maybe we simply need to narrow our investigation."

"Right." Molly props herself up on her elbows. "Work smarter, not harder. My mom says that."

"Yes. So far we've combed through the kitchen. The living room was surprisingly devoid of relevant memories, though I had no idea that Mr. Kern was so enamored of the widow next door."

Molly continues my train of thought. "Ugh, please don't remind me. The entryway memories were all proms, graduations, and farewells—*snore*."

"We should test the bathroom and the bedrooms," I suggest. "Those have always been emotional rooms of the house and have some original pieces like old pipes, fixtures, and windowsills."

Molly averts her eyes.

"What?"

"It's just . . ." Molly hesitates. "We need stuff. Shelves and windowsills are fine, I guess, but who clutches a bathroom pipe and pours their memories into it? I mean, it could happen, but in all my years of seeing dead people's memories, it's almost always an item like a cup or a watch that holds all the big feelings people put out there. Doorknobs are a close second—the whole psyching yourself up to enter or leave a room, I think—but really it's always *stuff*. Have you ever found any items in the house that came from the time when you were alive?"

I wasn't ready for this.

"I . . . I'd have to think about that. I doubt it." I hate lying to Molly, especially when she's trying to help me. She lays her head back on the floor and closes her eyes.

"Yeah, think about it. Day after tomorrow let's start in the bathroom. Who knows, maybe you fixed the pipe behind the sink and made a wish on a star." Molly laughs at the absurdity of that scenario and I force a laugh to keep up appearances.

I don't know how long I can keep my bones from Molly.

37
MOLLY

"How about you and me take a weekend road trip before school starts? See more of Texas? There are those Cadillacs stuck in the ground somewhere. Ooh! Or we could go to that water park in New Braunfels!" Mom finds me in the kitchen making a quesadilla for lunch. She's been working from home this week, which makes my Jade investigation a lot more difficult. More than once I've pretended to be talking to Eleanor on my phone instead of to the dead girl egging me on to touch the wall or poke the floorboards.

I'm about to say no—Jade and I are still deep in clue-gathering mode and we've gotten nowhere—but then maybe getting out of my haunted house might be the break I need to come back and really focus on our investigation and make some progress?

"That actually sounds like it might be good."

Mom looks so pleased. "Sweet. I'll ask around for recommendations on cool, cheap places to stay. I want some motel that looks like the set of a 1950s horror movie." And with that Mom practically skips out of the kitchen and up the stairs.

"You can't go away! We have so much to do!"

I turn to see Jade with her hands on her hips, momentarily looking more like an old auntie scolding me instead of a kid my age. "Jade, my dude, please enhance your calm."

This only seems to make her more upset. "Please don't make a joke of this, Molly. This is my existence we're talking about! You're about to go to school all day for months; we need to get as much work done as possible while you still have time for me."

Aaaaarrrgggggh. I'm not in the mood for this. I walk into the living room and throw myself face down on the couch. I hear the floorboards creak and feel a whoosh of cold air as Jade follows.

"Molly! I know you think you have all the time in the world, all living people do, but weeks and months go by fast. Before you know it, you'll be packing up and you'll leave without so much as a backward glance my way. Please don't go away even for a day."

This is too much. I sit up. "Look, Jade, I gotta have a life. I'm willing to devote most of it to helping you, but I need to be able to do other things. Like go on road trips with my mom or have other friends." Saying *other* friends feels so weird.

Something perks up in Jade. "So . . . we *really are* friends?"

"What? Of course we're friends. We've been over this before."

Jade suddenly looks very small and childlike again. She shifts her weight, looks at her feet. "You're the first friend I've ever had, Molly."

"Honestly, this is new to me too. I've never really had friends either, but I think I could? And that's because of you. So, really, if you think about it, you're, like, my *best* friend." It's my turn to look down.

"Really?" I hear Jade say. Her voice cracks a little. "I'd say you're *my* best friend too."

Neither of us knows what to say so we just sit in choked-up silence for a minute. Finally, after I swallow the lump in my throat I look up at Jade, ready to pour out my heart about how much she's changed my life for the better. But when I look up, her form flickers like someone flipped a light switch on and off. I can see through her to the staircase.

"What are you doing?" I ask.

"I—I don't know. I didn't do it. Everything went black, like I closed my eyes but I didn't, and now everything looks foggy and white." I can hear the panic in Jade's voice.

"What's happening?"

I open my mouth, but again I'm speechless.

38
JADE

"Maybe you're sick?"

"I'm dead!"

"Okay. Well, do you see any bright lights?"

"What?"

"You know, people say that when ghosts are done with their earthly business they go toward the bright white light to *the other side*. Jade, do you see any white lights?"

I look around Molly's darkened room. All I see is her face, the giant bag of marshmallows we are devouring, and the leftover pizza (again) that Molly brought me tonight. No lights to the other side.

"No. Nothing."

It is well past one o'clock in the morning and Molly and I are no closer to discerning what happened to me. I thought perhaps it was brought on by the emotion of being told I am Molly's best friend (I have a best friend!), but earlier tonight it happened again.

As Molly was explaining the social hierarchy of the modern American middle school and the different ways "theater kids" have been treated at her schools, the lights went out. At least, that's what it looked like to me. The world went black, then faded back in through the cobwebs again.

What was extra disconcerting was that one second I could feel the texture of Molly's blanket under my legs, but the next I felt like I was falling *through* Molly's bed. That's never happened before. It was as if I was more air than person, a feeling I never want to feel again.

"Do we need to do an exorcism?"

"Molly! That's to get *rid* of a ghost, not help one *not* fade away! Plus, isn't that for harmful spirits?"

Molly grabs a marshmallow and shoves the whole thing in her mouth as she thinks. I pick one up and nibble. I had no idea such a texture existed. If I wasn't so panicked I'd be delighted by these cloud-like, sugary treats.

"Nothing like this has ever happened to you before?" Molly asks.

"No."

"What's different now?"

I laugh. "Everything! I'm sitting on a bed with you eating *marsh-mallows* and you can hear and see me and are *talking to me*. Nothing about this has been part of my normal—until now."

"But something's got to be making this happen. Can ghosts suffer from malnutrition?" Molly asks.

"I hardly think that's the problem," I say, gesturing to our spread. "What if . . ." I'm afraid to say it. "What if it's just . . . my time."

"What do you mean?"

"What if ghosts only get a certain amount of time on earth and now my time is up."

Molly's dark eyes get even darker. This really seems to frighten her. "Maybe that's something we have to accept. Your . . . death. But I'm not ready to invite it in yet." I'm surprised by this superstitious streak. I drop it in the moment, but the idea burrows into my brain.

Molly chews a marshmallow "I'm figuring all this stuff out too. What is even happening in this house? You're dealing with the whole 'dead' thing, something I'm really trying to wrap my brain around. And while it's not the same, having a slumber party with my best friend—any friend—is not my normal either."

I hesitate. I'm curious about Molly's past, but everything about her tells me it's a tender spot. "Molly. If it's always been so hard for you to make friends and now you have a *best friend,* why are you so eager to leave Buckeye Creek?"

Molly lies on her back, her head hitting her pillow. She looks up at the ceiling, her mouth opening and closing as if she keeps trying to start a sentence, then rethinking it.

"I know it doesn't really make a lot of sense," she says finally, eyes still glued on the ceiling. "On one hand Buckeye Creek seems to have everything I've always wanted: friendship, my mom isn't researching the next move, and for the first time ever my *abilities* are a good thing. But school is about to start and that's a whole other thing."

"Why?" I ask.

"When I'm here in the house I can convince myself I make sense. I'm not the creepy girl, I'm not the Chinese girl, I'm just Molly. Molly who can talk to ghosts, but somehow that's exactly who I'm supposed to be here. Molly who can talk to ghosts is the best version of Molly." She pauses. "For now."

"For now? Why just for now?"

Molly sits up and sighs in exasperation. "Because when school starts, the best version of me is also the version of me that makes me a target. I can't just be Molly who helps ghosts anymore. I'll be back to being Molly who never fits in, Molly who might be the only Asian kid in the class, Molly who has to pretend that she only has normal teenage horrors to deal with when in reality the school's ancient gym bleachers zap her and she sees a basketball player from the '70s bleeding from a head injury on the bench, right before she screams, power barfs, and falls down in front of the whole school. *That* Molly Teng is the Molly who has to drag her zombie-fied butt to class even when kids won't sit next to her because, and I quote, they 'don't want to be in her splash zone.'"

Molly's eyes are distant, like she's reliving so many memories. She comes back to me.

"Living here might be the best and worst thing that's ever happened to me, but living here also never really lets me just BE NORMAL. At least in kooky old Bell Harbor, I got really close to just being a kid. People didn't look that hard at me for some reason. And if they did, they were okay with what they saw."

I take this in. Everything about me reminds Molly she is different. Her entire life she's wanted to blend in, and for as long as I can remember I've just wanted to be noticed.

Molly wipes her eyes and picks up a marshmallow. She holds it out to me. "But I'm here now, so I'm going to *really* be here. And I'm going to help you."

I take the marshmallow and force myself to smile and nod, but I feel let down. I haunt this house, and I haunt Molly. Molly scratches aggressively at her hair and lets out a big puff of air, as if she's trying to blow all the awkwardness out of the room.

"I've got to go to sleep soon, but I think we should keep looking for clues about who you are. That's got to be the key to all of it, don't you think?"

As much as I don't want to just pretend like everything is fine, I know she's right. "Yes, I agree, of course."

"We need things that people from when you were alive might have touched and left with a memory. Like the window seat or like when I saw your attic after I touched my bedroom doorknob. I saw . . ." Molly's brow furrows.

"You saw . . . ?" I hope to prod her into remembering.

"Just quick snippets of memory. Nothing that makes sense. Do you know where there might be more objects? Like antiques?"

I stiffen. "I might." I think about the sickening disappearing feeling and about how much Molly wants to leave. "I'll—I'll look around my attic and see if there's anything I can bring you." I know how vague and avoidant this sounds. Molly doesn't seem bothered, though. In fact she perks up.

"The attic! That's always been your domain! Why haven't we investigated there? Last time I was up there—when I met you—it felt like zap city. That's where we should go!" Her enthusiasm fills me with dread. If it could, my heart would thump out of my chest. I stand up and pretend to shake crumbs off my dress. As if I'd waste crumbs like that.

"That's quite the idea!" I say, hearing the panic in my voice. "Well, gosh, it's late, I should go back to my attic! I'll bring you anything I find. Maybe there's a corner I haven't looked at properly." The lie thuds between us.

"Okay . . ." she says cautiously. "Are you all right, Jade?"

"I'm great! Just tired! All right, thank you for the marshmallows. I'll find you tomorrow, good night!" I make myself disappear and slip out the door. In the dark of the hallway I try to calm myself. Whether I like it or not, I'm not going to be able to keep my secret hidden in the attic for much longer.

39
MOLLY

I climb into bed and try to drift off. It's almost two thirty in the morning and I can't tell what's more tired, my brain or my body. I feel like I have a whole bao in my stomach but the filling is rocks. I'm worried about Jade, and for the first time the realization hits me that I might not be able to help her. This spooky experiment could be a matter of life and death for Jade. Or death and death? Or death and . . . what's worse than death?

I can't even begin to know what Jade must be going through. I guess I can't blame her for behaving a little strangely.

As the sun starts to warm up the sky and the birds start to really commit to their concert, I fall asleep, wondering what Jade is doing in her attic right now. The bao in my stomach flip-flops.

———

"Ugh . . . Dot! Shoot . . ." My mom scolds herself as she almost drops one of the plates she found on my dresser. Awake but unwilling to open my eyes, I prepare myself for the interrogation. "Good morning, Mother dear," I say in a croaky morning baritone.

"Hey, kid." She stops wrestling with the plates and my bedroom door. "Sorry, I thought you'd be up by now, and then I thought I'd do some cleaning up while you snoozed and I found these plates. You okay, Molls?"

I open one eye and roll it over to her. "I'm really fine, Mom, I just got hungry last night."

"Two plates hungry?"

"Yeah." I wrench my other eye open. My clock says 10:13 a.m. Ugh. "Don't worry, Mom. I just went back for another slice and forgot my plate so I got a new one." I know it is a weak lie but it is the best I can come up with. Note to self: From now on, Jade and I share plates for Second Dinner Club.

Mom looks like she wants to dig into this excuse, but she also doesn't want to shame me.

"I promise I feel great," I tell her. "I've just had a really big appetite lately. I think I'm getting taller. My pants totally feel shorter." *Molly, stop talking.* Wanting to get Mom back on my side, I suggest, "Maybe we can go shopping for new outfits for our road trip?"

Normally a mother-daughter shopping mission makes Dot Teng downright chipper, but this time the guilty, uncomfortable look on her face just deepens. It's rare times like this that my mom actually looks like she's old enough to be someone's mom.

"Okay, Dot, spill it. What's up?" I ask.

She puts the plates back on my dresser and sits on the edge of my bed. "I don't think we can go on our road trip before school starts."

"Why?" I say, suddenly much more awake. I'm surprised how disappointed I feel.

Mom sighs and her eyes brighten even if her brows knit. "It's Bobbie; she's coming to visit us!"

Mom waits for me to react. I don't know what to do with my face, so I do nothing.

"I know, it's kind of bananas, right? If it was anybody else I'd say 'Forget it,' but she's a big reason why we—I—"

I appreciate Mom correcting herself.

"—decided to move here. This is huge. She's refused to speak to me for so long, understandably." Mom's eyes drop like she's fast-forwarding through past mistakes. "And now she's willing to come over here and stay for a few days. I think this is our chance to fix things, Molly. This is my chance to get my sister back."

Mom's right, this is huge. They apparently had some bonkers fight and Mom attempted to leap out of a moving vehicle just to get away from Bobbie. She and my mom really haven't spoken since then.

A little after Lunar New Year last year, Mom came home in a huff, went into the closet, then reappeared with a pile of mail that she threw in the garbage before locking herself in the bathroom and turning on the shower. Our code for "I need to cry alone." Looking in the trash can, I found a few greeting card envelopes and a small package that had just gotten returned to us. In Dot Teng style, she'd drawn little holiday-specific doodles on each envelope—a reindeer, party hats and noisemakers for New Year's, a rabbit for the Year of the Rabbit. They were all addressed to a Bobbie Teng in Denton, Texas. At least at first.

Bobbie's address had been furiously crossed out and a little white label, the kind you print at home, was stuck on every piece of mail. Each label said RETURN TO SENDER in an aggressive black font. The small package, the size of a book, had the same pointed postage on it. A not-so-subtle message from my auntie Bobbie.

So Mom's been trying. And failing. Until now.

"Is it okay, Molls? Is it? I promise we'll take a trip the first long weekend you have off from school. Anywhere you want that doesn't require plane travel or cash up front." She chuckles at her own quip.

I will my face to move and give my mom a reassuring smile. "Of course it's okay. I totally understand." I'm disappointed and I think Mom knows that. Getting away from the house for a few days before school starts honestly sounded great. I'd get to have some wacky, probably embarrassing fun with my mom and not worry about being all zombied-out for the first day of school.

But how can I say no?

She throws her arms around me. "Thank you for understanding. You're the best. Totally the best." Her voice is too loud and high, her attempt at sounding confident.

After she scurries out of the room with the plates, I climb out of bed and put on the cutoffs I've been wearing for days and a clean tank top with a neon armadillo on it.

All right, this is the sign I needed. Vacations can and *should* wait. If I'm going to help Jade, I need to commit. She's fading or disappearing or *something* and I'm the only one who can get to the bottom of it with her. She's scared and that scares me.

This is what friends do for each other.

40

JADE

Please let this work.

"This is my oldest possession. This comb was in the box with me. It's been my constant companion for as long as I can remember."

I hold out my red lacquer comb, the one I snatched away from Molly on that first day.

Molly's eyes light up. "The comb! I remember it from the stairs. This is perfect!" she says, and reaches for it.

I pull it back. "Please be careful, it's the most precious thing I have."

"I'm sorry, I didn't mean to be so eager. I'll be careful, I promise," she says, and holds open her hand, letting me extend the comb to her.

Grasping my comb in my fingers, I hover the comb above Molly's hand and place it on her open palm. *What will it have to say?* But instead of resting on her palm, it falls through, hitting the floor below without a sound.

Both of us stare at it, dumbfounded.

"What just happened?" Molly asks.

"I—I'm not sure," I say, and pick it up again. In my hand it's solid; I feel its weight and smoothness. I hold it out to Molly again; this time she tries to grasp it, take it from me. Her hands grab air.

"Is this . . . a ghost comb?" Molly asks, her fingers still trying to pinch the comb.

"It can't be. Can it? I was clutching it in the box; it must have followed me from life into death. I suppose it is." Perhaps that's why it's so dear to me. The fascination with this bizarre phenomenon only lasts a minute before I realize that the one item I hoped would provide answers, the one item I felt safe sharing, is not a real item at all. My choices have dwindled to one unavoidable option.

"This is unbelievable," Molly says, leaning in to look at it. "It looks just like a regular comb—an old comb—totally solid. I guess if it got put in the bone box with you, it's a ghost?"

That seems like an oversimplification, but apparently it's accurate. But is *everything* that comes from the box just a specter?

Molly looks up from the comb. "Is this all you have?"

I nod, attempting to conceal my nerves.

"Jade, why do I get the feeling you're holding something back?"

"I am . . . not."

"Liar!" she fires at me. "Come *on*, Jade! If I'm going to zap myself, you've got to give me the goods!"

The goods? How do I explain to Molly that the so-called goods might not be good at all? We've come so far, we're real friends! If—when—I give her the one object that might hold the key to this whole puzzle, I may be sacrificing our friendship for my past.

And future.

"I know, Molly, I know. I'm just afraid."

She softens. "I know, it's got to be really scary. I can't imagine what it's like to be fading away. Does it hurt?"

I wince a little; I can't help it. Earlier today while Molly and I were sharing more leftover pizza for breakfast, I started to bite a slice but my lips and teeth passed entirely through it. Then there was that falling sensation, like I was *inside* the chair I was perched on, even stronger this time.

"No, it doesn't hurt. I don't really feel anything, but that's what's most frightening really: I feel numb, like I'm *losing* feeling, I'm losing *connection* to this world."

Molly looks solemn. "I'm really sorry," she says, and reaches a hand out to me. "You're not alone, okay? We're going to figure this out together."

I nod. Right on cue my stomach growls. I want to believe her, but I also believe the monster in me. That creature that drives my stomach and my guts tells me I am very much alone and perhaps I deserve it.

"But," she says, her tone changing, "I can't help you if you aren't honest with me. We can investigate the whole house and I can get zapped by every button, bobby pin, and shoelace you've ever found, but I know the answers are in your attic. That's what I've seen—*I've felt*—from my very first day here."

This is the moment I've been dreading. When I have to make a choice: stay the Jade who Molly knows and cares about, the Jade who if she fades away will be remembered as good and *human*? Or tell Molly about what I've done, my first moments born into death; reveal my true nature, more monstrous than she could understand?

"Jade, I don't want you to disappear. Please, whatever it is, let me help you." Molly's eyes are liquid, searching.

Okay. One step at a time. I can always stop this before it goes too far. "Bring Second Dinner to the attic door tonight," I tell her. "We'll get to work. We should probably get some rest."

Molly nods and we sit in silence, each of us steeling ourselves for the night ahead.

41
MOLLY

The rest of the day feels like I'm barreling toward something ominous.

Jade and I retreat to our separate corners—she goes to the attic to do

whatever she does up there and I go down to the couch to watch videos

and attempt to turn my brain off. Don't judge me, I'm literally dealing

with someone's life, death, and death again.

And I know I sound like a broken record, but *this would never have*

happened in Bell Harbor. I feel a little guilty even thinking that because

it really seems like I came into Jade's life for a reason, but life was so

simple in Maine. Everything here just feels so unsteady and, well, BIG

LIFE AND DEATH. Bell Harbor was just living my life. Right now I

feel like other people's lives are counting on me.

Jade because, well, she doesn't want to disappear.

My mom because she really seems to like it here and wants me to

like it too, but she also wants to keep her promise about moving back

to Bell Harbor. I feel so *responsible* for her, more so than ever. I mean,

I usually feel a responsibility to be a good member of Team Teng and be all in on the narrative that it's *Us Against the World*, but now I also feel the weight of our future. *Her* future.

Mom's really been finding a place doing social media, content creation, and just straight-up helping small, mostly Asian American and immigrant businesses around Buckeye Creek. Places that hadn't necessarily thought about being on Instagram, TikTok, or even building a website are now getting more attention because of my mom. People like the Loh sisters or the Songs, who own a boba place, or her new client the Ahmads, who own a really amazing tandoori joint, are getting more business and buzz because of Dot Teng's social media stylings. Plus, it seems like my mom has found *her* people too.

She went on a date with Jami Ahmad and she blushes every time I ask if there will be a second.

Do I have the heart to take her away from all this? If we go back to Bell Harbor, will it be the same?

I've heard people say "you can never go back" and I never really understood it until maybe now. If we went back to Bell Harbor, would we be picking up where we left off, before Buckeye Creek left an imprint on us? Or would we be starting over brand-new AGAIN?

I wander into the kitchen and grab a fistful of stale corn chips. They are salty but they are not satisfying. Anytime I eat these days I can't help but think about Jade. What awaits me tonight? She's hiding something, and you don't have to have ghost powers to know it's a dark something.

I want to think I'm understanding and grown-up enough to be okay with anything she reveals, but what if I'm not? What if her revelation just confirms that I've got to get out of here and get back to Bell Harbor? I'll feel like such a failure—to everyone.

So much hangs on what Jade is hiding. More than she even knows.

42
JADE

I've been dreading the knock. When Molly laid hand to door, the gentle rap was like a bell tolling my fate. There is before and after that knock.

For so many decades I've longed for a friendly face to knock at my door, and now I fear what I may be inviting in.

I walk down the narrow staircase to the attic door—the atmospheric creaking of the stairs is not lost to me. I contemplate not opening the door, just letting myself disappear, never to be seen again. Maybe I'll fade away into nothingness; maybe it would be better to be forgotten than be remembered as the stuff of nightmares.

I gather up my energy to appear for Molly. As I reach for the door, my hand and arm feel light, too light. As I try to turn the knob to let Molly in, my fingers evaporate into wisps of greenish-white smoke. Crying out in surprise, I close my eyes and bite my lip in concentration, trying to pull as much energy from around me as possible to make myself solid. When I open my eyes, the smoke swirls into the shape of my hand again and I feel the weight of my fingers.

"Jade! What's going on? Are you there?" Molly hisses from the other side of the door.

Even though just moments before I'd been dreading seeing Molly, now the thought of being alone is too much to bear. There's disappearing and there's disappearing alone. I grab the doorknob—which thankfully my fingers make contact with this time—and pull the door open. Molly stands wide-eyed on the other side, holding a plate piled high with flat noodles. A box of cereal with rainbow-colored loops on it is pressed between her ribs and her elbow. The noodles are most likely another gift of food from one of the restaurants Molly's mother works for.

"I heard you scream." She looks unsure. I notice her breath appears in thicker clouds than usual—all the energy I need makes the hallway frigid. "Are you okay? You actually, literally look like a ghost right now."

"It happened again. Just come in," I say, stepping aside to let Molly past me and up the stairs. She starts to say something, but I look away and she changes her mind. Peering down the dark, still hallway to make sure her mother didn't hear us, I pull the attic door shut and lock it.

Molly and I sit on the floor of the attic, under the front window. It should be sweltering even at night, but I need so much energy from around us that Molly shivers a little. I've pulled the molding, bug-eaten rug from Celia Lotkin's bedroom out from the darkest corner of the attic and unrolled it. I thought it would be better than sitting on the bare floor. This spot gets the most light from the streetlamps—you can almost pretend it's actual moonlight. I needed a distraction and "decorating" for company was something to do. Plus, sitting on Celia's rug again, all these years later, feels appropriate. Celia told me to disappear and now it might actually happen.

The noodles glisten in the light from the streetlamp. They smell of sesame, chili oil, and onion. I wonder how long the scent will linger in my attic. *Longer than me?*

Molly wants me to talk to her, tell her what's going on, comfort her, but I can't. So I just eat to extinguish the growl in my stomach and to hopefully gain some strength. Molly nibbles—alternating between the noodles and the rainbow loops—but mostly she just watches me.

When the plate is empty I know I can't stall any longer. She knows too.

"Are you ready?" she asks. I nod. My stomach lurches but this time I don't think it's the monster. Is this anxiety? Everyone is right: It *is* awful.

I crawl over to the loose floorboard under the window, my fingers automatically finding the knot in the corner that serves as a little button. I push down on the knot and the other side of the board pops up. Molly peers over my shoulder.

I pull out my lacquer comb and put it on Celia's rug. I feel Molly give it its space. More items follow. I wordlessly show Molly all that I have in the world: buttons made of metal, wood, plastic; bobby pins; half of a faded cornflower-blue handkerchief; a tiny porcelain turtle with two legs broken off; a pink rhinestone; a stained purple ribbon that reads "Buckeye Creek Elementary School Science Fair, honorable mention, 1977."

I take my time, avoiding the inevitable, the reason we are sitting on a rotting rug in a dark attic. When almost all my belongings are on the rug, I pause. "Oh, Jade," Molly says, her voice heavy, and reaches for the rhinestone. I put out a hand to stop her and catch her eye. She stops.

"That's not why you're here," I whisper. I reach back into the floor, where my fingers quickly find the bundle in the darkness. My hands reappear, cradling my deepest secret, all wrapped up in a scrap of red satin I scavenged from a party dress. The satin glows in the light from the street, making my little bundle seem all that much more special and terrible.

I put the bundle between us on the rug and unwrap it. When I lift the last fold of the cloth, Molly leans in to get a better look, then inhales sharply and sits up. Her eyes search my face, questioning. When she speaks, her breath lingers between us like another ghost.

"Are those . . . bones?"

43
MOLLY

I don't know what I was expecting, but it wasn't this. Jade was apprehensive from the moment I arrived, but when she started pulling out all her stuff, I dropped my guard a little. I thought she was just nervous to show me her possessions, nervous for it to be real how long she's been in this house.

But when that shiny red bundle came out—the same silky red material that slid through my fingers in the Big Zap!—it was like the whole attic held its breath.

Lying on that old red satin scrap are three long brownish-white bones. Two pieces are about the thickness of my pinkie finger and about as long. The third is thicker than the other two and looks like it was probably longer when—oh geez, I can't believe I'm saying this—when it was inside a person. The ends are jagged and look like an animal gnawed on them.

"This is me."

"What?"

"This"—she moves a hand over the bones—"is me."

The realization smacks me in the head: JADE WANTS ME TO GET ZAPPED BY THESE BONES. I sit with that for a moment, my brain resisting the unavoidable truth of the situation. Sitting between us, laid out like the food we've shared so many times before, are Jade's bones.

These are Jade's earthly remains. If I don't help Jade, and she disappears forever, these three bones will be all that is left of her.

My head feels heavy and little pinpricks dot my vision. Holding a button or touching Mort's shelf in the dining room, that's one thing. But holding Jade's bones? Getting zapped by them? Listening to them?

I've never been so scared in my life.

Aren't bones the very core of a person? People say *I feel it in my bones*, like that's the most a person can feel. If one touch of Jade's hand on a doorknob turned me into a puking Molly-shaped puddle, what will a dead girl's bones do to me?

"Molly? Please, talk to me . . ." Jade's voice sounds like it's slipping away on the wind.

I think about getting up and running out and instating the *Ignore Ignore Ignore* plan again. This is not my problem, right? Jade can't be the first ghost to ever disappear! Maybe this is just how "ghost life" works.

You live, you die, you become a ghost, you die again. Then maybe you become the ghost of a ghost? Maybe it's not so bad!

There's that little girl who told Jade she wouldn't see her anymore. I could do that. Well, *could* I do that? Even in my state of fear sweating, that seems pretty cold.

Jade sits with her head hanging. Everything about her looks deflated, like there's a boulder crushing her.

I swallow hard, trying to find any spit in my mouth to make talking possible. I want to comfort her, tell her it's going to be okay and I'll help her, but those aren't the words that come out.

"Jade, why do you have these?"

And with that, like a dam breaking, a story pours out of Jade. A story about a box. A story about loneliness and fear and desperation. A story about survival. She acts as if she's confessing a crime.

"I had no choice, I had to . . . I was out of my mind with hunger, Molly. Please understand, please, please, please," she pleads. "The only thing to eat in that box, the only thing that soothed my terror in the most minuscule way, was eating . . . eating those bones . . . my bones."

My eyes travel to one jagged end of the biggest bone. Those are teeth marks. Jade's teeth marks. I think about the monster Jade is always talking about. There's an entire life and death in these bones and she wants *me* to talk to them. Every molecule in my body, *my bones*, screams, *NO*. What if it's more than I can handle?

"I can't," I blurt out without thinking.

Jade, who looks like she's actually shrinking, begins to cry softly. Her mouth hangs open as if she's wailing, but no sounds escape. Lustrous tears slide down her cheeks and I feel my ears straining, expecting to hear a cry, but all I hear is the hum of the house, my own ragged breath.

"I'm sorry, I'm sorry . . ." I say over and over again. I want to help her, but my fear is a leash yanking me back. "Maybe there's another way?" I add, but even I don't believe me.

Jade gathers her bones and clutches them to her chest, like she's protecting them from me. "I knew this was a bad idea, I knew, *I knew*! But you pushed me. This was *your* idea, Molly Teng!" With that, her head snaps up, lightning fast. Her eyes, giant white voids, glare at me, unblinking.

Jade's mouth spreads into a snarl, her lips darkening to crimson. Simultaneously her neck narrows and stretches to an impossible length, her head inching toward me. Hot breath threatens to burn my face. Tears run down her cheeks, drip into her mouth, and roll down—those are definitely fangs.

"Jade—let me explain—" I reach a hand to her. She recoils, and in a strangled voice she wheezes, "*Get out! Get out of my attic, Molly Teng.*

GET OUT!" Her white eyes are glued on me, glittering in the lamplight, but her face and body have become hazy, like the smoke from a candle blown out.

I spring to my feet and start to run, tripping over the rug and thudding to the floor. Crawling on my hands and knees, I make it to the stairs and scramble down, missing the last two steps and slamming into the door. Unlocking and opening the door, I turn just in time to see a wispy, transparent Jade floating at the top of the stairs, seething, teeth bared. She doesn't move, but a snarl emanates from her.

I yank the door open and dive through, pulling it shut and holding it closed. Growls shake the door from the other side.

What have I done?

44
JADE

I've spent five days curled up on Celia's rug. I eat cereal from the box Molly abandoned in the attic. Sometimes I am awake; sometimes I dream. Sometimes . . .

Early this morning I thought I was back in the box. I could barely move and every which way I pushed my body, I was only met with hardness and dark. I opened my mouth to scream, to call for help. "Mo—" I'm not sure if I was calling for my mother or for Molly, but immediately my mouth and throat filled with something rough, solid, and bitter. I choked and cried but I couldn't move. I thought it was the end.

I struggled and found myself lifting my head *out of the floor*. As I dozed, I had started to disappear and my head sank into the floor, hence my claustrophobia. It was the attic floorboards that filled my mouth when I cried out.

I've always been alone, but I've never felt so lonely. Perhaps this has always been my fate.

I let myself drift off again and hope I don't dream.

45
MOLLY

It's like Jade isn't here anymore. At first I worried that she'd disappeared, but when I knocked on the attic door while Mom was out, I was met with a low roar. I had to fight the urge to run again. That was almost a week ago. Occasionally, I hear the gentle creaking of the attic floor over my head. Last night before bed I knocked again, and with the growl came a gust of icy wind under the door. So she's still there, in some form.

The whole house feels heavy. Mom and I are both like exposed nerves. Maybe she's picking up on it from me; maybe we're just both feeling what Jade is feeling. Is she that powerful?

I keep telling myself that I set a boundary; I protected myself. What she was asking was more than I can handle. But do I know that for sure? After having some time to think about it, I wonder if I might be putting the fear cart in front of the fear horse.

I also didn't realize how lonely it is without Jade. I got so used to seeing her pop up when my mom left the house, and I loved our Second Dinner Club. I've never had slumber parties and this was like having one every night. Aside from the whole talking with a dead girl thing, it was like I got to be your average teenager for a while.

But what's so great about average? I've been wishing for normal for so long, but I don't even know what that really looks like. Would "normal" make me happy? Or is *normal* just the word people use when they've never taken a chance? I've never really had friends, but aren't true friends the people you take a chance on?

My stomach flip-flops at the word *friend*. I told Jade she was my best friend, and I meant it, then when things got hard I ditched her. Jade was so afraid to tell me about her bones, afraid I'd run away from her—and then that's exactly what I did. For lifetimes she might have been thinking about this worst-case scenario and I made it come true. Me, her best friend.

How will Jade ever trust me again?

———

I come downstairs to find my mom dragging a big box into the house that says DELUXE AIR MATTRESS. She sees me and yells, "Get the sheets from the car!"

I grab some brand-new purple sheets from the back seat of our car and bring them in. "Do I get new sheets?" I ask.

"No! I mean, not yet, probably later. These are for your auntie Bobbie. She's sleeping in the extra room while she's here. It's bad enough I don't have a real bed for her, I don't need her getting all judgy about our ancient bedsheets."

Ugh. Auntie Bobbie. I forgot she's coming tomorrow. Let the Awkward Olympics begin.

"I'm getting us Loh Kitchen BBQ for dinner tomorrow night—show off the Loh sisters a little. I figure since Bobbie is visiting, we might as well feast, right?" Mom seems so pleased with herself.

The past few days she's been cleaning and rearranging the house like it's her job. I swear she's gone to the local home goods store half a dozen times. All to impress Auntie Bobbie. "Hey, don't judge me! There will be enough of that when Bobbie gets here. I just want to, you know, show her how well we're doing. That we can afford the finer things."

"But we can't," I say, then immediately feel bad for rubbing it in my mom's face. We've actually been doing pretty well this summer and my mom works really hard, but looking around this big barely furnished house it's pretty obvious we're not exactly living in luxury.

"Well, Bobbie doesn't need to know that. Go start the water boiling, I'm making mac and cheese tonight."

Nothing says "the finer things" like boxed mac and cheese. But it actually sounds really good, so I go to the kitchen like a good daughter. Besides, I need some time to think, away from my mom's Bobbie nesting.

Having Auntie Bobbie in the house makes my plans more complicated. With her staying in the extra room, she'll definitely hear Jade and me in the attic at night (that's assuming Jade will speak to me again). My stomach wobbles when I think about the five days that Bobbie will be staying with us and all the time I'll be losing. All the time Jade will be losing.

The water starts boiling and my mind is pinballing around the same three thoughts:

I have to help Jade.

How do I do that?

What if I'm too late?

After all this time she's been invisible, I can't just let her disappear.

46
JADE

I hold my comb. I want its smoothness and weight in my shaky hands, to feel comforted by the belief that whoever gave me this comb cared about me and remembered me, even if I can't remember them. But the comb is disappearing too, just like my hands. My fingers look like vaporous tendrils floating away at the fingertips. Ghost girl, ghost comb—everything is fading away.

My stomach whines. I search for remnants of food in the rug, but I've found every speck, so I curl up and will myself to stay together just a minute longer.

Then another minute.

Then another minute.

Then another minute . . .

47

MOLLY

Mom sends me to Loh Kitchen BBQ to pick up dinner. It's late afternoon when I get dropped off by my Uber at the restaurant. Hazel is settling a bill with some customers, and I hear Rose bustling around in the kitchen. There's a lull between the lunch and dinner crowd, so aside from these lone diners, it's just me and the Lohs. I sit at a two-top by the counter and wait. I'm extra on edge from the Storm of Feelings at home that is Mom's nerves and Jade's rage, but being at the restaurant relaxes me. Something about the smell of food, the clatter of dishes, and hearing Hazel chat with their customers makes me feel safe.

Hazel waves goodbye to the customers and closes the front door behind them before coming over to my table and plopping down with a sigh as she shakes her long silver-streaked hair from her bun. "Oh, it's been a long day! Rose is finishing up your order; we wanted your food to be fresh. Just a few minutes, okay?"

"No problem, thank you," I tell Hazel, and continue the business of anxiously chewing on my lips.

Hazel watches me gnaw on my face for a bit, looking like she wants to ask me about it, but she reconsiders. Instead, with a sly smile, she pulls a tiny pink and green pack of Haw Flakes—Chinese hawthorn fruit candy—from her pocket. She rips open the pack, letting the candy loose on the table, and we sit in easy silence munching on the little red disks. It's really nice to be with someone who is comfortable with not talking. Everyone else in my life feels the need to ask me hundreds of questions anytime I'm within a ten-foot radius.

"Hey! Where's the new box of takeaway chopsticks?" Rose shouts from the kitchen.

"Ai-yah! Open your eyes—by the napkins!" Hazel shouts back.

A few beats go by before Rose pokes her head through the curtain. "It's not there. We're all out—hi, Molly!"

The sisters go back and forth in Canto and English for a little bit. I don't understand everything but I'm pretty sure they are accusing each other of losing the box of chopsticks. Finally, Hazel holds up a hand and says, "Wait, you know what? Go look by the condensed milk cans, sometimes Mary puts them there to joke around."

Rose disappears for a moment before we hear her go, "Ah! Wan dou lah!" Hazel turns to me with a satisfied smile. "She found them." Crisis averted.

"Is Mary in trouble?" I ask, assuming Mary is a server at the restaurant I haven't met yet.

For some reason Hazel finds this hilarious. She stops laughing when she senses my mood darken.

"Oh, Molly, I'm not laughing at you, sorry, sorry. Mary does whatever she wants!"

I'm so confused. "So . . . is she fired?" I ask.

"Ha! Nobody can fire Mary—Mary is our ghost!"

I don't mean to snap to attention but I do. Hazel notices and tilts her head, curious. I try to play it cool but I'm sure my face, and the shades of red it's changing, give me away. "You have a ghost?"

"Yeah. Why? You like ghosts?"

I build on the weirdness by not being totally sure how to answer this question. "I, uh, I mean, sometimes? I mean, yes. Yes, I do like ghosts. Mostly."

Hazel just stares at me in Chinese Auntie. I don't remember my own auntie, but I feel that stare down to my toes.

"So," I say, trying to sound less suspicious, "how long have you had a ghost?"

Hazel breaks the tension with a snort. "The real question is how long the ghost has had us. You see, not many people know, but this part of the International Village was where the first Chinese-owned business in Buckeye Creek was located in the 1890s. It was a laundry service."

My body involuntarily tenses. If this is an old, haunted building, why haven't I been zapped? "Wow, so this building was owned by a Chinese person back in the day?"

"Well, we're not sure if Mary owned the building. In those days, Texas, America, didn't like Chinese owning property. If she did, it didn't end well. We just know the laundry building stood near here and burned down by the early 1900s. This restaurant was built in the 1990s."

Okay, the '90s, so it's not SPOOKY old. I exhale. "So Mary was the name of the person who owned the laundry?" I can't help but do a quick scan of the restaurant to make sure Mary isn't eavesdropping.

"It's not that simple. When the ghost we call Mary was alive, many locals tried to chase Chinese people out of this town. Sometimes things got violent. The records for this area—Rose loves history—are not very good. All it says is the laundry opened, did business for about a year, then suddenly burned down. Too suddenly. From what we can tell, the owner died in the fire, so sad. She was buried in a nearby cemetery that's long gone, but the records end there. It doesn't even say the owner's name, just 'Chinese, female.'"

"How could it not say the owner's name?"

Hazel shakes her head. "To the people in charge, all Chinese were the same! Why bother with a name when you don't care about the person? So lots of times women were just called 'Mary' or 'China Mary.' There were China Marys all over America. Some became very successful businesspeople, but they were still 'China Marys.' So to honor the Marys and the woman who started her business here, we call our ghost Mary. We take the name back, like you say? She seems to be okay with it." Hazel sends a knowing look around the empty dining room.

I hear some porcelain teacups rattle on a nearby cart. It's probably just shaking from the giant trucks rumbling by, but maybe it's Mary agreeing with Hazel? I honestly can't tell anymore.

Hazel is staring at me again. I pull my attention away from the teacups.

"So you and Mary are . . . happy?"

Hazel shrugs. "I think so. Sometimes she moves things around, flips the lights on and off. Just to remind us, 'Hey, I'm here!' But we are careful to give her the respect she probably didn't always receive in life and she brings us good luck and good business." Hazel gets a funny look on her face. "You know, Molly, nobody, living or dead, wants to be forgotten. Otherwise you might end up with a hungry ghost."

I freeze. "A hungry ghost?"

"Yes. A ghost that has nobody to remember it, nobody to offer it food or comfort. That ghost is starving—both for nourishment and for memory."

That's literally Jade. From the moment I set foot in our house, she's been begging to be seen, acknowledged, remembered. She can never get enough food. I feel a little lightheaded with this new information. "So how do you take care of Mary?"

"We leave her food, we put up an altar for her—"

Hazel gestures at a little table by the back wall, with incense, a vertical tablet with words in Chinese, some oranges, a little cup. I always see mini shrines in Chinese restaurants, but I realize now that this one is different. It has a bracelet, an old black-and-white photo of what I assume was Mary's business, a little Year of the Pig figurine, and some handwritten notes. It feels more personal.

"She understands English but we think she prefers Gwong dong wa—Cantonese. The restaurant feels warmer, cheerier when we speak to her in her mother tongue."

"Have you ever seen her? Heard her?" I'm *this* close to asking if Hazel has ever been zapped.

"No. But once, when I was all alone here one night, the lock on the office door broke and I couldn't get out. From the gap under the door, I see a shadow, like two feet standing on the other side. I say, 'Rose?'

Nothing. Then I say, in Cantonese, 'Mary? Can you help me?' And I hear a little tap, tap, tap on the door. Then I hear the lock go click, click, and the doorknob turns all by itself."

My arms explode in goose bumps. Hazel continues.

"I grab the doorknob—it's icy cold!—and push the door open. Nobody there . . . that I can see."

"What did you do?"

"I looked all over to make sure there was no burglar tricking me, then I thanked Mary! I would have been stuck in the office all night. I put a full plate of dumplings on her altar before I left. And guess what."

I don't know what kind of response Hazel expects from me—shock? surprise? terror?—but I can't help but blurt out, "She ate all the dumplings!"

Hazel is taken aback but laughs and says, "Yeah. How'd you know?"

"I, um, I just figured," I lie (badly). I still don't know what to do, but I'm kind of freaking out—in a good way. I'm not the only one with a resident ghost! It's not exactly the same, but hearing practical, logical, self-possessed Hazel talk about a haunting makes me feel way less alone, even if I can't really say anything about Jade. I can't risk Mom finding out, not yet.

I want to ask more questions, but Rose comes bustling out of the kitchen with three giant bags of food just as my mom texts to ask my ETA. I try to give Hazel and Rose the money Mom gave me to pay for the food, but they are aggressive and loud with their refusal. "Respect your elders! You and your mom use that money to buy you some nice pants. Why are you always in ripped shorts?"

I agree and thank them over and over. When my Uber pulls up, Hazel walks me out. As I'm getting in the car she squeezes my arm and says, "There's a lot of food in the bags. More than enough for three. Share with a friend if you want." And she winks.

My mouth is still hanging open as she shuts the door and the car pulls away.

48
MOLLY

From the moment Auntie Bobbie walks in our front door, she looks unimpressed. More than that, she acts like she hates being here.

Greeting her at the door, I did my best to be the upbeat, respectful niece Mom told me to be under penalty of moving us to an emu farm and forcing me to make mother-daughter emu farm content with her until I'm eighteen. (Which honestly doesn't sound so bad.)

I wore my favorite yellow dress with the pockets and black lace around the shoulders. It's vaguely Gothic Lolita and I am very cute in it.

Auntie Bobbie apparently did not feel the same way. Maybe it's because she's ten years older than Mom, maybe it's because she sees me as an extension of my mom, or maybe she just hates *me*. Whatever the reason, when I met her at the door and said, "It's so great to see you, Auntie Bobbie! Welcome!" then opened my arms to hug her, she just stared at me like our vacuum cleaner came to life, rolled up to her, and started talking.

I got the full blast of the withering Auntie Stare. Wow, okay. I totally get it now.

"Well, look . . . it's Molly," she said, like my name tasted bad. Her mauve-lipsticked lips flattened into a tight line, her black eyes shrinking under her scrunched brow. She didn't even try to hide that she looked me up and down, judging me from head to toe. Then she walked into the kitchen, leaving me standing there with my arms open wide like a sad bird in an excellent dress.

Mom appeared at the front door huffing and puffing with a giant floral print weekender bag and three plastic shopping bags with what looked like fruit and various crackers in them. She pushed the weekender bag at me and said, "What are you doing? Go put this in the guest room for Bobbie!" Then she flitted into the kitchen all "What can I offer you to drink? Tea? Coffee? Lemonade?"

Lemonade? What are we, the local Marriott? I can't understand why Mom is trying to be someone she isn't—*we* aren't—for Bobbie.

After I wrestled Bobbie's heavy bag up to the extra room, I spent the rest of the evening watching my mom all but do an interpretive dance number to crack her sister. For dinner, the Loh sisters had made us the most beautiful crispy-skinned chicken I've ever seen. Its skin is glistening, golden, and perfectly crunchy, while the meat is melt-in-your-mouth tender.

I think of Jade the whole time, trying to figure out a way to share this with her without Auntie Bobbie catching me.

Bobbie just eats her food quietly, her face as bored as if she were eating a peanut butter and jelly sandwich. "Did that restaurant Fragrant Harbor close? When I lived in Dallas I'd make the trip just to eat there. It really was the best. Of course, this is . . . nice. A little underseasoned, don't you think?"

How dare she. I open my mouth to defend the Loh sisters, but my mom shoots me a warning look and interjects, "We haven't been to Fragrant Harbor yet! We should go while you're here."

"Yeah," I say flatly. When Mom kicks my shin under the table I add, "That would be . . . nice."

As my mom yammers on and Auntie Bobbie is just . . . there . . . I sneak glances at her, trying to find a resemblance. Even though Bobbie is in her late forties, she could easily pass for her early thirties. Both my mom and Bobbie have high cheekbones and long eyelashes, but while my mom's eyes are large, expressive, animated, Bobbie's eyes are small, round, and cold.

While my mom has long, wild, black hair, Bobbie's is a severe bob with gray strands running through it. Mom is in a pair of black jeans, chunky white platform sandals, and a white slouchy tank that looks like it has very artfully been splashed with black and red paint. Auntie

Bobbie's in gray pants, a white button-down, and brown nondescript loafers. This is the woman my mom used to adore?

I do notice one thing about Bobbie that screams Teng.

When Mom gets nervous she cracks her knuckles. I do it too. When we're both worried about something it's like the grossest rhythm section ever. My mom says she got it from her dad and that he got it from his mom. When Mom brought up some memory about Bobbie visiting her in Hawaiʻi, Bobbie cracked all the knuckles on her left hand, like someone running their fingers down a piano keyboard. She caught herself doing it and put her hands under the table before saying something about what an unfortunate time that was. Something in her response made my mom go quiet—a feat—and we all just listened to one another chew for a minute.

After we've all eaten our fill and are uncomfortably sitting at the table trying to navigate the silence, Mom turns to me. "Don't worry about cleaning up, Molls, I got it. You can go watch something up in your room."

"No worries," I mumble, and start to gather up dishes. Mom's voice stops me. "No, *really,* I've got it," she says, her head gently jerking toward the dining room doorway. I catch Bobbie roll her eyes a little.

I can take a hint. The grown-ups want to talk. That's fine with me; I hope they can work out whatever they need to work out. Auntie

Bobbie sucks, but I know my mom really wants her sister back.

I leave the table and go into the living room, but instead of going up the stairs I tiptoe into the kitchen. Part of the uneaten chicken as well as some rice, crispy shrimp chips, and vegetables are sitting on the kitchen table. I cautiously pull a plate from the cupboard and pile that shiny, beautiful food onto it. It's been a while; Jade must be hungry.

Watching a movie in my room is a perfect chance to coax Jade out of hiding, but I have to be careful. Creeping out of the kitchen clutching the sides of the plate in my hands, I climb the stairs oh so carefully so I don't make the staircase whine. It feels like it takes hours to reach the top of the stairs, but then I can walk normally—even if they hear me downstairs, they might just think I'm going to the bathroom. I go into my mom's room and grab a piece of computer paper from her printer. On it I write:

I want to help. <u>Please</u> come to my room for Second Dinner.

I mull it over, then I also write:

I'm sorry.

Mom has always taught me not to default to apologizing, that if I say sorry for everything I'll eventually believe everything is my fault and so will everybody else. Plus, if you're thoughtful about handing out your "I'm sorrys" you'll probably mean it instead of just blabbing it to everyone.

While I'm still not sure I'm ready to have Jade's bones speak to me, I really am sorry for making her feel like a monster, for running out on her.

I slip the note under the attic door and knock as loudly as I can without alerting Mom or Bobbie. They are having some sort of heated conversation downstairs, so I doubt they are even thinking about me. This works in my favor.

"Jade," I whisper-yell. "Jade, I put a note under the door. Please come see it!" I knock a few more times for good measure. I hear the floorboards groan in response from above, so at least I know she's still up there.

Back to my room, I flip around Netflix on my computer, looking for something distracting, and settle on a baking competition show. Just as I'm half-heartedly hitting play on the next episode, there is a featherlight knock on the door.

49

JADE

Molly looks taken aback when she clamps eyes on me. After the past few weeks of Second Dinners and late-night conversations—highlighted by the thrill of new friendship—I'm sad that a sense of trepidation now hangs between us.

Admittedly, I must look like an honest-to-goodness ghoul standing there in the shadowy hallway. Molly cracks the door wider for me to come in. As I enter, I instinctively place my hand on the door to hold it open, but my fingertips disappear into the wood. I yank my hand away like it's been singed. I look to see if Molly saw. She did. So many thoughts flit across her dark eyes.

Of course as soon as I enter the room, all I can see is the plate of food. I'm so weak and so hungry that my whole body begins to shake.

"It's okay. I won't watch. But I'm happy you're hungry."

"Thank you," I whisper as she grabs her laptop and goes to the opposite side of the room to watch something—her back to me, head-phones on her ears.

I make quick work of the meal . . . snarling and choking the whole time. My throat feels tight, like it's closing up, but I keep eating. It hurts, yet nothing on earth (or beyond) can make me stop.

When the plate is clean and crumb-less, I go over to where Molly sits on the floor by the wall and sit down facing her. She takes off her headphones.

"I'm sorry too," I say, the food in my belly clearing my head a little.

"You are?" Molly looks genuinely confused.

"I asked you to do something that I knew was scary for you and when you reacted in fear—*understandably*—I panicked. You confided in me the thing that scares you most, the 'monster' *you* live with, and I didn't listen. I should have, I just—I don't want to disappear so I didn't think it through."

Molly's furrowed brows are mountains over her eyes. She takes her time choosing her words. Finally she finds her voice and words tumble out like water over rocks. "I feel the same way! I'm sorry too! After all the things you've told me—about Celia, about the monster, about being so alone for all these years—I did the worst thing possible—I ran out on you! *I treated you like a monster.* Can you ever forgive me?" She stops to take a breath. We are both breathless.

Barely able to speak, I nod and whisper, "I forgive you. And you . . . forgive me?"

"Of course!" Molly practically shouts. "I'm going to be really honest with you," she continues. "The thought of getting zapped by your bones is terrifying to me. I don't know if I can handle it, but maybe we can figure out another way? There has to be some other clue to who you are. We'll scour every inch of the attic until we find it! I promise!"

It feels so good to hear Molly, my friend, say all this to me, but I can't help but feel dread creep in. I think I'm doomed.

I pull my legs into my body and bury my head in my knees. "I've lived in that attic for over a hundred years, Molly; there's nothing in there that I haven't found. My bones hold the key, I just know it." I keep my head buried, afraid to look at her. Saying such a thing out loud reminds me more than ever that I am dead and perhaps the dead are *supposed* to disappear.

I hear Molly shift, the floorboards complaining a bit under her, but she doesn't speak. Then she's very still, her breathing slows, and she says, "I've been doing a lot of thinking and I realized that your past, your life, is also my past. *My* history. The fact that you lived and died in Buckeye Creek maybe made it possible for me and my mom, and other people like us, to live in Buckeye Creek. I want to help you because you're my best friend, but I also want to help you because we deserve to know *our* history. We will figure this out together, Jade. I promise. You're not alone."

There's nothing adorned about the way she says these words. It is the most confident and resolute I've ever heard Molly. I don't know what she thinks she's going to do, but I believe her.

And she's right: I don't feel so alone.

Smiling through my trepidation, I lift my head to tell her I trust her, but freeze when I see what's behind her. As if the world is suddenly in slow motion, Molly turns to follow my gaze, a tiny gasp escaping her lips.

A woman with short dark hair, gray pants, and a white shirt is standing in the doorway.

And she's staring right at me.

5Ø
MOLLY

"Heeey, Auntie Bobbie." I try to sound casual. I don't. I sound like a little kid who's been caught coloring on the walls.

Unexpectedly, that's when I can see my mom in her. The rapidly blinking eyes, the chewing on one half of her lower lip, the shoulders sneaking up to her ears.

Her eyes and nose look a little red and puffy. Has Auntie Bobbie been . . . crying?

Then I remember how "spooky possessed child" I must have looked, sitting on the floor talking to nothing. How much did she see? Why was she coming into my room in the first place? I decide to play it cool.

"Ha ha ha! What's up?" I say like an alien who's doing their best human impersonation.

Her eyes stay glued to Jade. She can't see her . . . can she?

"Oh, I, uh—I was just using the bathroom. I just thought I heard voices. I'm sorry, it was rude of me to barge in . . ." She trails off. Her eyes float to the empty plate on my bed. I sneak a glance at Jade. Unsure, Jade says, "I should go," and starts to fade from sight.

"No, don't!" Bobbie blurts out, which makes both Jade and me snap our heads around to look at her. Auntie Bobbie's gaze rises to follow Jade as she stands. Looking at me, she quickly adds, "Don't let me interrupt your, uh, show," she says, gesturing to the laptop.

"It's fine," I say, but what I really want to say is "HOW MANY PEOPLE DO YOU SEE IN THIS ROOM?"

With a little nod Auntie Bobbie leaves the room, closing the door behind her. It isn't until I hear her creaking down the stairs that I exhale. Jade goes and stands vigilant at the bedroom door like Bobbie might come back. I stand up too and start pacing around the room.

"What was that?" I ask, feeling like my heart is going to beat out of my chest.

At the center of the room, Jade's face is a mix of awe and concern. "She saw me!"

"No way."

"Yes! That woman saw me! She's your aunt? Of course, that makes sense. It must run in your family."

"How does any of this make sense?"

"I don't know—I don't know the rules of the ghost world; it's not as if they give you a handbook. But just like I know my bones hold the answer to who or what I am, I *just know* that your auntie Bobbie is someone we need on our team."

"Oh no." I groan.

Jade ignores me. She's on a mission. "Don't you see, Molly? Your auntie Bobbie obviously has experience with ghosts. She saw me and heard me, but she didn't run screaming from the room. She was more concerned with *you* than she was with me. This is a woman who knows things."

The thought of stern, unimpressed Auntie Bobbie helping two teenagers—one her disappointing niece, one a hungry dead girl—makes me laugh out loud for real this time. Jade looks baffled and a little hurt at my outburst. I try to explain. "I'm sorry, I'm not laughing at you. It's just that I've known Auntie Bobbie for less than eight hours and I think she already hates me or disapproves of me or something. I can't imagine her wanting to help us. And even if she would, what could she do?"

Jade is practically vibrating. "Again, *I don't know*, but what's the harm in asking, Molly? In the worst case she denies everything. It's worth talking to her."

I'm exhausted, but Jade is right. If Auntie Bobbie can see Jade, she might know more than I do and she might be able to help us. If I don't talk to her, I'm closing off a way that could help my friend, and that's not fair. As much as the thought of talking to Bobbie turns my stomach, I have to do it.

Jade seems worn out too. She sits down on my bed and I notice she sinks a little too deep into the comforter. Like a watercolor painting dipped in water, the outline of her form starts to blur and bleed into the space around her; her long black hair looks like dark curls of smoke floating away.

"Jade," I say, but can't find more words.

She looks at me and there's no denying the fear in her eyes. "I'm losing myself," she says.

Okay, time to go all in, Molly.

"I need to rest," Jade says, her eyes fluttering. She lets herself fade from view. Before she's all the way gone I tell her, "Come meet me after midnight. We'll have a third dinner and figure out what to do next."

I see her nod her head, her hair swirling around her face in clouds of smoke. Then she's gone.

I wonder if my heart will ever stop pounding.

51
JADE

I drift into Molly's room well after midnight. I feel like I drift everywhere lately. Sometimes my feet and legs feel odd and when I look down they are just murky wisps floating above the ground. I am also rather aimless of late; it's difficult to differentiate between waking and dreaming sometimes.

I go to Molly and find her sitting cross-legged on her bed, the only light coming from her laptop. The streetlamp outside the house is broken. The house on Charlotte Street is still and dark; not a sound comes from Molly's mother's or auntie's rooms. It's remarkable how much more daunting the house feels without the warmth of the streetlamp. I hope they fix it soon.

Molly is wearing giant puffy headphones, so all I hear is the hum of her computer and her steady breath. I look over Molly's shoulder and notice that the time on the computer screen reads 1:17 a.m. I'm surprised. I thought I was earlier. Normally, I have an excellent sense of what time it is, but I've been off ever since I started disappearing.

I've started disappearing.

I can say things like "Since I've been dead" or "After I died" because even when my body went away, I remained. But I don't think I'll be able to say "After I disappeared."

The gravity of this thought sends a chill through me that ripples across the stillness of the room and makes Molly shiver. She looks around for me and startles when she turns to see me standing over her shoulder. I must look like a demon in the glow of her computer. She rips off her headphones.

"Jade! Don't sneak up on me like that! I've been so jumpy lately. I swear I'm going to crawl right out of my skin!"

"Sorry," I say, a little annoyed that Molly has the audacity to complain to me about feeling uncomfortable.

Living problems, I think bitterly. Anger wells up in me, then falls back down, like soda bubbles when the bottle is opened.

"Hey, I saw that! Don't roll your eyes at me," Molly says, a little prickly herself. Then softer, "Here, I brought you some almond cookies. Auntie Bobbie brought them. A Chinese auntie thing, I guess. At least, that's what I've heard. I've never really had an auntie."

"Neither have I," I concur. We both let out sighs. Our breaths are tiny clouds in the cold I bring with me everywhere.

I sit down on the air mattress and eat a cookie. My stomach leaps a little at the snack, but since I ate earlier the monster barely lifts its head. Molly sits down too and we eat together.

"I think the first thing we have to do is be sure that Bobbie saw and heard you," Molly says after she finishes her cookie. "We don't want to tell her too much if she didn't actually see anything and was just being weird and nosy."

"Okay, that makes sense. Though I have no doubt she saw me. How are you going to ask her?" I ask, reaching for my third cookie.

"Well, I was thinking, the easiest way would be for you to come with me tomorrow, when she's alone, and have you speak to her. If she responds—ghost-seeing genetics confirmed. If she doesn't, then that's all there is to it and we're on our own again."

"She'll hear me," I say. "And if she's anything like you, she's had years and years to learn more about her powers. I know she can help."

"I don't know if anyone can help, especially *her*," Molly says through a frown. She isn't usually this negative. Nervous, cautious, but not grim. I wonder if my gloom is influencing her? "But we'll try."

"All right, we'll have to keep an eye out for our chance," I say.

"My mom isn't working tomorrow, she wants us all to go do something, so it might not be until later," Molly says. Her voice is even but her are eyes worried. "If you want, you can stay down here tonight.

Things feel all sideways right now and I'm kind of creeped out. Is that dumb? It can be like a sleepover. I always wanted to be one of those kids who had friends come over and sleep in sleeping bags on their floor. I don't have a sleeping bag for you, but you can share my bed if you want?"

Molly sounds so young and hopeful and human, I'm reminded of the decades and experiences that separate us. Nonetheless, her offer stills any anger in me and replaces it with relief. I do not want to be alone either.

Molly closes her computer and the room is plunged into blackness. The other houses are fast asleep and clouds shroud the moon. I make my way over to the bed and lie down on my back—careful not to crowd Molly. Laid out with my eyes wide in the dark, I have to push down a surge of fear. I am reminded of the box.

"Jade?"

"Yes?" I return.

"Are you scared?"

"Yes. Very."

"I guess I knew that. It's kind of a ridiculous question. Like asking if you're afraid of death." Despite the nerve Molly's question presses, I'm very grateful to have her voice, a beacon in the shadows.

"Are you afraid of death?" I ask her.

She takes her time answering, thinking.

"I didn't used to be. I honestly didn't want to think about it, so I just didn't. But lately, yeah, it scares me. A few times, I've gotten so scared thinking about it, it keeps me up at night."

"Even with everything you know, everything you've seen, you're still afraid?"

"I am." Molly shifts; the mattress squeaks. "All the memories I've experienced, all the feelings I've felt from people long dead, what if that's all that's left of them? Maybe some people are ghosts and some people are just . . . gone. Nothing forever. It's totally unknowable."

Even though she can't see it, I nod my head. "That's how I feel too. The unknowable terrifies me. Will it hurt? Can I fight it? Or will the light just extinguish?" I hesitate; there's more to say, but I'm not sure how Molly will react. I listen to her breathe for a moment. "Have you thought . . . maybe it's kind of beautiful too? What remains?"

"What do you mean?" she asks.

"I mean, perhaps none of us are truly immortal—our beings, our thoughts will all someday cease—ghost or not. We'll all be gone, like you say. But somehow, if we are remembered, if somebody picks up our memory, the seed of who we are is planted in another person's mind and together our memories blend to form something old and new all at once. Life building upon a life that was."

"Oh, Jade," Molly whispers. "That's what you've been thinking about?"

"A little. It's daunting to touch these thoughts, but I also find it comforting. I never really thought much about dying—again—but I guess that's what I'm facing. In a way I feel a little silly—I'm a ghost who is afraid of death."

"But that makes so much sense!" The shadowy blob that is Molly pops up on an elbow. "I think it's totally normal to be afraid of death. I don't care if you're a ghost or flesh and blood or a three-toed sloth or whatever—most of us really, really want to live." She pauses. I can almost make out her mouth, open, carefully selecting her next words. "We can't imagine not being here."

"It's true. I really, really want to be here. But . . ." I lift myself up on an elbow—an elbow I hope stays solid—mirroring Molly. ". . . and I hope it's not upsetting to say this, but talking with you, knowing that you are afraid of dying too, makes me feel better? Like I'm not really alone? Not that I want you to die! But it may be the one thing you and I absolutely have in common: death."

Molly nods solemnly. "Morbid. But true." I see her eyes smile in the dark. "We're in a very nonexclusive, very *human* club." We laugh softly. It feels good.

"Molly?"

"Yeah?" Her voice sounds thick with feelings.

"Promise you won't forget me, okay?"

"Jade, don't say that, I—"

"No, please, just listen to me. I know you're going to do your best to help me, but in case it doesn't work, I have to think about the reality that I—I will not exist anymore. I have to—I want to find peace in this. If you are remembered, you existed, and you matter. Even if it's just for a glimmer of time. I want to matter." My voice cracks and I try to calm myself. The room gets very cold; it takes so much energy for me to keep my composure.

I barely get the words out. "Promise me, Molly. If I disappear, you will remember me."

"As long as I live. I promise. I'll twist our memories all up together and I'll carry them around with me—old and new. I could never forget my best friend," she says clearly and without any hesitancy.

This does give me some peace and my body eases back into the bed. "For what it's worth, Molly, I will never forget you either."

We lie in the dark together, listening to the house make little cracks and pops like an old skeleton. For so long it's been just me and the house on Charlotte Street, my one reliable companion. As much as I've always wanted to escape the house, I don't want to evaporate from her walls. Molly's breath starts to slow; she is falling asleep.

"Molly?"

"Yeah?" Her voice is low, a little raspy.

"I've had a lot of fun with you."

"No. I reject that. Don't say goodbye to me. Not yet."

I admire her optimism, even if it feels naive. "Okay. Then I'll just say good night. Is that all right?"

"Yeah, that's good." She turns over on her side and I hear her breathing become softer, steady. "Good night . . ." she mumbles, and then she is asleep.

"Good night," I say again, and let my mind and body drift.

52
MOLLY

I reach for my phone and look at the time: 7:08 a.m. Ugh, it's so bright in my room, the sun is like a laser going through my eyelids straight to my eyeballs. Squinting, I look around for Jade. She's nowhere in sight. Just to be sure, I whisper, "Jade?"

She must have gone back up to the attic. The plate of cookies is clean. No crumb left behind.

I pull the covers over my head and think about the night before—talking about death, Jade trying to say goodbye.

I start to fall asleep again, but the door across the hall opens, shuts, and footsteps move down the hall to the bathroom. I don't have much more time to lie in bed. Mom wants us to have breakfast with Auntie Bobbie, so the Loh sisters offered to make a special breakfast for us before the restaurant opens for lunch. I'm excited to see Hazel and Rose again and my mom hopes that if Bobbie sees how much other people like her, she'll soften up

242

and like her too. Doubtful, but I'm willing to play Mom's reindeer games.

Ugh, Auntie Bobbie. The memory of her standing in the doorway staring in Jade's direction pops into my head and makes my heart bounce like a rubber ball caught in my rib cage. Jade and I have to ask Auntie Bobbie to join our strange little team. I'm still not totally convinced it's a good idea, but if there's the smallest chance Bobbie knows something that will help Jade, we have to do it. Of course, getting help from someone who barely wants to talk to me might be a lost cause. I force myself to open my eyes.

Rolling out of bed, I drag myself downstairs and into the kitchen to make some coffee. As I'm spooning the grounds into the filter, a voice startles me.

"You're too young to drink coffee."

I jump and blanket the floor in coffee grounds.

Auntie Bobbie, already dressed in a matronly dark plum linen dress that falls below her knees, sits at the coffee table and watches me like the Queen of England as I clean up the coffee grounds. When I straighten up to throw them in the garbage, she says, "There are still some by the sink."

"Thanks," I say, trying not to let sarcasm creep into my voice, but I don't think I'm very successful.

I clean up the rogue grounds and get to work filling another filter with coffee—all the while very aware that Bobbie's eyes are scrutinizing me. I turn to her and try to look bright-eyed and bushy-tailed. "So . . . how do you like your room?" I ask.

"The air mattress is too soft and it's sweltering in there," she says, like she's complaining to the hotel concierge. It's all I can do not to roll my eyes and I open my mouth to say something a little snarky, but I'm cut off when she says, "Though I did wake up freezing at one point. I could see my breath. Odd, isn't it?"

Jade. Jade must have peeked in on her.

Auntie Bobbie and I lock eyes for a moment. In that instant it feels like everything is laid out on the table: She knows about Jade, she knows about me, the conversation is just beginning.

"Well, look at you two early birds!" Mom breezes into the room, snapping the wire of tension stretching between Bobbie and me. She pulls a mug from the cupboard and pours herself a cup of coffee while the pot is still filling. Coffee drips onto the hot plate and hisses.

"Bobbie? Molls?" She offers the cup to us but we both decline. She shrugs and sits down at the table opposite Auntie Bobbie. "So what are we gabbing about?" She's so eager it hurts.

"Auntie Bobbie was just telling me how much she likes her

room!" I say, seeing my opportunity to exit. "I'm actually going to go up and change, be right back." Mom doesn't think much of this and I hear her make some comment about what a weird age I'm at, but I know Bobbie is watching me as I walk out and go up the stairs.

53
MOLLY

Thirty minutes later, we pull into the International Village parking lot with its generic lantern-shaped streetlamps flanking the entrance. It's still early, but already aunties and older couples are streaming in and out of the Asian supermarket. Shopping carts clang and crash, people greet each other in Cantonese, Mandarin, Vietnamese, Korean, Hmong—nothing brings Asian elders together like fresh produce. This is the prime shopping time: before it gets too hot and while everyone else is at work. I remember my por por taking me to the Asian market once or twice when I was little. "The fruit gets picked over by late afternoon. If you want the good fruit you have to come early," she told me.

The restaurant smells like all the good things in the world when we walk in—sesame, onion, garlic, soy sauce—but floating above these comfort smells are rich scents. The smell of butter, eggs, sweetness. I press my lips together to stop from drooling.

Hazel and Rose come out with open arms when they hear the front doorbell ding. The restaurant is suddenly so much louder than you'd think five people could be. Everybody—except Auntie Bobbie—talks at once:

"Good morning! Good morning! Jo san! Jo san!"

"It smells AMAZING in here!"

"That's so nice of you! Sit, sit, are you hungry? Yes?"

"Ohmygosh, is that Lyle's Golden Syrup on the table?"

"Molly, you like yuenyeung?"

"You're the auntie, yes?"

"This is my sister, Bobbie! She's visiting for a few days."

"Sit, sit, Bobbie! Welcome!"

Bobbie sorta-smiles and politely thanks Hazel and Rose in Cantonese (how does she speak Canto so much better than my mom?), then allows herself to be herded over to a big round table the Loh sisters have set just for us. Our butts are barely in our seats when Hazel brings over a big pot of Sau Mei tea as well as three tall glasses of yeunyeung—a mix of coffee and milk tea that my gung gung, my grandpa, used to make.

Mom sighs. "Like what Dad used to drink," she says to Bobbie, her eyes hoping for a rekindling of some sort of nostalgia from her sister. Bobbie just smiles stiffly and nods. She sips the drink and pushes it away. I catch Hazel and Rose exchanging raised-eyebrow looks over Bobbie's head.

Then the parade of food begins. Rose places a big bowl of jook in the middle of the table and hands each of us small round bowls and spoons for the rice porridge. "You didn't," Mom cries out. "Is this bao yu jook? You remembered it's my favorite! This is way too much!"

"Nonsense!" says Rose as she ladles the thick white congee into our bowls, pieces of bao yu—abalone—peeking out from the soup. "This is a special occasion."

I know rice porridge doesn't sound delicious, but it's one of Mom's favorite comfort foods. The abalone is a pretty fancy (expensive!) touch, but really jook is just rice and water that you can doctor with anything from soy sauce to chicken scraps. Plus, the Loh sisters made us a giant plate of yau ja gwai, deep-fried airy sticks of dough that literally translate to "oil-fried ghost"—*my* favorite. And yes, I know there's probably some sign or symbolism in me *eating a ghost*, but I'm not going to think too hard about it.

Next comes soft white toast cut into perfect crustless triangles topped with creamy-but-fluffy scrambled eggs—an old-school Hong Kong favorite. A plate of French toast with the crust cut off is brought out too. Hazel dips a spoon into the green metal container of Lyle's Golden Syrup on the table and drizzles it on the toast.

The Loh sisters have made the breakfast of my mom's dreams. With every bite, it looks like my mom is being transported back to my por

por's kitchen. She makes all the yummy-food noises and tries to catch Bobbie's eye to share this moment with her. Bobbie eats in silence. (Though I do catch the corners of her mouth turning up when she takes a bite of the scrambled egg toast.)

Mom must have told Rose and Hazel that she needed to impress Bobbie, because they are really laying it on thick. "You know, we love Dot so much. My sister and I tell her she can never leave!" says Hazel.

"She eats everything," Rose tells Bobbie with a twinkle in her eye. "She'll eat three char siu bao, and I give her two more to take home to Molly. When I ask her later if Molly got the bao, she says 'Maybe . . .' and then asks if we have any extra!" Mom, Rose, Hazel, and I laugh. It feels good to be light and silly for a bit.

"Zan hai," Rose says—*really*, "Dot has been so important to us. She showed up talking about 'Instagram' this, 'branding' that, but now people drive from all over for yum cha—we have a line out the door on the weekends! And *D Magazine* is putting us in their Fall Food Guide. It's all because of Dot. She and Molly are like family to us."

I'm unexpectedly choked up by this and gulp down the last of my yeunyeung to stop from outright sobbing. Bobbie nods along, listening, and after all that she says flatly, "How lovely."

Hazel, really wanting to drive the point home, leans over the table and smiles warmly—but pointedly—at Bobbie. "It's *very lovely*. Dot has helped so many small businesses in the International Village and around Buckeye Creek. So many of us don't understand social media and some of us don't speak or write in English that well. Dot helps us have a voice—she's fearless!"

Something about what Hazel says strikes Auntie Bobbie as funny, and she snorts into her napkin. *Rude.* "It's nice to hear about my *fearless* sister," Bobbie says. I don't like the way she says *fearless*. Mom's face flushes red.

Not missing a beat (or Bobbie's sarcasm), Hazel smiles like the ray of sunshine she is and says, "It's not easy, but she doesn't give up. She helps people figure out what they want and then helps them do it!"

Bobbie forces a smile and asks for some hot water with lemon. Mom looks gratefully at Hazel.

Maybe I haven't seen it before, or maybe it wasn't there before, but as cartoonish as my mom can be, she really does care about people. She really does care about me.

"You sure you're related?" Rose whispers as she gives me another yeunyeung and Hazel pours Bobbie's hot water. We both suppress a giggle. I don't want Mom to be unhappy, but it's a relief to know we're all weirded out together.

We eat our meal—it kicks butt and definitely improves my mood— and leave after a cacophony of Chinese ladies arguing about the check.

"You have to let me pay you, this was SO MUCH food!"

"Ai-yah, no, it's our gift to you, to say thank you!"

Trailing "thank yous" behind us, we head out the door. I notice Bobbie lingering by the display at the entrance. She grabs a paper menu and stuffs it in her purse. *Huh.* I guess she didn't hate everything after all.

On the way out she squeezes Hazel's arm and, looking her in the eye, she says sincerely, "Thank you. This really was lovely." Hazel is taken aback for a moment, then just smiles and says, "It's good you came."

Mom squeezes my hand so hard. Maybe it's not the Hallmark moment she'd hoped for, but it was pretty wild to see Bobbie's icy veneer melt a little. This confirms it: The Loh sisters are magic.

I wish we could've stayed in the cozy Loh sisters' bubble all day long, but instead we go on the most uncomfortable tour of Buckeye Creek. Mom drives Bobbie around the town, showing her all the things she likes—art galleries, the vintage stores she drools over, restaurants she's working with. She wants *so much* for Bobbie to be excited about her new life. It's hard to see Mom fighting so hard to win someone's approval. Normally people just like her, and if they don't, she doesn't care.

On the way home we stop for a beverage break at a coffee shop in our neighborhood. I get my cold brew, then go across the street to check out a bookstore and give Mom and Auntie Bobbie some space to talk at each other or yell or have a dance-off—whatever estranged sisters do.

I take my time perusing the graphic novels and the dollar-book bin before crossing back over to the coffee shop. I can see Mom and Auntie Bobbie at a table in the front window. It doesn't look good.

Auntie Bobbie is gesturing all over the place with more animation than I thought was possible from her. She looks angry; Mom looks like she's pleading with her. I can't hear them but I swear that Auntie Bobbie's mouth is forming the word "Molly" over and over again.

Why are they talking about me? Why is Bobbie so obsessed with me but also seems to dislike everything about me? It's an unsettling feeling in a day full of unsettling feelings.

I try to be casual when I walk over to them. Mom looks like she's holding back tears and Bobbie's sphinxlike face is flushed.

"Want to go back home and chill for a while?" Mom tries to sound upbeat and easygoing.

I try to match her. "Sure, I could go for a midafternoon snooze. I didn't sleep that well."

When we get home we all go to our corners of the house. I flop onto the couch and close my eyes. I bet we're all doing the same thing: eyes closed, wishing we could just sleep away the next few days.

54
JADE

The sun had just started to disappear from the sky when Molly's mother zipped out the front door. She mentioned something about shooting video of a client's early-dinner rush before her dinner reservations with Bobbie and Molly. Auntie Bobbie went into the living room to look at a new book on the coffee table and Molly was in the kitchen doing the dishes from lunch.

These days I don't like to invisibly lurk around Molly and her mother too much—since I know them personally, it seems rude to spy—but I decided to stay close just in case there was a chance Molly and I could talk to Auntie Bobbie.

With Molly's mom out for a few hours, we might get our chance.

Stepping into the kitchen, I appear at Molly's side. I hear her breath catch. "Geez! People have got to stop sneaking up on me in the kitchen!" she says through clenched teeth.

"Now's our chance! Let's go talk to her!" I say, and start toward the living room.

"Wait, wait," Molly says, and steps in my path. "What are you going to say? We can't have you go in there and just shout, 'Boo!'"

"We'll walk in, stand in front of her, and see if she can see me. Then we'll test if she can hear me. If she can—and I'm sure she can—we'll ask her if she has any knowledge about ghosts."

"You think it's that simple, huh?" Molly says, wiping her wet hands on her shorts. "That woman does not like me. Even if she could help us, I'm not sure she would." She slides down to the kitchen floor and sits in a heap. I do the same across from her. Molly looks a little crushed.

"Are you okay?" In all the excitement of the past couple of days, I haven't really asked how Molly is handling her auntie's visit.

"I don't know." She lowers her voice even further. I have to lean in to hear her. "I just don't know why she's here. No matter what we do, no matter how many people tell my aunt that my mom is killing it at her job and helping people while she does it, no matter how polite I am— Auntie Bobbie just looks at us like we're trash. Like we're the trash queens of trash mountain." Molly puts her head in her hands like her head hurts.

"That *sucks*," I say in earnest, but also hoping Molly will find her usual amusement with my unnatural use of the word. She remains downtrodden. "Molly, if talking to your auntie is too hurtful for you, I can do it alone. I'm already asking so much of you; you don't have to do this." She lifts her eyes to mine and forces a smile.

"That's really sweet of you, but no. We do this together. If there's the tiniest chance my aunt can help you, then it's worth it." Molly releases a long breath like she's blowing away all the bad feelings. I'm over-whelmed with affection for my friend.

"Okay. Let's do this," Molly says, and stands up. I follow. "We'll go in there and I'll ask her if she wants a cup of tea. It should be pretty obvious if she can see you standing next to me or not. If it looks like she can see you, introduce yourself. If not, we'll just leave the room and it'll be like nothing happened. Got it?" I'm relieved Molly is taking charge because suddenly I feel like there are bees in my stomach.

"Jade? Are you with me?" she asks. I nod, noticing that my hands are trembling slightly.

Side by side, Molly and I go to the living room, where Auntie Bobbie sits on the couch reading a large hardcover book. The bees in my stomach travel to my head and I feel like I might fly away from nerves.

Looking up, I see Auntie Bobbie's eyes land on Molly, then flick over to me, then return to Molly. It's so quick, but I know she sees me.

Without thinking, without waiting for Molly, I blurt out, "Can you see me?" My hands fly to my mouth, but the words are already out.

Molly's head snaps in my direction, her eyes wide. All I can do is shrug. We both swivel our heads back to Auntie Bobbie, who is leaning back on the couch, an amused expression on her face.

"I was wondering when you'd ask," she says.

55
MOLLY

I don't know why I expect anything in my life to go according to plan. I don't know why I expect anybody in my life to be predictable. I am surrounded by chaos.

Auntie Bobbie sits on the couch, a smile crinkling the corners of her eyes. She raises her eyebrows and looks from Jade to me and then back at Jade.

"You can see her?" I squeak.

"Of course I can see her. Clear as I could yesterday. I was wondering when you'd come around to talking to me!" She laughs. I didn't know she could do that. As she turns her attention to Jade, her demeanor softens. Gently she says, "And what's your name, dear?"

"I'm Jade. At least, I think that's my name."

"And how long have you been in this house, Jade?"

"A hundred and twenty years, maybe a little longer," Jade tells her. It's like there are beams of energy shooting between Auntie Bobbie and Jade.

Auntie Bobbie actually looks like she's hurting for Jade. "That's a long time to be alone."

Jade is in awe. "It is," she says.

I can't keep my mouth shut. "I'm sorry," I interject. "Just to be clear, you can see her AND hear her and you understand her whole *situation*?"

A little bit of stern Auntie Bobbie returns when she talks to me. "I think the answers to your questions are quite obvious. I don't know exactly what Jade's situation is, but I know that she's been here for quite a while, and you wouldn't be coming to me unless you needed help."

"*Can* you help me?" Jade asks.

"I don't know. Sit down and tell me what's happening," says Bobbie. She gestures to the spot next to her on the couch. Auntie Bobbie is being so . . . motherly? Where has *this* Auntie Bobbie been?

I'm the only one still standing, so I plop down on the floor on the other side of the coffee table. I feel like I'm at the kids' table watching the grown-ups talk.

Jade pours her heart out to Auntie Bobbie. She tells her about her years in the house, the people she's seen come and go, waking up in the box, her bones, her hunger, the monster. Bobbie listens intently, nodding along and offering words of comfort at the hardest parts. "That sounds very painful," she says. "I understand."

Does she?

After Jade has told her story, she somehow looks smaller. She looks like she's sagging under the weight of her fears. Auntie Bobbie leans into Jade and ever so gently gestures for her to lift her head, her fingertips almost touching her chin but not quite. "Please hear me and understand, Jade: You did nothing wrong. Your circumstances are not of your own making. You are a victim of the time you lived in and the sorrows you've endured. Nothing more. All right?"

Jade nods solemnly. "Thank you," she says, her lips shaping the words when her voice cannot.

At this point, pieces of her hair look like they're blowing away, like ash. I can see through her body to the couch behind her. Auntie Bobbie notices too.

"You're tired, Jade, rest yourself. There's work to do."

"There is?" Jade asks eagerly. "You know what to do?"

"I'm not sure, but I do know that your story starts with your bones." Auntie Bobbie turns to me now. "Are you ready to listen to Jade's bones?"

No. But I can't bring myself to say it. I'm so scared.

As if reading my mind, Bobbie speaks, her eyes and voice so gentle I think of my mom soothing me after a zap. "This is so much for you to handle on your own. As much as Jade or me or your mom are here for you, this is something only *you* can do. It's your power. So it's your decision to make. I only offer support, Molly. Not judgment."

It's an unexpectedly emotional thing to hear her say my name. This different, compassionate Bobbie draws me to her. She gives me confidence.

"Me too," says Jade. "I trust your decision."

I focus on breathing in and out, in and out. As much as I don't want to commune with my dead friend's bones, I want Jade to be safe. If Jade's bones can tell us her story, tell us how to help her, then I have to do it. I *want* to do it.

"I'm in. Let's do it."

Jade's hands fly to her mouth and for a moment she's speechless. But her eyes say it all. I feel a little sick to my stomach, but also relieved. I made the choice I was afraid to make.

Bobbie nods, a knowing smile on her face. "Good." She turns back to Jade. "Tomorrow night, Molly and I will come to you in the attic and we'll see what your bones have to tell us. We shouldn't rouse any suspicions just yet by skipping the dinner your mother is so excited about tonight. Besides, you need some good rest, Jade; we all do. Tomorrow we look at your past."

"Okay, thank you," she says, looking at me with a luminous smile, before fading away. Bobbie and I sit in silence, listening to her telltale creaks on the stairs and upstairs floor.

"How do you know so much about this?" I ask.

"Because you and I aren't so different," Auntie Bobbie says, a kind of dreamy look taking over her features. "Oh, I'm not as powerful as you are, Molly. I see spirits from time to time. Occasionally they talk to me, but they never have much to say to me. Sometimes people's memories talk to me through objects—but it's just a feeling here, a fleeting image there. But your gifts are staggering . . . so I've heard."

"You mean—you know about me?" I ask. I always assumed my abilities were a secret from the family.

"Of course I know about you! Who do you think advised your mother when you started getting—what do you call them, 'the zaps'?— when you were little. This lady right here." I'm taken aback by all of this, but the kicker is how much she sounds like my mom with that last sentence, complete with a finger pointing proudly at herself.

"Then why—" I'm cut off by the sound of my mom's car in the driveway.

"We'll discuss this later," Auntie Bobbie says, picking up the coffee table book again. "I don't think your mom would like it if she came back home to me talking ghosts with her daughter. I promised I would never bring it up. But technically you did, so . . . I promise we'll talk more, just not right now." We hear my mom's keys clattering at the door. "It's long overdue and I'm sorry."

I open my mouth to ask *"WHAT IS HAPPENING? WHAT DID YOU PROMISE MY MOM?"* when my mom blusters through the door and the moment is gone. Bobbie's head snaps back to her book like nothing happened and I'm left sitting on the floor with my mouth agape. Mom comes into the living room carrying her camera bag and backpack. She looks at Bobbie, then at me.

"Well, it looks like you two are making up for lost time!" She can barely hide her delight in seeing us together. "Who's ready for dinner at Fragrant Harbor?" As Mom goes up the stairs to change, she tosses over her shoulder, "It's pretty chilly down there; did you two work some magic downstairs on the AC?" We don't respond.

For once I'm positive Auntie Bobbie and I are on the same page. We share an unspoken "ugh."

56
JADE

I thought someone was holding my hand, but when I open my eyes my hand has disappeared into the floor. I cry out and snatch my hand back, but to my ears my voice sounds like it's drifting away on the air. Holding my hand up, I can see the streetlamp's light slice through it.

These are my days and nights now. When I doze, disjointed images crowd my brain—the letter *C* ornately embroidered on a napkin, a cup being held to my mouth by someone else's hands, a woman whose face is hidden by her long dark hair, the sound of wailing. I would call these nightmares but they don't feel like dreams. They feel like my mind is draining itself of memories and I'm watching them wash away.

I'm running out of time.

I might already be out of time.

These are the thoughts that float away from me as I fall back into a tumultuous rest.

57
MOLLY

After a night of tossing and turning, I wake up to a silent house. Checking my phone I'm shocked to see it's almost eleven. Where is everybody?

I putter into the kitchen to find a croissant in a white paper bakery bag and a note.

> You looked like you needed to sleep in. Bobbie and I are running errands. We'll be home later. Let me know if you want anything while we're out!
> xo
> Mom

It's nice to have the house to myself for a while, but all the same I'm eager to talk to Auntie Bobbie. Apparently she knows way more about me than I know about her. And why did my mom make her promise to not talk about ghost stuff with me? It would have been so great, especially when I was younger, to have someone who really understood the zaps.

I finish the croissant and go upstairs to take a shower. Grabbing a clean towel from the hall closet, I glance at the attic door and pause. Jade looked so hopeful but weak yesterday. I suddenly remember that I forgot to feed her when we got home last night and instantly start to worry. How could I have done that?! I swear, with everything going on, things are just falling out of my brain.

Dropping the towel, I run downstairs and find one of the conchas—those sugary Mexican pastries that look like shells—Mom stashes in the cupboard. Wrapping it in a paper towel, I go back upstairs to the attic door and knock. Silence.

"Jade!" I call, not having to worry about anyone hearing me. "I'm sorry I didn't give you anything to eat last night. We got home late from the restaurant and I was wiped! I'm leaving something at the door."

Putting the wrapped concha on the floor outside the attic door, I grab my fallen towel and go to the bathroom for my shower. When I draw back the curtain I can't help but look to the bathroom mirror, hoping that maybe Jade left me a message. There's no message and I feel a twinge of concern. These days I'm always afraid that the last time I see Jade will be the LAST TIME.

Just as I finish getting dressed I hear the front door slam and Mom call up the stairs, "Molls! We're back! I got cookies from Cynthia's, that diner by the casket store!"

Why Mom feels the need to yell "casket store" up the stairs is beyond me.

But I remember the concha and hurry out the bathroom door to grab it before Mom sees, in case Jade didn't take it. Mom already thinks I've developed a food-hoarding habit or I'm sleep-eating or something; I don't need to give her more evidence.

The wrapped concha is still there, totally untouched. I hear the floorboards squeak behind me and turn to see Auntie Bobbie standing at the guest room door.

"She's not eating?" she asks.

"Not always," I say, unable to keep the worry out of my voice.

Auntie Bobbie opens the bedroom door and goes in, leaving it open. "Come on," she calls impatiently from inside. I go in still cradling the concha.

I notice I'm getting crumbs on the floor, so I sit on a chair by the mattress and rest the pastry on my lap. Like the first day Bobbie arrived, she looks me up and down again. Her eyes narrow like she's trying to see into my brain.

"What do you want to know?"

Wow, Bobbie just gets straight to the point.

"Um, so, you see ghosts too?"

"Yes."

I wait for her to elaborate. She does not. I continue. "Why did Mom make you promise not to talk to me about this? It would have been amazing to know I wasn't alone."

Bobbie actually looks nervous. "I know. I apologize. It's just, your mom wanted you to have a normal life, unburdened by the 'family secret.'"

"What do you mean 'family secret'?"

"Many women in our family have what's called 'ghost-seeing eyes.' Eyes like yours and mine. Your great-grandmother could also see ghosts, but nobody really talks about it anymore."

"Whoa, if this is a thing in our family, shouldn't someone have told me? Is this why you disapprove of me?"

"Disapprove of you? Is that what you think? That's not it at all. I'm sorry if it's seemed that way. I just get so frustrated sometimes. I see a girl with so much potential for good being squelched by fear and mis-understanding of what she's capable of. I always wanted to tell you. From the very beginning I insisted upon it, actually. But your mother refused; she wanted to protect you. And now you've spent your whole life believ-ing you are some kind of abomination when in fact you have a gift. I blame your mother for this—this isn't protecting you, it's lying to you."

I'm gobsmacked. All the same, a surge of protectiveness wells up in me. Bobbie is not being fair. My mom is the only person who has ever made me feel safe and not like I'm from another dimension.

"You're wrong," I say firmly. "Mom is doing her best and has always been there for me when I'm scared, when the zaps turn me inside out. She doesn't have answers, but I've never expected that from her. I know she's scared of the ghost stuff but she's never judged me for it. How many parents are accepting of their kids even if they don't understand them?"

"Of course, and I'm not here to turn you against your mother. I just think that if I'd been guiding you in your life you wouldn't have had to navigate any fear of your powers at all," says Bobbie in a measured, careful tone. "But Dorothy told me to leave you alone, to stay out of your life, both of your lives. So I did—entirely. Maybe I was bitter, maybe I acted in anger, but hearing my little sister tell me to get out of her life wounded me to my core."

"She kicked you out of our lives? That's what you've been fighting about?"

Auntie Bobbie hesitates. "Among other things, we've been arguing about the decisions we've made. But, Molly, understand that I removed myself from a situation where I wasn't wanted. I also may have said things I didn't really mean, cruel things. Things I regret. Molly, your mother loves you ferociously, never forget that. But she also has a habit of running away from things. Our family, our history, our powers. She thought that if you didn't center your abilities, if you weren't inundated with 'all the family ghost talk,' you'd find your own way around it and wouldn't be weighed down."

"Weighed down by what?"

"Responsibility. To the dead."

As soon as she says the words, I know this is what I've been dancing around from the moment I met Jade. *What is my responsibility?* Just having this conversation feels like I'm betraying my mom, but I'm also so curious as to what Auntie Bobbie can reveal to me. Hoping my mom can forgive me, I press on.

"Responsibility? What do we owe our dead?"

Bobbie sighs. She cracks her knuckles like she's preparing to reach inside my brain. "Most people believe that we are divided: There's the living and there's the dead. Someone dies, we mourn them, we bury them, we tidy their grave. The end."

"But that's not the end, is it?"

"No. It's just the beginning. What the living do impacts the dead. It's not so much that we owe them anything, it's more that to care for the dead is to care for our past. Without our past, our history, we are just dots floating in a void—nothing connects us. Our ancestors— whether by blood or experience—give us context."

I think of the Loh sisters and their ghost. Mary isn't their relative by blood, but I bet she shared Hazel and Rose's deep determination.

Nineteenth century or twenty-first century, it's not always easy to be Asian in Texas. Sometimes it's impossible to fight a place that calls to you, but sometimes you have to fight to call that place home.

My head feels like a bag of moths—dozens of thoughts careening around my brain. "Have you seen ghosts like Jade before?"

"Not quite like Jade. I've never interacted with a ghost on such a *human* level before. Mostly I'll see them pass by or we'll exchange a few words—"

"What do they say?" I'm too eager and interrupt. Bobbie looks only mildly annoyed.

"Sometimes they ask about their family; sometimes they're confused and ask what I'm doing there. But the one thing they have in common is the loneliness. Perhaps that's what I feel so strongly, the loneliness. They are all alone, searching for something or someone."

I nod. I know that loneliness.

"Sometimes they just want to know their child or spouse is well and safe. Other times they are bewildered, searching for a loved one. Then there are the ghosts that are just so *tragic*. They're the ghosts that have been forgotten, have nobody to mourn them. When nobody remembers them, they're lost."

I remember Jade's frightened plea the other night: *I'm losing myself!* I remember what Hazel said.

"Jade is a hungry ghost," I say.

For once I've caught Auntie Bobbie off guard. "You know about hungry ghosts?"

I tell her about the Loh sisters and Mary. She seems pleased, but worried still.

"I see Jade, I hear Jade, I give her food—she's my best friend! But why is this happening to her?" I ask with a tad more desperation than I intended.

Auntie Bobbie exhales heavily, her eyes far away in thought. "Hungry ghosts can become tortured, angry spirits, bringing bad luck to the places they haunt. Or they can become sad, mournful ghosts who make a home unlivable. Nobody wants to stay in a house with a suffering spirit."

I think about how tense and cranky everyone in the house has been lately. About all the tenants this place has had.

Bobbie's face darkens as she chooses her words. "Jade is unusual. She's been in this house for so long, just *surviving*, seemingly from sheer force of will. I've never heard of a ghost like Jade. Does she know anything about her family?"

"She barely remembers anything from life. She just knows being a ghost."

Auntie Bobbie shakes her head, her face contorted in thought. "How odd. That poor girl."

"Auntie Bobbie . . . how do you know so much about this?"

Her eyes are bright with tears, but she holds my gaze. "It's not just Jade, Molly, it's not just Mary. So many Chinese ghosts are wandering, lost and alone in this country, from the beginning."

"Why? What beginning?" I ask.

"Thousands of Chinese people built the Transcontinental Railroad that joined America. Chinese men came to America to earn money to send back to their families. Many didn't know if they would ever see their families again, but they made the sacrifice to give them a better life. Some found success, some started businesses, some were able to go back to their families if they wanted. Many did not. Many died alone, forgotten. There were also the countless people that died in the treacherous conditions of building that railroad—killed in explosions, crushed while tunneling through mountains, falling off cliffs."

A shadow passes over Auntie Bobbie's face. "So many nameless, blotted-out ghosts haunt that railroad. Nobody bothered to properly record their names. Some were just names like 'Ah Ching' or 'Ah Sing,' repeated over and over again—the rich men who ran the railroad couldn't be bothered to learn our names, let alone keep a record of our lives or deaths."

"Like Mary," I whisper. She nods.

"Occasionally, when you meet a ghost and can't help them, it's . . ."

She swallows hard, composing herself. She finds her voice again.

"It's never been easy for us, seeing our ghosts die, be erased from history . . . they don't deserve that. It erases *us*. We should do better by our ghosts." She takes a deep breath and sits up taller.

I want to ask Bobbie more, but I hear my mom coming up the stairs. "Why am I sitting in the kitchen alone eating cookies?" she calls out.

"Go," Bobbie says, standing up and wiping any leftover tears from her face. "Go be with Dorothy. I'll be there in a moment. I'm sorry if I've complicated things between you and your mother. I just see that you and Jade need help and this is something I can do. For my family."

"Okay," I say, so overwhelmed by everything that I can only do as I'm told. "We'll go to Jade tonight?"

"Yes, yes, of course. Just knock on my door." And then, "Maybe . . . wait until after Dorothy goes to sleep." It's weird to hear an adult, my mom's older sister, talk about sneaking around behind my mom's back. Somehow this makes me feel a little guilty.

I start to leave Auntie Bobbie but pause at the bedroom door. "You're wrong about me and my mom. Maybe it took some time, but I'm here and I'm trying to do good now. That has a lot to do with my mom," I say. Then gentler: "But thank you for telling me about our family. I wish we could have talked sooner too." And I go out the door to be the good daughter.

58
JADE

Having all eyes on me is strange and alarming.

Molly and her auntie Bobbie stand in my attic, looking at me, their eyes shining in the light of the streetlamp, which thankfully glows brighter than ever. Concern radiates from Molly and her auntie. I am moved and I feel fortunate, but dread also nips at the edges of my mind. Do they know something I don't?

Part of my fear comes from the fact that I can no longer appear fully solid to Molly and her auntie. The room is so cold, I try to find every little bit of energy in it, but I remain transparent. My hair looks like it's melting away around my shoulders, the lamplight cuts through my body and I see the wooden beams we stand on beneath me; my hands and feet are almost gone, engulfed in smoke. I float, I drift, everything feels dulled. I don't have much time left.

"Jade, can I see your bones?" Molly asks.

I look to Auntie Bobbie; she bobs her head, as if to say, *Go ahead.*

Somehow I trust this woman. Adults normally don't see me or won't, which has always made me wary of them, but I am safe with this austere woman, I know it.

With the trust I feel toward Molly and Auntie Bobbie, you'd think it would be easier to comply. But I hesitate. If this doesn't work, if I learn nothing that can help me, is there anything else I can do?

"Your bones hold the answers," Auntie Bobbie says gently. "Let Molly hold them. It's okay, Jade."

I glide over to the loose floorboard and kneel on my transparent knees to open it. I press the knot on the board, but my fingers—mostly wisps—push right through. It barely jiggles. I close my eyes to focus and the board lifts a little, but once again my fingers go through and the board snaps down.

"Can I help?" Auntie Bobbie is next to me.

I nod. "Please." My voice is thin, more air than sound.

She presses the floorboard down and it pops open, revealing my treasures. She checks with me again to make sure it's all right if she reaches in. I nod.

The light from the window makes all my earthly possessions look enchanted. My comb in particular glints like a jewel in the light. If oblivion awaits me, I hope this gift can come along.

Bobbie finds the bundle of red satin and places it carefully on

Celia's rug. Molly kneels next to it, her hands in her lap. As if unwrapping delicate china, Bobbie opens the bundle to reveal my bones. I can't help but gasp—they glow in the lamplight. Usually off-white, a little brown in color, my bones shine bright, almost translucent now.

Molly lifts her hand, reaching for my bones. I intercept her with the gauzy tendrils that are my fingers. She looks at me, confused. "I know you're scared. I want you to be sure," I say, struggling to give my words some weight. "If this is too much to ask, if this could hurt you, I don't want you to do it. If this is how being a ghost works, then I have to go. You have a choice, my Molly, my best friend."

Her face crumples a little and she looks like she might break down but she does not. "I want to do this. I'm not going to just let you disappear without a fight." She looks at Auntie Bobbie. "Besides, we have help."

I want to ask what has transpired between auntie and niece, but a fragment of my hair floats between us and disintegrates, an oddly lovely reminder that that too might be my fate. "Thank you," I say, and Molly turns back to my bones.

"Remember, Molly, we're here with you," Auntie Bobbie says reassuringly. "You are just witnessing the past; you *will* come back."

Molly breathes deeply and closes her eyes, hands hovering over the largest bone. Slowly, she lowers them.

Her fingertips only graze the incandescent surface when her whole being goes rigid and her eyes fly open. Molly's pupils fly back and forth as if taking in a world before her, a world none of us can see. One that she is very much on her own in.

I hope we aren't making a mistake.

59
MOLLY AND JADE

I'm in the attic but not *quite* the attic. It's daytime. Sun shines through the window, which has white curtains now. I feel the heat in the room, but I'm cold. It's silent. The distant hum of the air-conditioning unit is absent; no cars roar by.

I turn my head to look around the room and I feel long, heavy curtains of hair brush my arm. I run my fingers through my hair. My hands are so small, so delicate. There's so little flesh on my arms, they feel so light. This yellow dress . . .

I'm not me. I'm Jade. These are Jade's hands, Jade's hair, Jade's dress.

It hurts to breathe.

I'm sitting on a bed under the slope of the roof, near the window. It's hard and squeaks when I shift my weight. The sheet over my legs is rough, thin, and grayish white. A faded blue, rectangular rug is in the center of the room, and under the opposite slope of the roof is a dresser that leans a little to the left. A pitcher of water and a cup sit on top of the dresser next to some partially burned candles in holders.

My breath comes in rasps. A layer of sweat coats my skin as I shiver in the heat. My vision starts to darken and little pinpricks of light dance in front of me. My head feels like a heavy bucket with water sloshing around in it. I start to fall back onto the bed and it feels like I'm moving in slow motion. My head hits the lumpy pillow behind me hard, forcing searing, painful coughs that pound in my chest and tear at my throat.

It's that rasping sound from my first zap at the window seat!

Instinctively, I cry out. It's Jade's voice.

"Ma! Ma!"

Nothing happens and I wonder if I'm calling for anyone real.

"Ma!" I use all my strength to call out. The pillow I lie on smells of sour and sweat. Turning my head, I see a tin cup on a stool by my head. I reach for it but the effort is too much and I knock the cup to the ground. It makes a clanging sound and water splatters. Panic grips me and it gets harder to breathe.

I hear movement on the floor below and the sound of the attic door being opened and shut. Light footsteps fly up the stairs, a head of dark hair appears, rising above the floor, climbing to the top of the stairs. "Pui Yu! What do you need, my baby? Are you okay?"

Pui Yu. That's me. Precious Jade. She's calling me by name.

When the woman turns to me, I feel dizzy. She looks so much like Jade, her giant, dark, searching eyes, her delicate features. I can't tell her age at all; she seems caught between being very young and very old. Her plump cheeks are betrayed by deep lines on her forehead and at the corners of her eyes. There's a groove between her brows like worry has carved a canyon. But despite all the pain that lies across her face, she is undeniably beautiful. I wonder what life has doled out to carve such concern into her features?

She speaks Cantonese, except for the last part, which she says in accented but natural-sounding English. The woman rushes to me, she is so tiny, barely five feet tall, I bet, but I want nothing more than her protection. I reach for her with trembling arms.

My mother. I want my mother.

Seeing the spilled water at the side of my bed, she scoops up the cup, saying under her breath, "You need to drink more water." She goes to the pitcher to refill the cup.

I feel such an all-consuming affection for this woman. I'm desperate for her to be near me. This tiny woman with shiny black hair parted in the middle and pulled into a smooth, tight bun. Dark circles like smudges ring her eyes, but when she smiles at me from the dresser she is all brightness. Her love for me is palpable; it fills the room and is as sure as there is a sun in the sky. She wears a charcoal-colored dress,

Western style, with long sleeves and an apron. She works in this house, she cooks and does laundry—the knowledge just floats into my head. I work here too, for a family . . . a family with blond hair and blue eyes . . . or at least I used to, until I got sick.

Now I'm only allowed in the attic. Until I . . .

She puts her hand on my chest and furrows her brow. "Your chest, does it hurt?" she asks in English.

"Yau di tung," I answer back in Cantonese, without even thinking. "It hurts a little." I'm lying so she doesn't worry. She knows.

Her smile only falters for a blink and she opens one of the dresser drawers to look for something. She reveals a glass bottle that fits into the palm of her hand. It has a label and words on it, but I can't see what it says. She comes over with the cup and the bottle and sits on the bed next to me. My breath comes in great rattling gasps.

"Some water," she says in English, and tilts the cup to my lips to drink. I choke. She wipes my mouth with her apron. It smells like grease and food. Removing the lid from the bottle, she supports my head and tells me to "be my good girl and drink your medicine." I do as I'm told—it's bitter and burns my throat. I cough even harder.

Sensing my growing panic, she puts the medicine and cup on the stool and hurries back over to the dresser to get something. When she returns she's holding a shiny red lacquer comb.

She tells me to lie on my side and when I do, facing her, she runs the comb from my scalp to the ends of my hair, gently picking apart snarls with her fingers. Soon the comb slides easily through my hair—Jade's hair—and despite the feeling that my throat is getting smaller and smaller and the room is growing dimmer and dimmer, I feel safe.

I don't want to leave, but I feel myself leaving. I cry out and her arms encircle me.

My mother hums a song, a tune I'll never remember but will stay with me forever. I reach for her hand and she catches mine, her hand so frail but holding mine so tight. She leans in close to me and I feel wetness fall on my cheek—her tears. My breathing grows shallow.

She holds me tight and whispers in my ear, "I will never leave you. You will always be with me, my precious, my Jade. When you are a ghost"—the word catches in her throat; she takes a breath and continues speaking in her smooth, youthful voice—"I will remember you and I will take care of you, just like I do now, yes? Then one day we will be ghosts together and won't we have fun? We will fly like birds! Where will we go, Jade?"

The memory dissolves into blackness; snatches of life punch through the dark like fireworks: A wail. My mother's face. Loud footsteps on the attic stairs, other people. My mother closes my fingers around the comb; she kisses my palm. I'm floating; I hold on to my mother's hand as tight as I can, for as long as I can, but it slips away.

The next memories come in big, blinding scraps like disjointed clips from a movie. It makes my stomach lurch.

A mustached man and a blond-haired woman with steely blue eyes in an old-fashioned green dress. Her lips curled in disgust.

My mother—I mean Jade's mother; the feelings are so confusing—pleading.

My body is lifted.

A hand grabs my foot, tries to hold on.

The wooden beams of the attic ceiling spin. A scream.

Darkness. The whole world seems to tip, then suddenly right itself. I'm still again.

I can't see, but I can move. Barely. Every direction I try to go I'm met with a wall. It smells like metal. But there's something else in the dark with me, something rattling around like pieces of a kit that needs to be assembled. There are so many pieces, large and small. I grab one of the larger pieces; it feels familiar. I gasp.

It's Jade's bone.

I'm Jade in her box of bones. And I'm starving. Starving in a way that feels like white-hot fury. My stomach growls so loud it sounds like a wounded animal in my ears—until I realize I am the one who's growling. The growl shakes my body and grows into a shriek.

This is more than I can take. I thrash around, slamming myself into walls and bones. I'm not human, I'm just hunger.

Then for a moment I feel weightless, I'm suspended in midair, like when a roller coaster drops.

CRASH! My bones and I are sprawled on the floor of the attic. In my hands I'm clutching the large bone with the teeth marks in one hand and some smaller bones in the other. I am wild; the world is too bright and dangerous.

I hear footsteps on the attic stairs, more than one person. One set is very heavy and loud. Terror surges through me. My head is swirling but my gut tells me to scurry into a corner of the attic, where the roof meets the floor. I'm like a feral animal, snarling, bones in hand.

The blond-haired woman from the earlier memory, now in a long lavender dress, appears along with a tall man in a dirty blue shirt with the sleeves rolled up. I now see that the attic is almost empty—the bed is gone, the dresser, the curtains. Only the stool remains, a rumpled bedsheet piled on the floor, a broken candle, and a lingering familiar scent that clings to the space. My mother. Jade's mother. But where is she?

The woman stands in the middle of the room and that same repulsed expression returns to her face when she sees the bones. The man looks up to a wide, flat beam above their head.

"She must have stashed it up there before she died and it fell from all the furniture moving around," he says.

The woman dramatically shivers, clutching her necklace. "Such filth. These people really keep the most dreadful things. Throw everything out."

"Ms. Cullum, ma'am, I think these are bones, shouldn't we—" says the man hesitantly.

"I know exactly what they are and I don't care. Throw them out with anything else you find here. I want no evidence that I ever had a Chinese in my house. I will never understand my husband's fascination with those people." With a sniff she turns and leaves.

The man shrugs and starts roughly shoving Jade's bones back into the gray metal box, throwing the broken candle in as well. He turns for a moment to make sure there's nothing else in the attic, and when he does, something catches my eye glinting in the sunlight on the floor by the stool.

The lacquer comb.

Without thinking, like I'm on autopilot, I run over and grab the comb, then scurry back to my corner. The man goes to the bedsheet on the floor. He puts the stool, the box, everything in the center, then bundles it up. He throws it over his shoulder. I lean in, watching the last remnants of Jade's life get swept away, when the floorboard creaks beneath me. The man pauses as he turns to leave and looks around the attic. His eyes land right on the corner where I'm crouched; I swear he's staring at me. His eyes narrow a little.

But he seems to think better of it. Shaking his head, he goes down the stairs and the attic door slams shut. I hear it lock.

Then I am alone—Jade is alone.

With just her bones and the comb from her mother clutched in her hands.

60

MOLLY

I'm back in the attic alongside Auntie Bobbie and Jade. My head is throbbing and every part of my body feels like it's run a marathon. Even my teeth ache.

If everything else was a zap—all the knickknacks, doorknobs, chairs—this is like being struck by lightning. Every cell in my body is lit up. I wonder if my hair is standing on end.

I collapse on the rug and lie on my side, trying to catch my breath. Jade and Bobbie are saying my name, asking if I'm okay, but they sound very far away. I know my mouth is moving, but am I talking? I'm very grateful that Jade's presence makes everything so chilly. I feel like I'm going to be sick; I curl up in a ball and try to breathe. I concentrate on how the old rug feels rough on my cheek.

One thought circles round and round in my head: *I want my mother.*

I don't know if it's leftover memories from Jade or the fact that any-time I feel this terrible, my mom makes it better. Maybe it's both. Fear and rage and loneliness rush through me, though I can't tell which feeling is mine and which is Jade's. Something wet is on my face. I'm crying and I'm reminded of my mother's tears—I mean Jade's mother's tears—on my cheek.

Jade crouches on the floor next to me. I can see through her pale skin and dark hair to the attic beams behind her. *The beams Jade saw when she died.* "Molly! Please speak to me! Are you okay? What did you see?" She reaches a misty hand to me and her icy touch soothes me. I swallow hard and force sound out of my mouth.

"They took your bones." And just like that, my energy is spent.

The world churns, then sharpens and I find myself in my bed. Weak yellow light from the bedside table lamp casts shadows around the room. Auntie Bobbie, in an oversize gray T-shirt and blue-striped pajama bottoms, sits with her knees drawn into her, reading a book in a chair by the door. The chair from her room. In such cozy, casual clothes and her hair a little mussed up, it's eerie how much she looks like my mom.

I move and the mattress squeaks.

Auntie Bobbie looks up from her book and sees that I'm awake. "Hello, Molly, how are you feeling?"

"Did you throw me in front of a bus? Because that's what it feels like." I gasp as a current of fury courses through me and then is quickly replaced by the most intense sorrow I've ever felt. Is this grief? My eyes start to well up.

I look around the room, searching between the light and shadows for Jade. Knowing who I'm looking for, Auntie Bobbie speaks up. "She's been at your side for the past few hours. She needed to rest. She'll be back soon. You should rest too. We'll talk when she returns."

Even though it's tempting to close my eyes again to avoid the nausea rising in my throat and the ferocious emotions bopping through my body, I force myself to sit up. "But I know what happened!"

Auntie Bobbie stands and comes over to me. She kneels down at my head and brushes my hair off my face. Her hands are warm and smooth and she smells a little like spearmint or Mentholatum. *Big Chinese auntie energy*, I think, and smile. She returns the smile.

"I'm happy to see some color in your face. I don't want your mom to worry."

MY MOM. I sit up taller. "Does she know? Is she okay?"

"She doesn't know a thing," Auntie Bobbie assures me. "I was able to get you down here without waking her. My sister is still like a vampire—she's dead to the world when she sleeps."

"Do vampires snore?" I say without thinking.

Auntie Bobbie chuckles. "You need to drink some water. I'll be right back."

"Wait," I say. "How long was I . . . um . . ."

"Seeing the past?"

"Yeah."

"I'd say about a minute."

"WHAT?!" I yelp, making my head throb again. I felt like I was gone for hours; how did all that happen in ONE MINUTE?

"Shhhhh!" Bobbie's eyes fly wide. She points in the direction of my mom's room.

"But how?" I hiss.

"I don't know, but obviously you have a lot to tell us. Jade will be back soon. Rest," Auntie Bobbie instructs, and goes down to the kitchen for water.

I must have dozed off again, because I wake up when the side of my bed dips. My eyes flutter open and I see Jade, or what's left of Jade, next to me. Her body and hair are just an undulating mist. Only her face, though see-through, is clear. Her eyes still shine.

"Molly, are you okay? I was so scared, you looked, you looked—"

"Dead?" I say. I don't know why I thought this would be funny. Judging by Jade's face, it is not. "Sorry, I didn't mean to scare you. But, Jade, the things I saw. Your life, your—" I hesitate. Can I really say this to a person? "—your death. I think I saw your death."

Jade recoils ever so slightly. "I was wondering," she says softly.

Auntie Bobbie is back from the kitchen, stepping carefully so as not to creak or thud across the old floor. She carries a glass of water and a plate piled with crackers and half a leftover "Calzone à la Dot," aka the dish my mom makes for special occasions (her secret ingredients are sour cream and a lot of MSG).

She puts the plate on the bed between Jade and me, and sits down at the foot of the bed with us.

"The crackers are for you, Molly. I figured you needed something to settle your stomach."

I'm horrified. "Did I barf on you?"

"Don't worry about it," she says with a wave of her hand. "Jade, some food would probably do you some good as well."

Jade and I reach for our respective snacks—I notice the effort it takes for her to grasp the calzone in her wispy hands. Not gonna lie, I'm a little afraid I'll see her chewed-up food go down her throat and be digested in her stomach, but luckily it vanishes as she eats like normal. As normal as a ghost eating a calzone anyway.

After a while, Auntie Bobbie speaks.

"Okay, Molly. Tell us what you saw."

61

JADE

Molly's gaze holds mine. She takes a deep breath and begins recounting my life and death through her eyes.

It's almost more than I can bear.

She tells of the room that once was my attic, the sensation of moving from life to death, and a woman who vowed to love me beyond forever.

My mother. Molly saw and spoke to my mother. Again something wells up in me. Is it anger again? That's part of it, but I'm not angry at Molly, I'm . . . jealous. I'm so jealous that Molly has these memories and I don't.

Somehow all I have is the memory of my name. My mother doesn't even have that. What was her name? What happened to her? Where are *her* bones?

Molly describes being inside the box with my bones, screaming to be rescued. But this is where our memories diverge. I remember crashing to the floor but being so overwhelmed and frightened that I was more animal—more monster—than human. Snippets of memory pepper my recollection of that day, but my memories of being a ghost begin after. During the night, searching for food.

The blond-haired woman and her blond-haired family did not live in the house for very long. Cullum was the family's name, George and Meredith. Those early days, my "toddler days" of death were very confusing. I was either huddled in the attic or prowling for food at night.

I had always wondered what happened to my bones, the box where my ghost was born. Now I know: Meredith Cullum threw them away, *threw me away*, like garbage. I'm gone; any evidence that my mother or I existed is gone. All that remains of me are a few chewed-up bones in a hole in the floor. All is lost.

"How could anybody be so horrible?" Molly asks.

"Because we often weren't seen as human," answers Auntie Bobbie. "We were hated, we were killed, all for the crime of being Chinese in America."

Auntie Bobbie's words ring true to me—there were definitely times in the house when I heard snippets of people talking about "those Chinamen" or "the Chinese must go!" but most people who lived in the house, people who looked like the Cullums, seemed unconcerned with the plight of people struggling to make a life in Texas, in

America. People who didn't look like them were an annoyance to be utilized, avoided, or expelled. Little did I know what was going on beyond the walls of the house on Charlotte Street.

"You were another victim of the Chinese Exclusion Act, Jade."

"Chinese *what*?" Molly interjects. "I've taken American history classes all over the country; how have I never learned about this?"

"Because history is written by the people who make the rules," Auntie Bobbie says. "And Chinese people did not make the rules in this country. Other people made rules about us." She continues:

"From 1882 to 1943, America decided that if you were Chinese, you were not welcome in this country. You could never become an American citizen; you always had to carry your papers with you or risk deportation. Like so much of our Chinese American history— our names, our bones, our ghosts—we've forgotten that the only time Americans decided to create a law banning a race of people from American soil, it was against Chinese people. First they went after Chinese women in 1875, then it was all Chinese who could be considered a laborer. So most everybody."

I feel all 120 years of my existence as I watch Molly learn what I know I lived. Even if it's locked up in my brain somewhere, an ache deep down inside me confirms what Bobbie is saying.

"Like I told you, Molly, it's so important for us to remember our dead, to care for their remains. Part of a proper burial, especially for those who were so far from home, was to dig up their bones after they had been buried for a while—it was someone's job to gather every single bone, if possible—and send them back home to be buried and honored by their loved ones. This is how a ghost finds peace in the afterlife. They are remembered, they are fed, they are home."

"But"—and even Auntie Bobbie seems depleted now—"even if a person's bones were properly exhumed and cataloged, they didn't always make it home. Because of the hatred that grew up against our communities, many of those containers of bones were destroyed or lost."

I can barely move. All these years in my house I've thought *my* fate was cruel. But to be a starving, lonely ghost trapped in a box for all eternity? I can't imagine that. For all I know, as I sit with people who are trying to save me, there are ghosts out there who will never know any such kindness.

"After Chinese people finished building the Transcontinental Railroad," Auntie Bobbie continues, "we were favored for a while, dependable, talented, hard workers who could build more railroads around the country for less pay. A lot of people only think of the coasts when they think of Chinese immigration, but hundreds of Chinese people came to Texas in the 1800s and early twentieth century. Even as Chinese hatred grew and railroad work dried up, Chinese people still found work all over the state—cooking, doing laundry, or working in white Americans' homes. Like Jade and her mother.

"But it wasn't long before any illusion of goodwill gave way to blame and jealousy. People claimed the Chinese were taking their jobs, poisoning their communities. Eventually, the president signed the Chinese Exclusion Act into law."

Auntie Bobbie turns to me. "I'm so sorry your bones never made it back to your family, wherever they are."

I don't know what to say. I am a piece of buried history. Swept under the rug of the past.

Once again, Molly looks like she is going to throw up.

62

MOLLY

"Now we know what happened to Jade's . . . remains. What can we do?" I ask, afraid of what Auntie Bobbie will say. I'm still reeling from everything Auntie Bobbie has told us, but I try to pull myself together and not dry heave.

She cracks a couple of fingers. "Let me think about this. Jade died in this attic. Most of Jade's bones were thrown away. All she has is the bones she was clutching when she fell out of the box. I've never heard of a hungry ghost disappearing like this, but if there's nobody left in her family who remembers Jade . . ."

"It will be like I never existed," says Jade plainly, matter-of-factly. "I will cease to exist." Her whole body seems to billow in an unseen wind. Jade is trying to put a brave face on, but it's a flimsy mask.

"We don't know that, Jade," Auntie Bobbie says. "There might be something we can do."

"I knew my bones would have the answers. I just wasn't prepared that the answer would be my second death." Jade flickers. She's giving up.

"No," I say, and stand up to pace around the room. I feel light-headed, but I need to get my blood pumping to my brain, I need to think this through. "I'm not going to just watch you disappear into nothing! You were here. You ARE here!"

Then I remember the promise I made to Jade.

"I'll remember you. I'll take care of the bones you have left. I'll feed you. Why can't I be your family? Your home?" I turn to Auntie Bobbie. "That'll work, right?"

"But so much of me is gone . . ." Jade objects.

"Well, we don't have all of your bones, but we have some of them. They're still part of you. What if we honor them—put them in something beautiful, like a chest or a—a—"

"—an urn," Auntie Bobbie joins in. "You can put Jade's remaining bones in an urn, just like you would if someone were cremated now, and we can make an altar for her in the attic. Like we would for family—"

"—like Hazel and Rose did for Mary!" I cry out, unable to contain the hope bubbling up in me.

"Perhaps it will be evidence that we claim Jade as one of ours. An adopted sister . . . or niece. Her bones will always be in our family's care." Auntie Bobbie smiles reassuringly at Jade.

"Yes!" I can't contain the relief I'm feeling at this idea, that it might actually work.

Jade stands up and comes up to me, looking me square in the eyes. "You'd do that for me? You'd care for my bones? You'll keep feeding me? What if you move?"

"You're my best friend, Jade. You're a . . . sister." I pause for a moment to let the word settle in. It feels good. "I need you. And . . . maybe I won't move." Both Jade and Bobbie raise their eyebrows in surprise. "Calm down. I haven't committed to anything yet; one life-and-death decision at a time, please." I smile for what feels like the first time in years.

Jade's eyes light up, though fear still holds her features hostage. "All right. Let's try it."

63
MOLLY

Dot Teng wants to have a pancake breakfast. I have never loathed a pancake more.

After the longest night ever, falling asleep as Jade went to rest and the sun appeared to torture me, I don't even have the luxury of sleeping in.

As Mom scurries and chatters around the kitchen, telling me to measure ingredients or grab plates and pans, Bobbie and I barely speak or even make eye contact. We probably look as awkward as we have for her whole visit, but a part of me feels really bad about keeping up this deception in front of my mom. Even though Auntie Bobbie is still very much a mystery to me, I feel like I have a connection to her now and I know Mom would love that.

But would she be okay with us bonding over a ghost?

I haven't forgotten what Auntie Bobbie told me about my mom keeping our "family secret" from me. But did she really think she'd be able to keep it from me forever, especially if Bobbie is back in our lives? *She* wanted this. I can't help but be a little angry that, just like with all our moves, Dot Teng didn't stop to think if what was best for me was really just best for her.

But there is so much to do for Jade, I don't know how I'm going to carve out time to have a BIG CONVERSATION with my mom. We have to get an urn for Jade's bones, create an altar for her, stay with her to make sure it works.

Stay with her in case it doesn't work.

If Jade continues to disappear, there's no way I'm letting her die alone.

Auntie Bobbie says she'll handle getting what we need, but I can't help but feel like I'm drowning all the same.

As we eat our pancakes, Bobbie actually asks Mom about her work. Mom tells Bobbie about a project that she's spearheading, an online directory of all the local Asian and immigrant-owned restaurants in the area—in English as well as the native languages of the restaurants listed. "So people who have trouble with English can still find comfort foods. I was thinking of calling it 'A Taste of Home.' Do you think that's good?" She can barely hide how much she wants her big sister's approval.

Mom and I watch Bobbie, unsure what's going to happen. Putting down her fork, Auntie Bobbie's face softens into a smile and she says, "I think that's a wonderful name and a wonderful project. I'm happy to see your food obsession is making this world better. I'm very proud of you."

Mom and I have to take a minute to scrape our jaws off the floor. Auntie Bobbie just stares at us, though she does look really amused. When we recover, Mom is straight-up bouncing in her seat. "Thank you, Bob, that means so, so, so much to me." *(She calls her Bob?!)*

And from there the floodgates open. I take advantage of the best mood my mom has ever been in.

"Mom, I think it's time we were honest with each other." It's like my mouth is moving on its own and I can't stop it. I don't want to stop. "Our house is haunted."

And just like that, I tell her everything that's happened from the moment we moved into the house on Charlotte Street.

I tell her about seeing things.

All the zaps.

Operation Ignore Ignore Ignore.

Finding my first real friend in Jade.

Learning about the family secret.

Trying to save Jade.

When I'm done letting the events of the past couple of months pour out of me, I feel free. Mom might freak out, but at least I can be honest with her now.

She sits blinking and nodding like she's replaying my monologue over and over in her head. Then out of nowhere she abruptly stands up. Auntie Bobbie and I watch her walk to the door and shove her feet into some sneakers. She then grabs her purse, which is hanging on the upward swoop at the end of the staircase banister. As her fingers graze the wood, she pauses and looks at it like it might bite her. She peers up the stairs into the darkness for a moment before turning toward the front door.

She reaches for the doorknob, then stops and looks at us. "I gotta get some air," she says numbly, and goes out the door. We hear her car start and drive down the street.

Auntie Bobbie and I look at each other, completely baffled. "Is she . . . mad?" I ask.

"At this point, you know her better than I do, but if I remember my sister, she just needs to process. I'm sure she'll be fine," Bobbie responds, but for the first time since I've met her she sounds unsure.

We silently clean up the kitchen, then sit at the table again, not sure what to do. Finally, Bobbie stands up. "Well, whether Dorothy likes it or not, we have things to do. I'm going to go get the items we need. Do you think you'll be okay here or would you prefer to come with me?"

Feeling both distraught and utterly spent, I tell Auntie Bobbie I'd prefer to stay home—in case Jade needs me.

"Okay," she says, and grabs her keys and purse. "It's going to work out, Molly. Remember, you don't have to do these things alone anymore." I give her a half-hearted thanks and she goes off to run errands for the dead.

But that's what Auntie Bobbie just can't understand. Not knowing where I stand with my mom? That's the loneliest I've ever felt.

64
MOLLY

I wake up when I hear the front door shut and feel a whoosh of hot air. After Auntie Bobbie left, I put my head down on the kitchen table, just to shut my eyes and seal out the world for a minute, and I must have fallen asleep. I have the puddle of drool under my face to prove it.

"Hello?" I call out groggily, but nobody answers. Instead I hear someone pounding up the stairs. I'd recognize those footsteps anywhere.

My mom goes into her bedroom; she opens and closes drawers, walks around the room. After a few minutes I hear her on the stairs again, this time coming down. I sit up in my chair and brace myself. I have no clue what is going on in my mom's head right now.

She walks into the kitchen and makes a beeline for the chair opposite me. Sitting, she crosses and uncrosses her legs a few times, trying to get comfortable.

She says nothing, just reveals a tiny toy horse she's holding in her hand. It has a mane and tail made of real hair, and I think I see eyelashes. Its wooden hooves make a *click* sound when she puts it on the kitchen table.

It's the toy horse from my First Big Zap!

"Wait, is that—" I start, but mom holds up a hand to stop me.

"Let me go first or I might never get through it. Okay?"

I nod. She takes a deep breath. Her eyes hold mine. It's just Mom and me; the world falls away. It's like we're in the hair fort again.

"Sorry I walked out; I know that was kind of alarming. I needed some time to gather my thoughts. I'm not mad at you, okay? I just want to be clear about that. I'm almost never mad at you, but I'm almost always afraid."

I freeze. So it's true, my mom is afraid of me. My heart is a rock and it has fallen into my guts. It's hard to breathe. My face and hands start to tingle. "You're afraid of . . ."

"Hey." Mom instantly sees me start to panic and grabs my hand, knocking the horse over. It clatters on its side; we both watch it for a moment, a memory rising to the surface. Our eyes meet again.

"Not of you. Never *of* you, my Molly Mei. I'm sorry I've made you think that. Keeping Bobbie away from you, not telling you about our family, *totally avoiding* talking about the zaps—I thought I was protecting you, but I can see now that I only made you feel weird and alone. I promise I'm not afraid of you."

"You're not?" I ask. I need her to say it a thousand more times just to be sure.

"No way! You're basically my hero, kid! Not only do you have to deal with *me* as a mom—I'm sure I'm in some textbook somewhere as the How Not to Parent poster child—but on top of all that, you've become this thoughtful, compassionate person while living with your . . . powers."

There's that word again. POWERS. Like it's this amazing thing.

"Plus," Mom goes on, "you've been carrying this huge CHINESE GHOST SECRET the whole time we've been in this house! How is that even possible? Bobbie always said you could use your powers to help people, living *and* dead people . . . but I always thought that was more than a kid could handle. I'm sorry I underestimated you."

I don't know what to say. "What made you decide to ignore my . . . powers?" I try out the word.

Mom picks up the toy horse. "Because of this little guy. He was my por por's, your taai por's—your great-grandmother's—before he was your por por's. You were, like, four or five in Honolulu and the whole family was visiting from Hong Kong. My uncle Michael brought a whole box of junk from my mom's childhood home in Kowloon Tong before it was demolished."

Mom looks like she's seeing a movie replay just for her. It's odd to see her so small and contemplative, but I like it. I feel like I'm finally being let into her world.

"Bobbie and your por por were like kids going through that box. They were giddy! You know, Bobbie actually spent some of her childhood in Hong Kong; maybe that's why her Canto doesn't suck like mine. Anyway, she found this horse and asked if she could give it to you. I knew what she was doing, but I let her anyway. I really thought maybe all the 'episodes' before—the mini zaps—were just flukes and this was the way to prove it to her."

"Hold on," I interrupt. "Auntie *Bobbie* gave me the horse? And you *knew* it would zap me?"

"I thought it *might* zap you. Bobbie saw it as a chance to start your ghost education or something. Oh, I wish you could have known Bobbie back then, Molls—I idolized her. She was so confident, so unique. And when she listened to you it felt like you were the most important person in the world. Even though I was an adult with a kid of my own, it was hard for me to go against her. So I didn't. But I really thought there was a good chance you'd be fine and then everyone would leave us alone."

"Everyone?"

"The women in our family. The aunties. It's a family thing. Ghost-seeing—"

"—eyes. Yeah, Auntie Bobbie talked to me about it."

Mom's face darkens for a moment, but she shakes it off and pushes on.

"I'm sorry you heard it from her and not from me."

"It's okay, millennial. Stop apologizing." I try to lighten the mood. No matter what, seeing my mom hurting is my kryptonite. "So what's with this horse?" I instinctively lean a little bit away from it. I really don't want to get zapped right now.

"Like I said, it was my por por's. She was holding it when she died." Then she quietly adds, "And I was there too."

"What?"

"I was at your taai por's house in Hong Kong for a visit when I was six or seven—you would have loved her, Molls. She was so funny, told such good stories, and cared so hard about everybody she met. Her house was always bustling with family and chosen family. You actually look just like her. Anyway, she was playing with me on her porch overlooking the garden. Everything was bright and warm and smelled like city and sea. That summer in Hong Kong was the best and worst of my childhood.

"My por por and I were laughing as she made the horse leap over her potted plants, when all of a sudden she stopped mid-leap and the life drained from her face. I'll never forget her eyes as she fell. They stayed on me; it was like every single emotion she could feel flew from her to me—fear, love, anguish, regret, joy. Wonder. I can't do what you do, but I feel like I lived in that moment for days."

"I know the feeling," I whisper.

Mom nods. "She was holding this horse when she fell. When she died. It hit—"

"—the green tile floor." I finish her thought. "The horse clattered when it hit, but it didn't break. It was you crying in my First Big Zap, 'Wake up!'"

"Wake up!" Mom says it with me. We sit together in this shared memory. Me, Mom, and the little wooden horse.

Her voice is low and smooth when she speaks again; she's trying hard to keep it together. "Molly, that zap hit you so hard. I was terrified. Sure, I handle your zaps now, but I've had to teach myself how to do that. It's the hardest thing in the world to see your kid disappear for a little bit, even a few seconds. Sometimes, when you're in a zap, your eyes look like my por por's did that last time she was with me." She's trying so hard to keep her voice steady. "I'm always a little bit afraid I'm not going to get you back.

"I was so angry with Bobbie." Her voice gets even deeper. It reminds me of Jade's growl. "She knew what she was doing—what she was doing to you—and she did it anyway. To prove to me that you needed her guidance, that you were special. I knew that! Zaps or not! And while now I see that maybe she wasn't totally wrong, back then I was so young and so scared that I just reacted. I shut her out. Shut everyone out, really. I thought by sheer force of will I could stop the ghost stuff from taking over your life. If we didn't talk about it, if I didn't make a big deal out of it, maybe it would fade away. But I was wrong and now you're stuck in this mess. If you want to grab our stuff and go back to Bell Harbor tonight, I'm in. We can be out of here by midnight." I can see her already mentally packing.

There's so much happening I need to get up and walk around the kitchen, breathe in and out. I can't believe what I'm about to say.

"No. There are things we need to do here."

"Not what I expected to hear," she says.

"Bobbie was right, but not all the way right," I say. "Yes, it would have been nice to know that I wasn't the only spooky, zappy ghost-seeing girl in the world, but I get why you did what you did. You were taking care of me. Like you've always taken care of me. Bobbie might be a guide, but you're my home. All those times I 'went somewhere else' during a zap, I always knew, deep down, that you were waiting for me. That I'd be safe."

She starts to say something but I can't stop.

"What Bobbie *is* right about is that I can do good things for people. Living people. Dead people. Our people. *Our ghosts.* Jade needs me. I'm the only person who can help her, the only person who sees all the wonderful and mysterious things everybody else can't see. I think you know what that's like."

"But it's so much to take on, Molly. You're a kid trying to save another kid—from what? Death? The unknown? Being a ghost of a ghost?" Mom does not look convinced.

"It's overwhelming and sucks sometimes. But I'm not alone. I've got you, I've got Auntie Bobbie, I've got Jade. For the first time in my life I've got a community. And you do too! You have the Loh sisters, Jami Ahmad, all those restaurant owners who freakin' LOVE YOU—Mom, we have reasons, plural, to be here. If I've learned anything over the days and weeks, it's that it's hard to be us—Team Teng, Chinese American, weird ghost ladies—in Texas or anywhere!

"For once it doesn't feel like we're floating around waiting for life to happen to us—life *is* happening. And yeah, it's hard, and yeah, I really didn't want *Buckeye Creek, Texas*, to be the place that feels like home, but I can't resist it anymore. We're here for a reason."

Mom is not looking at me; she's sitting slumped in her chair, nodding.

"Mom? What do you think?"

Without warning she stands up and comes over to me. She puts her hands on my shoulders. Her smile is like the sun breaking through a storm.

"Welcome home, Molly Teng."

65
JADE

Molly comes to my attic as the sun is setting and tells me she wants to surprise me. "But I know what you're doing; you're making me an altar. What's the surprise?"

She rolls her eyes the way only teenagers in any era do. When she does, I notice the dark circles under her eyes and feel a pang of guilt for what I'm putting her through. She answers, "Yes, but . . . I want to make it special and I have something extra for you." Molly bubbles with excitement.

I'm so tired and it's so hard to appear to Molly, so I agree to stay out of the way.

———

When I open my eyes the attic is glowing.

Paper lanterns hang from the beams, casting an otherworldly mix of light and shadow around the room. Even the light from the streetlamp streaming in through the window feels magical.

Under the slope of the roof where Molly said my bed once was, there is a small square table with more candles, red and yellow flowers, burning incense, and a plate of gummy worms, dumplings, and little oranges. A tall piece of wood with black ink brush writing on it sits at the center of the table, next to a pale yellow ceramic urn.

Across the room, a single blue lantern hangs from the rafters, just below where my bone box was hidden. Under the lantern is a narrow single bed with a fluffy white pillow and a pale pink blanket. Next to the bed is a wooden stool, with a candle and a tin cup. My room! She rebuilt my room!

My attic has never felt more special.

"Molly! This is all for me?"

"Of course! After all these years you deserve to have a beautiful place to call your own."

"But how did you do this? Won't your mom find out?"

"That's kind of part of the surprise," Molly says, and stomps her foot twice. On cue, the attic door opens and two sets of footsteps come up the stairs. Something about this feels so familiar, like an echo of the past. My body instinctively tenses; a growl rumbles in my throat.

Auntie Bobbie and Molly's mother appear. Bobbie's eyes are on me and she smiles; Molly's mother's eyes sweep the room.

"What's happening?" I ask Molly, taking a step back.

"It's okay, Jade," Molly says, looking from her mother to me. "Auntie Bobbie and I told Mom everything. She helped us do all this." Molly gestures around the room. "She kind of knew something was up."

Molly's mother steps forward and follows Molly's gaze to me. "Well, I was a little shocked *how much* was up, but I trust Molly." She looks over to Bobbie. "And I trust my sister."

She looks back in my direction. "I'm sorry you've been alone so long, Jade, but you're not alone anymore. You always have a home with Molly and me. We've decided—Molly's decided—that we're going to stay for a while. We're part of something in Buckeye Creek; we've got things to do. Plus, we have family here *and* we could always use another member of Team Teng." Molly and Bobbie simultaneously roll their eyes.

I can't believe what I'm hearing. I look to Auntie Bobbie, remembering what Molly told me about her mother not wanting Bobbie teaching Molly about ghosts. "So she's not mad about . . . the ghost stuff?"

"No, Dorothy isn't mad about Molly learning about ghosts," says Auntie Bobbie, glancing at Molly's mom, transmitting to her what I'm saying.

"I've never seen Molly with so much purpose," Dot chimes in. "I wanted to protect her, shield her from ghost things so she would have an easier time, but I can't pretend she's someone she's not. My daughter doesn't just see dead people, she helps dead people. That's pretty astonishing."

I go to Molly, saying softer, just to her, "But, Molly, what about Bell Harbor?"

She shrugs. "Bell Harbor was easy. Yeah, it felt safe and Buckeye Creek feels a little dangerous, but like Mom said, there's work to do here. For the dead *and* the living. I want to stay, Jade. I want to stay with you."

I can't hold it in anymore—I weep with relief. Teardrops fall through my hands and make little dots on the wood floor.

"OH MY GOD. Are those tears on the floor?" Molly's mother stares at where my feet should be.

"Yeah, Jade's crying. Happy tears, I think. Right?"

"I am," I sob. "I am."

"I'm sorry to interrupt but we should really put Jade's bones into her urn." Auntie Bobbie comes to my side. "The poor girl is literally going up in smoke."

"Can we get your bones?" Molly asks. I nod. My hands and arms are just wispy outlines; I certainly need her help.

We go over to the loose floorboard and open it. I reach in with both hands and use every last bit of energy I can find to lift the bones. They fall through my hands for a second, but I catch them, the red cloth falling to the floor.

"Let me help," says Molly, and reaches for the largest bone. Her hand touches one end as I hold the other, and suddenly I'm engulfed in light. I see image after image fly in front of my eyes like a flip book. I see Molly—the first day she walked into the house; Bradley and Tómas curled up in front of the TV; Celia laughing at my *Wizard of Oz* antics; my attic.

A dresser.

A bed.

A woman with deep smile lines around her eyes and long black hair that falls around her shoulders.

Laughter. Her hands cradle my face. The faint smell of incense wafts from her skin. ". . . and then one day I'll show you the ocean! We'll be warm in the sun and cool in the water and we'll swim free like all those shiny fish!" She makes a fish face, sucking her cheeks and puckering her lips. I giggle and she gives me a kiss on the forehead. I believe her; we'll go together someday.

The flip book flips again and I see my mother once more. This time she's coughing, holding a handkerchief to her mouth. When she pulls it away it's stained with red. She collapses.

The box, the floor, the man taking the pieces of my life away in a sack.

And just as the memories seem to be fading away, I see my bone box, tucked onto a ceiling beam. I am looking at my own bone box from the outside. Two small diaphanous hands reach for it, cradles it like they did my face, and the box falls with a crash.

The images blur and like a light being snapped off, I'm plunged into darkness. Like when I woke up in the box, my eyes are wide open but I see nothing. I feel like I'm floating but I cannot feel my limbs. Is this it? Is this my end? Are we too late?

But then as if it's from a great distance, echoing across the void, I hear voices.

"NO!"

"Where is she?"

"What happened?"

"JADE!"

66

MOLLY

She's gone.

It didn't work.

Jade is gone.

When I came out of the zap, it's just me holding Jade's bone and all that is left of her is a column of black smoke. Then it disappears. There is nothing left of Jade.

I fall down, trembling. How could this happen? We built her a home, we made her our family, we memorialized her. But it was all for nothing.

Jade died anyway.

Mom's arms are around me, but I feel nothing. My mind flies over the talks, the food, even the arguments we've shared—through it all I never really believed she'd go away. Jade has become such a major part of my life. With her gone it feels like there's a huge, gaping wound where she once was.

No. No. This isn't right. I stand up. My hands continue to shake.

"Molly." Mom reaches for me, steadies me. I let her.

"This is wrong," I say.

"Molly, death comes for us all," Bobbie says gently.

"I know that. But that's not what I mean. What I'm saying is that this is wrong. Jade was here for over a hundred and twenty years; I can't just let her go unacknowledged. I can't just let her disappear without a word." I stumble to her altar, still gripping my mom's hand.

I speak.

"My best friend, Jade, died a long time ago. She died again tonight. She was not alone. When she was alive, people like us were either hated or erased. So many people didn't see us as human beings with families and hopes and dreams. But Jade had all of those things, and she still does. You are part of this family, Jade, wherever you are, now and forever. You may not have been seen by people in life and you may not have been seen in death, but *I* saw you. And you saw me. Jade, is . . . was . . . determined, she was full of curiosity, and even though she went through more than I will ever understand, she still found joy in so many things. Marshmallows. Gummy worms. Sharing a meal. I mean, you were REALLY ANNOYING when ignored"—I laugh at our little joke—"but you made these first months in Texas the most exciting of my life. So I'll take it all—the happiness and the sorrow. Every inch of who you were. I could never forget you, Jade, even if I tried. *And I did try.*"

Nobody says anything. There's nothing to say.

Bobbie, her hand on my shoulder, turns me to face Jade's altar. She bows three times, then steps aside and gestures for me to copy, counting "Yat, yih, saam"—*one, two, three*—as I bow. I remember Mom doing this at her mother's grave.

Suddenly a roar fills my ears. I put my head in my hands, afraid I'm about to faint, but then realize that the roar isn't coming from inside my head; it's all around me.

And it's not a roar. It's a growl.

Coming from all four corners of the room, the growl fills the room. It circles us, getting louder and louder, shaking the altar.

Mom, Bobbie, and I cling to one another, the growl swirling around us like a tornado, hot wind lifting our hair.

I know this growl. It's the monster. Jade's monster. It's all around us, surrounding us. Sour breath fills my nose. My heart pounds; the entire house rattles. "Jade!" I scream into the cacophony. I glance at the beams of the attic and hope they don't crash down on us. This beast had been living in Jade this whole time?

The growl becomes sharper, higher; it turns into a shriek. Then, just as I begin to legitimately worry that my eardrums will burst, it's gone.

Our hair floats down, the ringing in our ears quiets. Once again we are in silence.

And there stands Jade.

67

JADE

I'm back in my attic with Molly. She is holding my bone. My hand, no longer smoke, is suspended in the air as if reaching for Molly.

"Jade!" she cries.

"What's happening?" her mother asks, concern in her voice. Everyone looks utterly baffled.

Molly runs to me. "Are you okay? You were gone. Where did you go?"

"I don't know, I was floating in darkness. I couldn't see or feel anything. I heard the monster, the growl. I heard you call my name. I also heard what you said, Molly. About me. Thank you for seeing me."

"Always," she says. Taking a breath, she goes on, gesticulating wildly. "The monster was all around us; it was awful. It screamed at us! I can't believe you shared a body with that thing. But I think it's gone. Look at you!"

I examine my arms, my legs, my hair. I'm me again! I look down and all of me has returned. I've never felt such elation at having feet!

"I think you're free!" Molly beams. "You have a family who will never forget you. You aren't a hungry ghost anymore."

With those words I'm reminded of what I need to tell her. "Molly, I saw my mother," I say, the words tumbling out. "I remember her. Her name was Yum Yiu, but she also had an English name . . . it was . . . it was . . . Eli—Elizabeth! I remember, I remember her, Molly! Jade and Elizabeth, we were Jade and Elizabeth! We lived in this house. We worked here. She loved me, she loved me so much. We were going to swim in the ocean! She died after me. Her ghost freed me from my box so I wouldn't be trapped forever. That's how I fell! She's out there, Molly! I feel it, I feel her. She never forgot me. I'm not the only ghost!"

Molly tries to keep up, to tell her mother what I'm saying. She looks pale and I notice she's perspiring a bit despite the cold—I'm sure she feels a little ill—but she carries on.

"How?" I ask her.

Molly looks at the bone in her hand. "Like that day we both grabbed for the doorknob and touched it at the same time. I think the same thing happened now, only because it was your bone, somehow I zapped *you* and unlocked *your* memories." Molly looks to Auntie Bobbie. "Is that possible?"

"Apparently it is," she says.

"Let's hurry up and give your bones a good home," Molly says, and moves toward the altar.

Holding my bones like a baby chick, Molly carries them to the yellow urn. Bobbie opens the top and Molly carefully places my bones inside. They stand back from the table.

"This is your name written in Chinese," says Bobbie, indicating the slim tablet on the table. "Normally we'd write your birth and death dates on here as well as where you were born, but we don't know those things. Yet." Bobbie raises her eyebrows as if to ask me if I'm up for the challenge of completing my tablet. With my new family, with my returning memories, perhaps I am.

"Dorothy's friends—"

"—Rose and Hazel Loh—" Molly adds.

"—helped us make this for you. It's your spirit tablet, so you'll always have a place in our family."

I don't know what to say. I reach for her and she reaches back—our hands touch! As Molly's warm hand holds my cold one, I feel like a flower unfurling, blooming, my roots crawling into every corner of the house—my house. But I don't feel stuck; in fact, I feel like I could fly. I wonder . . .

I look to the window and my feet lift off the ground. Floating over with just a thought, I reach for the glass.

My hand glides through it to the warm Texas breeze outside. My arm follows, then I'm going through the window, to the other side of the glass, to the world beyond the house on Charlotte Street. The air on my skin feels like every part of me is breathing for the first time!

I want nothing more than to explore the big wide world, find my mother, but I stop. I drop back to the attic floor and return to Molly. My stomach twists. Do I know how to exist outside this house? What if I can't? How can I leave Molly?

As if reading my mind, Molly speaks. "It's okay, Jade, you should go. This is your home; we're your family. You'll always have a reservation at the Second Dinner Club. And I mean, come on, you're a ghost, you can do whatever you want!"

The lump in my stomach melts and again I feel myself getting lighter. "Go," Molly says. "I can't wait to hear about your adventures." She looks to her mom and back to me. "I love an adventure."

I squeeze her hand one more time. She squeezes it back. Her hand feels so good in mine, but it's time to let it go. I turn toward the window, take a running start, and leap.

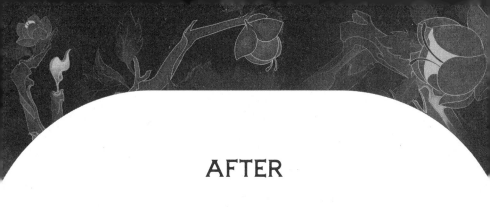

AFTER

SUBJECT: Books and TG

BTeng@gmail.com

Hello Molly,

I ordered you some of the books you were asking about, the one about Chinese America and the one about Polly Bemis. Excellent reads, but kind of dense. We can talk about them when you come for Thanksgiving—if we can tear your mother away from her work.

Oh! And tell Dorothy to stop waffling and just bring Jami!

Hope school is going well. Say hi to Eleanor for me. Don't forget to dust Jade's room.

Love, Bobbie

Before I forget, I put a reminder in my phone to dust Jade's room after school tomorrow. I really do miss her. Eleanor's made me braver about the living, but everything that's happened with Jade has made me braver about being Chinese American. Before Jade, I really didn't think that much about our culture, our past. Honestly, there were times I wished I looked like some blond-haired, blue-eyed kid. But not anymore. Now with Auntie Bobbie around and learning about the world Jade came from, I'm kind of obsessed with Chinese history (and ghosts).

I close my laptop and roll onto my side in bed. It's way past eleven o'clock and I need to sleep, but I also need to proofread my English essay one last time. Ms. Flores is a stickler for typos—last time I forgot a "the" and an "is" and she docked me half a letter grade. Bonkers, right?

I really should have done this sooner, but all week Eleanor and I have spent every spare moment working on our Halloween costumes. We're going as fire ants—not the insects that ate my leg, but ants dressed as firefighters. In the past I would be too embarrassed to wear a giant helmet with antennae and a shiny red uniform with a bunch of legs sprouting out of it, but when I'm with Eleanor I don't care (as much) what people think.

I heave myself back to sitting and take a bite of the Loh sisters' char siu bao that I've been picking at all night. I'm about halfway through the essay when I hear a creak on the attic floor above me. The house makes noises all the time, especially now that it's getting colder, but I can't help but wonder if it's more than just old floorboards whining. My whole body tenses for a moment, listening, but the house quiets again.

Blah. Back to my essay on *Huck Finn*.

My eyes start to get heavy but I'm jolted awake by another noise. Another creak. This one is on the attic stairs. Could it be?

I hop off my bed and peek into the hallway, the dim light from my room splitting the dark. I look toward the attic door. Still shut, just like I left it earlier today.

I go back to my bed and my essay, but I'm barely a sentence in when I see my breath fog in front of me. I smile.

ACKNOWLEDGMENTS

Writing a book is hard. They don't tell you that. Or maybe they do and I didn't listen. Point is, there's no way I could have brought this story to life without a whole bunch of excellent people.

There would be no *Hungry Bones* without my editor, Anna Bloom. Thank you for not giving up on me after that first email . . . and that second email . . . and that first DM . . . and the second. But you are so much more than a relentless communicator. Thank you for your impeccable eye, for believing in Jade and Molly from the very beginning, and for loving ghost stories just as much as I do.

Thank you, Anjali Bisaria. Knowing your smarts and energy were at the other end of all those drafts and emails was always a bright spot for me.

Thank you to my agent, Kirby Kim. My friends say your name sounds like a superhero's and I think that's very fitting. You were like a superhero to me when you took me under your wing (cape?). Thank you for your confidence, for answering all my questions, and for making me feel like a real, live author.

Emily McCombs, I would not be a writer if it weren't for you. Thank you for showing me how to be brave in my writing (and everywhere else). Joy Nash, thank you for answering every "But could I possibly?" with a defiant, "Why not?! You're the boss of you!" Amy Lubinski, you heard every rant, you cheered every victory. Thank you for always being a part of my story (all the way from the "book" I wrote for you in sophomore year Spanish).

I haven't shut up about all things book for years now. Liz Lark-Riley, my first "publisher," thank you for always wanting to hear more, even about the boring business stuff. Bethany Umbach, thank you for the ferocity of your friendship and for your equally ferocious daughter. Eleanor Louise, thank you for sharing my name and lending me yours for a few pages. Jennifer Grace, my favorite lawyer at law/puppeteer, thank you for always recognizing the nonsense. Leah Okraszewski, dear SW, thank you for your expert ear, compassionate heart, and complete lack of BS.

Robert Wong at Manoa Chinese Cemetery, thank you for that hours-long chat about ghosts, ancestors, and bones.

Sarah and Denise Leung, my original "Loh sisters." Thank for every single memory I cannibalized and for all the CBRs. Hazel and Rose, you wild and brilliant girls, thank you for being a part of my story.

I would never have written a single word in lockdown if Allison Meier and Bess Lovejoy hadn't let me "sit by them." The same goes for Landis Blair and his unending supply of Forgiveness and Dignity. Corinne Elicona and Megan Rosenbloom, thank you for every encouraging text and thoughtful note.

Dr. Lindsey Fitzharris, thank you for introducing me to Kirby and for generously being an open book about all things book. Tracey Hung, thank you for taking on the mind-numbing task of checking my Canto. Dr. Lucy Coleman Talbot, thank you for never needing me to explain and for always understanding my ghosts. Thank you Nuri McBride for cheering so loud I can hear it all the way in BK and for always understanding the aunties.

Sayo Nakagawa, thank you for always rooting for me, for your curiosity, for your concern every time I disappeared into this book. I miss our Kahala Mall lunches. Debra Pasquerette, thank you for always supporting my big, bonkers endeavors in the biggest, most bonkers way. I miss the stoop and the grill.

Thank you to the women of The Order of the Good Death for the years of helping me become a better writer. Sarah Chavez, I would never have landed on a title without you. Ericka Cameron, encouragement and superior cat names, things you give in abundance. Caitlin Doughty, where do I even begin? It's probably somewhere in the millions of words I've overwritten for you over the years. Thank you for answering that first awkward email and giving a hag a chance.

Vera Rogals, Juliet Rogals, and Trixie Symmonds: Thank you for being the smart, spirited, compassionate weirdos who inspired so much of who Molly is. I'm honored to be your auntie.

Thank you to the Creepy Corneristas. I'll leave the porch light on for y'all. Or will I?

Auntie Bobbie, thank you for making it possible for me to write this book.

Mom and Dad, thank you for telling ghost stories instead of fairytales. Thank you for saving the weird little books I wrote and stapled together in elementary school. Thank you for being excited to have a writer in the family. Thank you for loving me and my stories.

Alex Rogals. Thank you for reading every word of every draft, for talking (arguing) with me late into the night over a section, a sentence, an idea. I trust you with every story in my head. Thank you for always believing in me.

And, of course, to my Auntie Molly. Thank you for your ghost-seeing eyes.